POOR DARLING

POOR DARLING

Christopher Nicole

Severn House Large Print
London & New York

X000 000 020 8321

This first large print edition published in Great Britain 2003 by
SEVERN HOUSE LARGE PRINT BOOKS LTD of
9-15, High Street, Sutton, Surrey, SM1 1DF.
First world regular print edition published 2002 by
Severn House Publishers, London and New York.
This first large print edition published in the USA 2003 by
SEVERN HOUSE PUBLISHERS INC of
595 Madison Avenue, New York, NY 10022

British Library Cataloguing in Publication Data

Nicole, Christopher, 1930 -
    Poor darling. - Large print ed.
    1. Princesses - Fiction
    2. Bodyguards - Fiction
    3. Suspense fiction
    4. Large type books
    I. Title
    823.9'14 [F]

ISBN 0-7278-7223-0

Printed and bound in Great Britain by
MPG Books Ltd, Bodmin, Cornwall.

Careless she is with artful care,
Affecting to seem unaffected.
                    William Congreve

The Attempt

'The performance ends in five minutes.' Seated behind the wheel of his car, Rosen spoke into his mobile in a low voice. 'Are your men in position?'

'Yes,' Burke said. 'But we will not take her on the street. It is too risky; she may be hurt.'

Rosen blew through his teeth.

'She is no use to us dead,' Burke pointed out.

'She will be even less use to us once she gets back to the palace,' Rosen said. 'We shall have to plan all over again.'

'She will not go back to the palace. Not immediately, anyway. I know this girl. I have studied her for two years. It is her birthday, and she is celebrating with her friends. She will go to a disco. What is more, to do that, she will ditch her guards, and become utterly vulnerable. Because she believes she is invulnerable. Follow her and report when she goes in. We will take her there.'

'You will be telling me next you know which disco she is going to.'

'I do,' Burke said.

Rosen listened to the click of the other phone going dead, and resumed watching the façade of the opera house across the street from his car window. It was a brand new building, built with the sultan's almost brand new money, inspired by his determination to create a new Paris – he had been educated in the French capital – out here in the wilderness.

And in there, at this moment, was his pride and joy, not to mention his heiress. Rosen only hoped that Burke was not being over-elaborate.

But Burke was the expert. As well as the commander of the mission.

'That was good,' Cerise said. 'Don't you think it was good, Highness?'

'I think it was boring,' Karina said.

She spoke English, as her entourage was required to do; the princess was half English and had been to school in England.

Her companions, two young women and three young men, cast anxious glances at each other. Being invited to be the princess's companions, especially on such an occasion, was a great honour ... but the invitation carried with it the risk of exposure to Karina's well-known moods.

Now they trailed behind her down the broad staircase of the opera house and into the lobby. They were surrounded by people, all hoping to be photographed in close proximity to the famous young woman, even if she was paying no attention to any of them. Her security guards hurried in front of her to make sure no one came too close.

Princess Karina continued to move with unconscious arrogance. Quite apart from her beauty, she had tremendous grace, and seemed to glide down the steps. An average five and a half feet in height, she had a full figure for an eighteen-year-old, amply delineated by the crimson evening gown, worn off the shoulder with two straps round her neck. Neither she nor her two female companions wore wraps; in the heat of Kharram, even in April, they were simply not necessary. Her black hair was loose; straight save for a slight wave, it rested on her shoulders and then drifted down her back. Her features were symmetrical, each well matched to the other in that delicious mixture of Arab and English ancestry, but her lips, which could be very firm, also had a slightly petulant droop, as if nothing in her life was quite as good as it should have been. Her companions could be forgiven for wondering how her life could possibly be improved.

The group emerged on to the porch, and now there were cameras flashing and TV video recorders busy.

'Did you enjoy the performance, Princess?' someone asked.

9

'Not particularly,' Karina said with that devastating honesty which distressed so many people.

'What does it feel like to be eighteen?' asked someone else.

'The same as it did to be seventeen,' Karina said.

'And where are you going now, Highness?'

Karina turned a smile on the camera; she knew her parents would be watching at the palace.

'Home to bed,' she said.

She had been descending the porch steps as she spoke, and had reached the foot. The door of her limousine was open. Karina turned back to the waiting throng and smiled and waved, then ducked her head and got into the car. Her five companions followed, and a detective-captain got into the front beside the driver. There were also four motorcycle outriders, two in front and two behind.

They drove away from the crowd outside the opera house, and Karina leaned forward. 'Tell your people to leave us,' she instructed the detective.

'Highness?'

'I wish to enjoy myself, and that is not possible when I am surrounded by flat-footed policemen.'

'But ... it is forbidden. You told those reporters you were going home to bed.'

'That was for Mummy and Daddy.'

'But they will expect you.'

'They won't get worried for at least an hour. I will be home by then.'

The detective-captain drew a deep breath. 'I cannot permit this, Your Highness. It is my responsibility...'

'I am giving you an order, Captain.'

'The danger...'

'What are you talking about? Do you know where I am going?'

'You have not told me, Highness.'

'Exactly. I have not told anyone. I do not know myself. Therefore, how can anyone know? Therefore, how can there be any danger? Anyway, what danger have I ever been in? Who do you suppose would dare interfere with me? Dismiss your people.'

The captain sighed, then spoke into his mobile. There was some hesitation on the part of the outriders, then they opened their throttles and surged past the limousine and into the night.

'Tell me where we are going,' Karina said.

'Turn left at the next corner,' Cerise suggested.

The driver looked at the captain, who nodded. The car turned left on to a broad, tree-lined, brilliantly lit avenue known as The Thoroughfare.

'You are not going to Quadrino's?' one of the young men asked.

11

Karina looked at Cerise.

'It is the best,' Cerise said. 'Amalda dances there, in the back room.'

'So that is where we are going,' Karina said. 'Are you turning chicken?'

'No, Highness,' the young man said hastily. 'But to turn up there in this limo...'

'That is a good point,' Cerise said. 'It is only a couple of hundred yards, now.'

'Stop the car,' Karina commanded.

Again the driver and the detective-captain exchanged glances, then the car pulled into the kerb and stopped.

'We will walk from here,' Karina said.

'You will walk on the street in the middle of the night? No, no, Princess. I cannot permit that.'

'You will do as you are told,' Karina snapped. 'No one will know who I am.'

'You are in evening dress.'

'So? Many people go from the opera to a disco. I will not be noticed.'

The captain pulled his nose.

'You will remain here,' Karina said. 'Until we come back to you. If we need you, Cerise will call you on her mobile. Understood?'

'Yes, Highness,' the captain said, understanding that he was putting his job on the line.

One of the young men was already out of the car, holding the door for the princess; tall and slender, and wearing a little moustache,

12

he was only a few years older than Karina herself.

'You are our host, Henri,' Karina said as she stepped on to the pavement. 'Cerise has the money.' She glanced at her lady-in-waiting.

Cerise, a tall, busty, sharp-featured, black-haired woman in a green gown with a plunging décolletage, several years older than the princess, patted her large shoulder bag – incongruous both on the occasion and with her outfit – and smiled reassuringly.

'I will see you later, Captain,' Karina said, and set off along the pavement, her companions to either side.

The captain gave another sigh.

Rosen parked a hundred yards behind the limousine, watched the young people disembarking. As it was a typical Saturday night in Kharram, warm and dry, the streets, glowing with light, were packed with both vehicles and people – since the oil strike everyone in the country was at least moderately rich – and no one was paying any attention to his modest little car, which was now sandwiched next to the kerb between two much grander vehicles.

He thumbed his phone. 'As you said,' he commented, 'she has dismissed her guards, and now she is leaving her car. I think she must be going to Quadrino's.'

'That is what we expected,' Burke said. 'But make sure.'

Rosen pocketed his mobile and got out of the car.

'A table for six,' Henri told the maître d'.

'In the back room,' Karina said.

The maître d' frowned at her, not immediately recognising her, although her face was certainly familiar; his initial reaction was that she was a night-clubber who had caused trouble in the past. 'The prices in the back room are doubled,' he remarked.

'That is no matter,' Henri said, resuming control.

The maître d' gave a stiff bow, and led them into the first room, which was crowded with young people dancing to a five-piece orchestra with a great deal of noise and laughter. He was a strict Muslim, and although happy in his well-paid position, did not approve of the official government stance in Kharram, which permitted drinking alcohol, although not in public, and which therefore turned a blind eye to places like this officially private club, allowed to open on the Christian weekend.

They threaded their way through the throng, and reached a door at the rear of the room. This was guarded by another dinner-jacketed man, extremely large and aggressive-looking. But he was in the maître d's employ, and at a nod from his superior opened the door.

This gave access to a small lobby, at the rear of which there was another door. The security guard carefully shut the first door behind them before opening the inner door. While he was doing this, the six bodies of the revellers were pressed together in the confined space, the young men snuggling up to Karina. No one was ever sure how far they could go with the princess, or how far anyone had gone before. It was of course unthinkable that she could not be a virgin, or that she would not be a virgin on her wedding night, but she was allowed so much freedom by her doting father and her liberated mother that it was always possible to dream of an inadvertent fumble at breast or buttock which might go unnoticed, or certainly unpunished.

The inner door opened to emit another gush of sound and laughter, and music, but this time the mingled odour of sweat and perfume was overlaid with that of alcohol, and the dancers were more frenetic in their movements.

The newcomers were met by a waiter.

'Table for six,' the maître d' said.

'On the floor,' Karina told him.

The waiter looked at the maître d', who waggled his eyebrows and then hastily withdrew, closing the door behind him.

The waiter gestured the party to a table on the edge of the dance floor. 'This table is two hundred dinars an hour,' he said, to leave them in no doubt of the cost – a Kharrami dinar was worth roughly fifty English pence. 'And the champagne is twenty dinars a glass.'

'Suppose we do not wish champagne?' Cerise asked.

The waiter shrugged. 'We serve nothing else.'

'Of course we wish champagne,' Karina said, and sat down. 'And Amalda. When next is she on?'

'She does another performance at two o'clock.'

Karina looked at her diamond-encrusted Cartier wristwatch; it was just past midnight. 'We cannot stay that long. Have her do a show in fifteen minutes.'

'She will not do this. She has only just finished her last performance.'

'I wish a show in fifteen minutes.' Karina snapped her fingers, and Cerise opened her shoulder bag and took out both a card and her purse. From the purse she took a hundred-dinar note, and this, together with the card, she placed in the waiter's hand. 'Tell her, if she pleases us, there will be several more of those,' Karina said.

The waiter glanced at the card and did a double take. Then he began to bow.

16

'Stop that,' Karina snapped. 'We do not want publicity.'

Already heads were turning in their direction, but thus far the interest was caused by the beauty and elegance of the women rather than any recognition of the princess. Hastily the waiter stood straight. 'I will see to it, Highness.' He scurried off, signalling to the bar to produce the champagne.

Rosen strolled along the pavement towards the entrance to Quadrino's, the six young people in his sight through the bustling crowds. He was a big, heavy-set man with thinning dark hair and curiously soft features. He passed the waiting limousine, gave a casual glance at the interior, and then walked on. He did not pause in his stroll as he reached the nightclub's entrance; the door was open and he could see the princess and her entourage talking with the matre d'. He continued on his way until the next corner, and stepped round it into a darkened alleyway.

He stood there for a moment, just to establish that he was not being followed. A woman walked by on the street, glanced at him, and continued on her way.

Rosen thumbed his mobile. 'They have gone into Quadrino's,' he said.

'As we expected,' Burke commented. 'They will have gone through to the inner bar.'

'I do not know this,' Rosen said. 'Do you wish me to check that out?'

'No. I know this. I have told you, I know her habits. That inner bar has a door at the back. This leads to a corridor which goes past the kitchens and storerooms to a street door. This door opens on to Parrot Street. That runs parallel to The Thoroughfare. Go there. You will be joined.'

'You wish me to go in?'

'No. You cannot go in. The door is barred on the inside. You will wait there for people to come out.'

'Will I have enough support?'

'You will have enough support, Rosen.'

'There is also the matter of the limousine.'

'Where is it?'

'Parked two hundred yards west of the nightclub.'

'How many men?'

'Only two. But one is Captain Farsi. He will certainly be in touch with Police Headquarters.'

'We will see to it. What time do you have?'

Rosen looked at the luminous dial on his watch. 'I have zero zero twenty.'

'That is correct. Be in position by zero zero forty-five. It will happen then. Out.'

Rosen looked up to see a woman standing there, and realised she was the woman who had passed him on the street a few moments earlier.

'Hello,' she said.

Rosen licked his lips. There could be no doubt that she had overheard most of what he had said. At the moment she had obviously made nothing of it. But tomorrow...

'Would you like a good time?' she asked.

He peered at her in the gloom, trying to decide what she looked like. Definitely she was a Kharrami, both from the way she spoke the language and her dress, which was a haik, or long outer garment. But in common with most Kharramis, who were probably the most liberated women in the Arab world, thanks to their sultana, she did not wear the yashmak. She was quite pretty, and quite young as well. And very eager. He supposed she probably had a family at home to support.

'One hundred dinars,' she said. 'And I will do anything you wish.'

He sighed. Pretty women were his weakness; he could not keep his hands off them, and when on a job, especially a job like this one, his sexual instincts were close to being uppermost. Thus he would dearly have liked to take what this woman offered. But when one worked for Rosen, business came first, and he was on a schedule.

'Then turn around,' he said.

'The money first.'

Rosen extracted his wallet from his inner pocket, took out a hundred-dinar note, and gave it to her. She had a pocket of her own, in her haik, and she placed the note in this. Then she smiled at him, turned round, hitched the haik to her waist, and bent over; she wore nothing underneath.

Rosen stepped against her, drawing his knife from its sheath on his belt beneath his jacket as he did so. She gave a little start when she realised he had not dropped his pants. Because of the start her head came up, and Rosen grabbed her hair with his left hand to expose her throat still further. Now he passed the knife across it with a quick slash, at the same time stepping away from her. Only a few spots of blood landed on his hand as she plunged forward to hit the ground. She still moved as blood spread around her, but she could make no sound and he knew she would be dead in a few seconds.

He waited for the movements to cease, then stooped beside her, taking great care not to step in the blood, cleaned the knife on her haik, replaced it in its sheath, and removed the note from her pocket. There were three other notes beside it. He took these as well, reflecting that if he did not, whoever found her body certainly would. He placed all the money in his wallet, and stepped on to the street. He did not suppose that the discovery of the body of a murdered whore would make much of a stir beside the other news that would be filling the media tomorrow morning.

'This is not very good champagne,' Karina remarked.

'It is the best we have,' the waiter protested. 'French.'

'Is there any other? If it gives me a headache I will have this place closed down.'

The waiter gulped, but was rescued by a drum roll.

'Here by special request,' the bandleader announced, 'Mademoiselle Amalda has returned for another show.'

The other patrons were surprised but gratified, and clapped. So did the royal party. Amalda sidled into the room from the door at the back. Barefooted, she wore a bolero jacket which did not button across her chest, and sheer harem pantaloons with nothing beneath. Her hair was thick and yellow, spreading past her shoulders; as her eyebrows were black it seemed likely that the hair was dyed, but so thoroughly had the job been done that there was no trace of darkness at the roots even when she began dancing, throwing her head, and her hair, around in the same manner as she threw her extremely voluptuous body.

Unrestrained by the skimpy bolero, her breasts swayed and jumped, hard nipples pointing aggressively at the audience. Billed

21

as a belly dancer, she also rotated her stomach, but she had an additional gimmick in that her pants did not seem to fit properly, and had constantly to be gripped and pulled up to stop them slipping far enough to expose her buttocks and pubic hair, already darkly delineated beneath the thin material. As the audience had seen the act before, and could anticipate the climax, they cheered every hitch.

As Amalda's garb prevented her from pursuing the normal belly dancer's routine of getting close enough to her clientele for them to tuck notes into her waistband, they threw their offerings on to the floor, again in anticipation of her climax, when, dripping sweat, she stopped dancing and dropped to her hands and knees to collect the money, now definitely allowing her pantaloons to slip down her thighs. As she did so, she looked at the royal table, and Karina crooked her finger to beckon her.

Hands filled with notes, Amalda made to stand up, but Karina shook her head. Amalda dropped back to her hands and knees, and approached the table on all fours, breasts swaying to and fro. Karina held out a hundred-dinar note, and Amalda reached for it, but again Karina shook her head. Amalda withdrew her hand and opened her mouth, and Karina placed the note between her teeth. Karina nodded, and

Amalda at last rose to her feet. Her pantaloons gathered around her ankles, and to rapturous applause she stepped out of them, gathered them up, and hurried from the room.

Because of the heat, Captain Farsi had his window rolled down, as did the driver.

'What do you think?' Ahmed asked.

'About her? I think she needs a damn good ram up her ass,' Farsi said disagreeably. He hated having his careful arrangements disrupted on a whim.

Ahmed grinned. 'It will happen.'

'The sooner the better,' Farsi said, and turned his head. 'Do you want something?'

The man stooping beside his window said, 'Yes.' He thrust the elongated barrel of a silenced pistol against Farsi's forehead, and squeezed the trigger. The detective uttered no sound, merely slumped in his seat; his head fell against the rest. The bullet had made only a small entry, but in its exit into the interior of the car had carried with it most of the back of Farsi's head.

Ahmed, who had turned towards his friend, had been shot in the back of the neck by the man standing at *his* window. He fell forward across the detective's knees, but his murderer grasped his shoulders and pulled him upright again. Except to a close look, the two men in the darkened interior

23

appeared to be relaxing.

'Thank you very much,' Farsi's killer said in a loud voice. 'Good night.'

He left the limousine and walked along the street, his companion at his side.

Rosen hurried along Parrot Street. This was narrow and all but deserted, certainly when compared with the crowds on The Thoroughfare. He looked right and left, while trying not to appear too obvious about it, but was still surprised when three people suddenly appeared from the shadows to stand on either side of him.

One of them was a woman. 'What kept you?' she asked.

'I had a slight delay.' He peered at her. She was clearly a Caucasian rather than an Arab, wore a neat blood-red suit over a white blouse, and high-heeled shoes. Her hair, which he knew was long and pale brown, was concealed beneath her matching blood-red turban, and she also wore blood-red gloves. The outfit suggested that she belonged in an upmarket cocktail party rather than on a street. 'What are you doing here?' he asked. 'You were not to be involved until after the snatch.'

'As you say,' she agreed. 'I am to look after our friend. You do not suppose Burke would deliver a beautiful princess into your grubby hands, even for a moment? When she is

24

returned, *if* she is returned, she must be intact.'

Rosen snorted. 'And if she is not to be returned?'

'That would be a different matter. But that is also negative thinking.' She studied her watch. 'Two minutes.'

Rosen looked at the two men. But they were underlings. Sonia was as important as himself. And Sonia ... The adrenaline was still flowing through his arteries; he found himself wondering what it would be like to cut Sonia's throat while her naked backside was pressed against him. He did not even know what her naked backside looked like.

From the front of the nightclub there came a blast of noise.

The entire building shook, and some plaster fell from the ceiling, even in the inner bar.

'What in the name of God...?' Cerise began.

'That was a bomb!' Henri said.

They all turned to look at the princess, who was looking at them, open-mouthed. One of the other women in the room screamed as her companions rose to their feet. A table was knocked over with a crash of shattering glass. The band dropped their instruments and fled to the back of the room, pushing the door open.

'We must get out,' Manfred said, and

actually had the temerity to grasp Karina's arm.

'It can be nothing to do with us,' Karina said. 'Out there.'

'Listen!' Henri said.

For a few moments following the blast, there had been silence from the front of the building. Now there came a series of shrieks and gasps, punctuated by the sound of shots. And the gunfire was coming closer.

The other people got the message, and fled.

'There is a way out the back,' Cerise said. 'We can get to the street.'

'Come *on*, Your Highness,' Manfred shouted, pushing Karina out from behind the table and towards the door.

The others followed, and behind them the door to the lobby crashed open.

Karina looked over her shoulder. 'Bastards!' she shouted. 'When my father—'

'That's her!' said one of the masked men; all three were carrying handguns, but they had stopped firing.

'Quick!' Manfred begged. Now he threw both arms round the princess and half carried her through the doorway into the corridor. This was still full of fleeing people, mostly staff from the kitchen. In their midst was Amalda, unrecognisable in jeans and a shirt. The back door was open, and people flooded out, the royal party bringing up

26

the rear.

On Parrot Street the fleeing people scattered left and right. The street itself was now quite crowded, and immediately outside the door was a car, virtually filling the narrow thoroughfare. Its door was open, but was guarded by a large man who resisted the attempt of anyone to get in by the simple method of pushing them away, as hard as he could. 'Find your own way,' Rosen shouted.

'My limo!' Karina gasped. 'Cerise, call Farsi.'

'This way,' Manfred said, still holding Karina's arm. 'Get away,' he told the people who had suddenly appeared in front of him, then gasped as Sonia thrust a pistol into his waist and squeezed the trigger.

Manfred went straight down, his fingers relaxing in death. Even so he all but took Karina with him, and she fell over his body. But before she could hit the ground Rosen seized her shoulders, dragging her up and thrusting her into the back seat of the car in almost the same movement. She lost her breath and panted as she was pushed against the far door, banging her face, while Sonia and Rosen piled into the car behind her. Then it roared away into the night, horn blaring.

'That was highly successful, don't you think?' Sonia asked Rosen.

'We're not clear yet,' he said. 'How far to the change?'

'Five minutes,' the driver said over his shoulder.

'There,' Sonia commented. 'Listen!'

Behind them sirens wailed and there was a great deal of noise.

'They still have no idea what has happened. And the police will not yet know the princess was even in there.'

Karina snorted.

'Ah,' Sonia said. 'You can speak, then? Up you get.' She grasped Karina's shoulders to lift her and turn her. The princess's hair was dishevelled, and her face was bruised. And she was clearly more furious than afraid. 'A bomb,' she said. 'There was a bomb! You!'

'That made it easy for us.'

'And you shot my friend!'

'He got in the way, darling.'

'I am going to stand in front of you when they cut off your head,' Karina said.

Sonia slapped her face. Karina brought her hands up, but had her wrists grasped by Rosen. 'And you, you bastard,' she said.

'You are a bloodthirsty little girl,' Sonia said. 'We will teach you different.'

Karina spat at her. Sonia's lips drew back in a snarl, and she raised her hand again.

'Do not,' Rosen said. 'Burke does not wish her marked. You said so yourself.'

Sonia lowered her hand. 'And as you said,

28

maybe her daddy won't play ball.'

'My daddy will cut off your head,' Karina threatened again, her tone still filled with anger and outrage.

'All he has to do is sign a piece of paper,' Sonia said, 'and we can all be friends.' She leaned forward, grasped the bodice of Karina's gown, and pulled. The straps round Karina's neck snapped, and the bodice fell down, exposing her breasts. 'Listen, Rosen, would you not like to feel her up? Teach the arrogant little bitch a lesson? I'll hold her arms, and you have a good *feel*.'

Rosen licked his lips, but as he did so the car turned a corner into another darkened street and parked behind another vehicle, alongside which there lounged a man.

'All change,' the driver said.

'You can do it later,' Sonia decided, and opened her door. 'Come along, Your Highness.'

She was outside of the car. Rosen released Karina's wrists, at the same time pushing her towards the opening. Despite her man-handling, Karina still wore her high-heeled shoes; they had straps round her ankle. Now she stamped down on Rosen's foot with all of her strength. He gave a yell of pain and anger, but before he could react Karina was propelling herself forward, leaving the car like a rugby footballer in full charge. Sonia gave a shriek, and then was struck in the

29

stomach by Karina's shoulder, a tremendous blow which winded her and had her sitting on the ground, gasping for breath.

While she was thus defenceless, Karina scooped her dress to her thighs and kicked. The toe of her shoe caught Sonia on the chin, and she fell over, now banging her head on the side of the car.

The driver gave a startled exclamation and tried to reach for Karina, but he in turn tripped over Sonia and landed on his hands and knees. Karina paused long enough to unbutton her shoes and throw them at the other driver, who was coming towards her. While he ducked and stumbled, she ran into the darkness.

'What are you saying?' shouted Yusuf ben Idris, Sultan of Kharram. He seized the police chief by the front of his tunic and shook him to and fro, for all that the startled official was by far the larger man. 'What are you saying? That my daughter has been blown up by a bomb?'

'My poor darling!' cried the sultana, speaking English – as she was inclined to do when under stress. 'Karina!'

Known to her subjects as Our Lady Fatima, the sultana had been born forty years ago, in London, as Vanessa Bland. In her it was possible to discern the beauty she had bequeathed to her daughter; it was difficult

30

to accept that Karina had inherited anything worthwhile – apart from her title and fortune – from her father, who was short and plump, with a round face half concealed beneath his drooping white moustache and beard. It had been Vanessa's looks and languid air of sophistication which, together with the fact that her father was a prominent arms dealer, had first attracted the sultan, and had, in fact, so infatuated him that when he had failed to inveigle her into his harem as a concubine, he had actually proposed marriage.

In seeking to marry an English girl he had not been in the least unique amongst Arab potentates, and his people had approved – the more so as when the marriage had taken place, Kharram had been one of the poorest of the Gulf States, and, although anyone with the least knowledge of world affairs knew that the days when Great Britain might send a gunboat to rescue one of its citizens in distress had long vanished into history, the common people still liked to think that she might maintain an interest in them.

Their affection for their new sultana, if slightly muted when she had given birth to a daughter instead of the required son, had bloomed all over again when, within three years of the wedding, the Big Strike had been made, and Kharram had suddenly found itself in the top ten per capita of any national wealth list. That the money actually all belonged to the sultan had not offended anyone, because Yusuf ben Idris had wisely and quickly ensured that all his people benefited.

He had thus retained his popularity even when he insisted on remaining married to the Englishwoman, despite the fact that not only had she never produced a son and heir, but had indeed borne her lord and master no children after Karina at all; it was not politically correct in Kharram to speculate that the fault might lie in the husband rather than the wife.

Vanessa herself was nowadays regarded with a mixture of distaste by most male Kharramis and affection by most females under thirty. A child of England's swinging sixties, she had grown up in the women's-lib, female-oriented seventies and eighties, and regarded any attempt to suppress her sex's natural instincts as abhorrent. Herself always refusing to wear the yashmak, she had soon had all the young women of Kharram following her lead. She had in fact dragged feminine Kharram into the twentieth, and now the twenty-first, century virtually by their bra straps – not that many Kharrami women ever wore such western garments.

This laissez-faire attitude had applied even more to her only daughter than to herself; it had simply never occurred to her that in so basically contented a community as that of Kharram anyone could possibly bear the royal family any ill. Now she was attempting to reject the very idea. 'But she wasn't in a nightclub at all. She was on her way home.'

'I'm afraid, Your Highness,' the police chief said, 'that the maître d'hôtel at Quadrino's, who escaped both the blast and the subsequent shooting, is positive that the princess was one of a group of young people who entered the club shortly before the outrage.'

'Quadrino's,' Yusuf muttered. 'A den of iniquity. You will close it down, Colonel Bartruf.'

'I do not think it will be in a position to reopen for a very long time, Your Highness.'

'You do not know the bomb was meant for the princess,' Vanessa said. 'It could have been...'

She looked at her husband, eyebrows arched; there had never been a terrorist attack in Kharram.

'Yes,' Yusuf said. 'It was probably some sort of gang warfare. We know that Quadrino's is a den of iniquity. They have offended some gangster...'

'Unfortunately, Your Highness, the princess's limo has been found. Inside it were the bodies of Captain Farsi and Ahmed the driver. Both had been shot through the head.'

'I do not understand,' Yusuf said. 'Her car was found ... but she was not in it?'

Bartruf suppressed a sigh; he could appreciate that his sultan was distraught. 'It seems clear, Highness, if the evidence of the maître d'hôtel is to be believed, that Princess Karina left her car to walk to the nightclub.'

'She did this alone?' Vanessa demanded. 'Was not Cerise with her?'

'We believe she was, Highness. In fact, it seems that Her Highness had five companions, according to the maître d'.'

'And where are they? Are you saying that they are all dead?'

'We do not know, Highness. The work of identifying the bodies is continuing. But—'

'Bodies?' Yusuf muttered.

'There are thirty-seven known dead, Highness. And forty-four have been taken to hospital. Not all the injuries were sustained in the bomb blast. Several have suffered gunshot wounds.'

'Oh my poor darling,' Vanessa muttered. 'Lying there, in the midst of so many dead people...'

'Where is she?' Yusuf demanded. 'May she not be in hospital?'

'She has not yet been identified, Highness, either amongst the dead or the wounded. But, you see...' He licked his lips. 'Not all the bodies *have* been identified. Or will ever be identified, I am afraid.'

'Oh my poor darling,' Vanessa repeated. 'Blown to bits.'

'Well...' Bartruf looked embarrassed.

'What are you doing about it?' Yusuf barked. 'What are you doing here? Why are you not arresting people? You must know who these terrorists are.'

'I felt you should know what happened, Highness. As for the terrorists, it is a matter first of all for our forensic department to examine what they can find of the bomb and endeavour to identify where it might have come from, by whom it might have been made...'

'You do not know who these people are?' Yusuf demanded. 'You, my chief of police, do not know who these people are?'

'Well, Your Highness, there is no record of terrorism in Kharram.'

'Do you not have a record of everyone who enters the country?'

'Yes, we do.'

'Well, on that list you will find the names of the terrorists.'

'Several hundred people enter and leave Kharram every day, Highness.'

'So? Go through those lists, Colonel, and connect with other lists, Interpol...'

'Scotland Yard,' Vanessa said, patriotic to the last.

'Yes, yes, Scotland Yard!'

'Yes, Highness. About the dead...'

'What am I supposed to do about the dead?'

'They are your subjects, Highness. Your people. I think you should visit the scene, express your outrage and your sympathy for the bereaved...'

'The bereaved! You tell me I am one myself.'

'To show yourself, to your people, at such a time...'

'Well...' Yusuf humped his shoulders. 'I suppose if I must...' There was a sudden noise in the hall, and he turned to look at the door. 'What is it?'

The doors were opened by one of the palace footmen, and Cerise stumbled in, falling to her knees on the carpet. 'Highness!'

Yusuf stared at her in consternation. He had last seen Cerise earlier that evening, just before she and Karina had left for the opera. The lady-in-waiting had been the height of chic perfection. Now he looked at a distraught creature, whose hair was a tangled mess, who had lost her shoes, whose dress was torn – she was having to use one hand to keep the bodice in place – and whose face was bruised and blackened. 'What in the name of Allah...?'

Vanessa was on her feet. 'Cerise? What are you doing here?' Her tone suggested that she should be lying dead somewhere.

36

'I came as quickly as I could,' Cerise wailed. 'They hit me, and threw me into the ditch. I was unconscious. People trod on me. It wasn't until a policeman found me...'

Colonel Bartruf knelt beside her. 'You were with the princess?'

Cerise's head jerked up and down. 'Yes. I was with her. Please, could I have something to drink?'

The footman had remained standing just inside the open doors. Yusuf pointed at him. 'Fetch something.'

'Brandy,' Vanessa recommended.

Yusuf cast an anxious glance at the police chief. If it was an ill-kept secret that he and his wife pursued western customs inside the palace, it was nonetheless a secret.

But Bartruf merely nodded. 'The young lady certainly needs something. You say you were with Princess Karina when the bomb went off. Was she hurt?'

'No, no,' Cerise said. 'None of us were hurt by the bomb. We were in the back room. We tried to get out the back of the building, but there were people waiting for us. They took Karina...'

'Took her? What do you mean?'

'Oh, my poor darling!' Vanessa resumed.

The footman reappeared with a silver tray on which there was a goblet of brandy. Cerise grabbed it and drained it at a gulp, the glass clattering against her teeth as her hand shook.

Bartruf looked ready to shake her. 'What do you mean, took her?'

'They put her in a car. Manfred tried to stop them, and one of them shot him. A woman. She shot him, just like that.'

Bartruf raised his head to look questioningly at the sultan. Yusuf looked at his wife.

'Manfred von Dornstein,' Vanessa explained.

'The German ambassador?' Bartruf was aghast.

'His son.'

'Ah.' That was bad, but not as bad as it might have been. The last thing the colonel wanted was for any foreign power to muscle in, start investigating his procedures and, more important, his methods. 'This Herr von Dornstein...?'

'He's dead,' Cerise wailed. 'I told you. The woman shot him. Just like that.'

'And they put the princess in a car?'

'Yes,' Cerise panted, regarding the empty goblet.

'Fetch another,' Yusuf instructed, and stood above the young woman. 'You say they took my daughter away in a car.'

'Oh, my poor darling,' Vanessa commented.

'Then she may still be alive?'

'Well, yes,' Cerise said. 'She was still alive when last I saw her.'

38

'Being driven away in a car.' Yusuf looked at Bartruf. 'My daughter has been kidnapped. Why?'

'They will rape her before they murder her, my poor darling,' Vanessa wailed.

Both Yusuf and Bartruf looked at her impatiently.

'Do you think that is what happened?' Yusuf asked.

'No,' Bartruf said. 'To kidnap a princess is a very serious business, involving the most severe repercussions. To kidnap her simply for, ah, carnal pleasure would be madness.'

'Then tell me why they should do this thing?'

'Well...' Bartruf scratched his head.

'I can tell you why they did it,' Karina said from the doorway.

Everyone stared at her, for she looked even more dishevelled than Cerise, being also barefoot with a torn gown and scattered hair and a bruised face. Unlike Cerise, however, she looked neither afraid nor distraught, but was actually smiling at them. Nor was she making any effort to keep her torn bodice in place; Bartruf found himself gazing at a pair of small but perfectly shaped breasts – he hurriedly averted his eyes.

'Karina!' Vanessa screamed, and launched herself forward.

Karina fielded her easily enough, but

accepted a hug.

'My poor darling! Are you all right?'

'Never felt better.'

'But ... your clothes...?'

'Karina!' Her father replaced her mother. 'What has happened to you? Why are your clothes torn? Why—'

'I have had an adventure,' the princess said, and looked past him. 'Cerise! Are you all right?'

'Yes, Highness. Well, as all right as you are. But...' Cerise looked totally bewildered. 'They took you away!'

'And now I am back. The others?'

'They got away. Except for Manfred.'

'Manfred,' Karina said. 'Yes. He was a hero. He tried to save me, and...' She looked at her parents. 'They shot him.'

'We know,' Yusuf said. 'But you! They put you in a car!'

Karina nodded. 'They were going to transfer me to another car. But I got away.'

'Oh, my poor darling. Did they...?'

'Not really,' Karina said. 'I fought them! I kicked them! It was tremendous!'

'Oh, my poor darling!'

'Weren't you afraid?' Cerise asked.

'Afraid? Why should I be afraid? It was an adventure.'

Her father was concentrating upon essentials. 'You escaped them ... with nothing on?'

40

'Of course I had something on, Daddy. This.'

'You are virtually naked. You have been walking the streets of Kharram, virtually naked. Cover yourself up.'

The footman returned with a tray and the second balloon of brandy. Karina seized it and drained it at a gulp. 'I could do with another of those.'

'Bring two more,' Yusuf commanded, as Cerise was left with an empty outstretched hand.

Colonel Bartruf gallantly took off his tunic to wrap round Karina's shoulders.

'I am sorry, Daddy,' Karina said. 'My dress got torn while I was fighting them.'

'What do you mean, you fought them? You mean they laid hands on you? On the Princess of Kharram?'

'They thumped me about a bit,' Karina explained, and sat on a settee. 'I think they meant to do more, but they never had the time.'

Vanessa sat beside her. 'My poor darling.' She glared at her husband, and his police chief. 'Those thugs laid hands on my daughter. What are you going to do about it?'

'Ah...' Bartruf cleared his throat. 'Can you describe these people, Your Highness?'

'Of course. Two of them, anyway. One was a man, one a woman. Neither was Kharrami.

41

The woman was very good-looking, very well-dressed.'

Bartruf had produced a notebook and was writing.

'She shot Manfred,' Karina said. 'He stepped in front of me to protect me, and she shot him.'

'Oh, my poor darling!'

'You saw her face? Can you describe it?' Bartruf asked, ballpoint pen poised.

'She was Caucasian, good-looking. Sort of pointed features.'

'What colour was her hair?'

'I do not know. She was wearing a turban.'

'You said she was Caucasian,' Yusuf reminded her.

'Yes, Daddy. Caucasian women often wear turbans.'

Yusuf raised his eyebrows. Although he had been married to a Caucasian for very nearly twenty years, he had never become familiar with their way of dress. 'What about her age?'

Karina shrugged. 'Thirty something, maybe.'

'And the man?' Bartruf asked hopefully.

Another shrug. 'Caucasian. Maybe forty. Well built. Quite good-looking. Dark hair.'

'What language did they speak?'

'English.'

'You are saying these people were English?'

'I am saying that they *spoke* English,'

Karina said.

'Were they American?' her father asked.

The second brandies arrived, and again Karina tossed hers off. 'They did not speak with a recognisable American accent. There was no accent at all. But the words they used were English.'

Yusuf looked at Bartruf.

'When you came in, Highness, you said you knew why they did this thing.'

'Yes,' Karina said. 'They wished to kidnap me to make Daddy sign a paper.'

'What paper?'

'They did not tell me.'

Everyone looked at the sultan. Who looked back for several seconds, then snapped his fingers. 'The concession! By Allah! I did not think they would dare go this far.'

'You mean these people were employed by Worldoil?' The police chief was bewildered.

'No, no,' Yusuf said. 'These people are *opposed* to Worldoil. They wish the concession for themselves.'

'Who?'

Yusuf pulled his beard. 'There are three other consortiums in the bidding. But they all surely know I have made up my mind.'

'One of them does not seem prepared to accept it.'

'You mean there are people who would kidnap an innocent young girl for the sake of an oil concession?' Vanessa inquired.

Karina snorted.

'There is a great deal of money at stake,' her husband pointed out.

'Then they will try again,' Bartruf said.

'Oh, my poor darling.' Vanessa once more threw both arms round her daughter, who was starting to look somewhat irritated.

'And the next time,' Bartruf said, 'they might not be so caring about her life.'

Vanessa uttered a shriek.

'There must not be a next time,' the sultan announced.

'The princess will have round-the-clock protection,' Bartruf agreed.

'Doesn't she already have round-the-clock protection?'

'Yes, Sire, she does. But ... may I ask, Your Highness, what you were doing in this night-club?'

'That den of iniquity,' Yusuf put in.

This time Bartruf could not resist a little sigh as he continued, 'When your security guard was seated in your car, several hundred yards away?'

'I told him to stay there. I wanted to enjoy myself. It is not possible to enjoy oneself when Captain Farsi is about.'

'Captain Farsi is now dead, Highness.'

'Oh! I am sorry. How did he come to die? He wasn't involved.'

'He was involved by the simple fact that he was your bodyguard. Someone shot him

44

through the head at point blank range.'

'Oh! Well, as I said, I am very sorry.'

'I have no doubt that his wife and family are even sorrier,' Bartruf said severely.

Karina looked at her father, her expression indicating that not even the police chief had any right to speak to her like that. But Yusuf was also in a censorious mood. 'There are thirty-seven other people dead,' he said.

'Thirty-eight if you include Ahmed the driver,' Bartruf said.

'And Manfred,' Cerise said, starting to cry.

'Are you saying I am responsible for all of those deaths?' Karina demanded.

'Yes, I am saying that,' Yusuf said. 'Had you stayed with your car, retained your out-riders, and come straight home as you had said you were going to do, this would not have happened.'

'It was my *birthday*!' Karina shouted. 'I wanted to have fun!'

Now Vanessa also burst into tears.

'You see, Highness,' Bartruf said placatingly, 'it is impossible for my men to give you the protection you need if you keep going off on your own. Now, if you were to promise...'

Karina glared at him, and then turned to her father. 'Wouldn't the simplest thing be to sign their paper? Worldoil don't *have* to get the concession. These other people might be better.'

'That is absurd,' Yusuf snapped. 'I have

made my decision. Anyway, do you suppose I am going to allow myself to be dictated to by a bunch of thugs? That is no way to run a country. You remember that.'

'You would prefer me to be killed,' Karina riposted, 'when they try again.'

'It must not happen again,' Yusuf declared. 'It will not happen again.'

Karina's glare turned into a look of alarm. She was well aware that her father, for all his cuddly, roly-poly exterior, could be quite ruthless. 'What are you going to do?' Vanessa asked, equally concerned; she even stopped crying.

'Arrange things,' Yusuf said. He snapped his fingers at the waiting footman. 'Get me Sir William Bland on the phone. He lives in England.'

The Squad

Breath coming in great gasps, the woman staggered up the hill, mud-stained trainers splashing through the wet earth. Mud also flecked her red tracksuit, within which she was as wet as the steady drizzle outside. But the end was in sight. From the top of the slight rise she could see the Land Rover waiting on the road that ran through the next shallow valley. She splashed down the slope, the rain continuing to settle on her yellow hair, plastering it to her scalp and neck. The straight hair, which she wore shoulder-length when it was dry, combined with her piquant features, her five feet four inches of height, and her trim figure to make her appear at least ten years younger than she was. In fact, Jessica Jones was thirty-five, and jogs like this, while necessary to maintain the full fitness required of her job, often left her wondering why she still did it.

She panted up to the car, unlocked the door, reached for the thermos of orange juice, and realised that her mobile, which she had left on the seat, was ringing. She picked it up. 'Yes?'

'Sergeant Jones?' It was a woman's voice, somewhat severe.

'Yes.'

The woman listened to the heavy breathing. 'Are you all right?'

'I'm fine,' Jessica said. 'Just a little short of breath.'

'Are you alone?' The voice became suspicious.

'Yes, I am alone,' Jessica said wearily.

'Very good. The commander wishes to see you.'

'This happens to be Sunday, Mrs Norton. My day off.'

'This is an emergency.'

'Sh ... oot. When?'

'Immediately.'

Jessica scratched her wet head. 'What exactly does that mean?'

'What I said. Now.'

'I see. Well, it can't be for three hours.'

'Three? Are you joking?'

'I'm afraid not. I happen to be in the wildest part of Essex. I now have to drive into town and get changed before I can come down to the Yard.'

'I will tell him that you will be here at twelve o'clock.'

Jessica looked at her watch; it was just past ten. 'Can't be done.'

'Yes it can, Sergeant Jones. If you skip going to your flat to get changed. Twelve o'clock sharp.' The phone went dead before Jessica had the time to blow her a raspberry.

Jessica did have a towel to use on her hair, and on her body when she took off her track-suit in the back of the Rover. She also had a dry suit to change into, although her under-wear remained uncomfortably damp, and she did what she could with her comb. But she still felt an utter mess as she drove towards London as rapidly as she could. Not that she supposed it was going to matter what she looked like. In the commander's mind she was Sergeant Jones, one of his best people. She had never been sure he even understood that she was a woman.

She preferred not to consider what emergency might have arisen for him to require her presence so urgently; she had learned long ago that attempting to anticipate what might next be thrown at her was the fast track to the psychiatrist's office.

Scotland Yard wore its usual air of bustling efficiency, which was not always exemplified by results. As Jessica was well known within the hallowed precincts, her appearance in a tracksuit and dirty shoes, with untidy hair and the odd fleck of mud still visible on her face, did not cause undue comment – until she reached the Special Branch and the commander's outer office. There his secretary gave a double take. 'Sergeant Jones?'

'You said I was to come as I was,' Jessica explained.

'But what on earth were you doing?'

'Keeping fit. Don't you ever keep fit?'

Mrs Norton looked down her nose. Fitness was not part of her remit. She thumbed her intercom. 'Sergeant Jones is here.'

'About time,' Commander Adams growled. 'Send her in.'

'Good luck,' Mrs Norton suggested.

Jessica drew a deep breath, knocked, and entered the inner office, as she did so gazing at the heavily built man with the lantern jaw behind the desk. She often felt that Commander Adams had got where he was because he looked the part rather than on account of any outstanding talent. But he was there, and he was her boss, and he had to be accepted as such. 'Good morning, sir.'

'Is it? What on earth have you been doing?'

'Running twenty miles, sir. Keeping fit. I would have changed, but I was told not to.'

'Yes. Hm.' He looked at his leather-upholstered armchairs, as if wondering if he dared risk allowing her to sit in one. 'This is Sir William Bland.'

Jessica turned. She had not noticed the other man in the room. Now she gazed at someone who was hardly less imposing, as regards the heavy shoulders and lantern-jawed stakes, than the commander, although he was clearly several years older. There was also something vaguely familiar about the name, although she could not immediately place it. 'Sir William!' She held out her hand.

Sir William Bland looked at it somewhat distastefully, then glanced at the commander. 'Sergeant Jones is one of our top people,' Adams said. 'As she has explained, she has come straight from the training field.'

Bland took Jessica's hand, reluctantly. 'And she is your recommendation?'

'There is no one better suited.'

Jessica began to feel vaguely alarmed. She instinctively felt it would be an unpleasant

50

experience to get too close to this man.

'Sergeant Jones,' Adams went on, 'is not only an expert in protection, but is also highly trained in all aspects of intelligence and counter-intelligence. She has even trained with, and spent some time working with, the SAS.' Jessica almost blushed; the commander was not given to such fulsome praise. At least he had not gone completely overboard and claimed that she was also highly successful at her job, which would have been a downright lie in view of some of her more recent disasters, even if none had been her fault and she had emerged from each one with enhanced credit.

'Then I will take your word for it,' Bland said, and sat down.

Jessica glanced at her boss, received a quick nod, and seated herself also – in one of the precious armchairs. Adams sat behind his desk. 'I am assigning you to the protection of Sir William's granddaughter,' he said.

Jessica could not prevent her eyebrows from rising. As Adams could see. 'Her name is Princess Karina of Kharram,' he explained. 'And she is the sole heir to Sultan Yusuf.'

Jessica looked at Bland. 'She is coming to England on a visit,' Sir William said. 'And will be accompanied, in the first instance, by her mother, the sultana. My daughter,' he added, to cross the last T.

Jessica shifted her gaze back to her boss.

'The matter has been cleared with the Home Secretary,' Adams said. 'Sultan Yusuf would have liked to send his own people with her, but he has been persuaded not to do this. Sir William understands that we cannot have trigger-happy Arabs roaming the streets. In their place, the Home Secretary has agreed that we should provide round-the-clock protection. You will pick a team of four, including yourself. In view of the princess's, ah, well, of Arab views on women, all of your team will have to be women.'

'Yes, sir. May I ask what sort of timescale is involved here?'

Adams looked at Bland. 'It may be for some time.'

Jessica sighed. Tom was due back from an overseas assignment in a couple of days, and she had hoped for some time together, especially as she had a birthday coming up. But there was another consideration. 'Then I will have to recruit a double team, sir. My people cannot be expected to work round the clock, day in and day out, for an indefinite period without relief.'

Once again Adams looked at Bland. 'If you are worried about the cost,' Sir William said, 'do not be. The Government of Kharram will bear all expenses.'

'Very good,' Adams said. 'You may recruit a back-up team, Jones.'

'Thank you, sir.'

'There is the other matter,' Bland said.

'Yes,' Adams said. 'What Sir William wishes you to know, Jones, is that this is not an ordinary protection assignment. The princess is coming to this country because she has recently been the object of a kidnapping attempt in Kharram.'

'For that reason,' Bland said, 'she is travelling incognito and in secret. Her name will be Karen Smith, and she is accompanied by her mother, Vanessa Smith. Her real identity is to be revealed to no one, not even the members of your team.'

Jessica gave him an old-fashioned look. She was starting to remember where she had heard his name before. 'Are you suggesting, Sir William, that my team cannot be trusted?'

'No, no,' he backtracked hastily. 'But a single careless word...'

'The point is, JJ,' the commander said, using her office nickname to placate her, 'that while the would-be kidnappers appear to have wanted the princess alive, they do not appear to have had the same consideration for anyone else. The kidnap attempt cost forty lives.'

'Forty!' Jessica was aghast.

'They used a bomb to distract attention.'

'Good lord!'

'Does this information frighten you?' Bland asked.

'Frighten me? It appals me.'

'Well...' He looked at Adams.

'It will not distract Sergeant Jones from her duty,' Adams said. 'She is well acquainted with bombs. In fact, only a year ago she was blown up by one. Fortunately, she wasn't seriously hurt.'

Bland was looking increasingly sceptical.

'However, sir, I am sure you will appreciate that I cannot ask any of my people to undertake any duty which may involve risk to their lives without putting them in the whole picture,' Jessica said.

'Absolutely,' Adams agreed. 'I'm afraid we will have to leave it to Sergeant Jones' discretion to decide just how much her team needs to know, Sir William. I may say that I have the utmost confidence in her judgement.'

Bland snorted. But he said, 'Very well. Princess Karina and her mother arrive this afternoon at six o'clock. I will meet you at Stansted.'

'Six o'clock?' Jessica asked in dismay. 'This afternoon?'

'Does this disturb you?'

'It's a bit short notice. Certainly when it comes to recruiting a team.'

'But we'll manage,' Adams assured his client.

'There's a heck of a lot I need to know,' Jessica protested.

Bland raised his eyebrows.

'As for instance, where the princess will be staying. The place will need to be inspected, and the management and staff interviewed.'

'My granddaughter will not be staying at an hotel,' Bland said. 'She will be staying at my country home, at Liphook in Hampshire, where my staff will look after her. With your assistance, of course.'

It was all Jessica could do to prevent herself from pulling a face. Because that meant...

Sir William seemed able to read her mind. 'I have arranged live-in accommodation for yourself and your, ah, ladies.'

'And with the princess...?'

'There will be her mother, my daughter,' he felt it necessary to repeat, 'and a lady-in-waiting.'

'Will there be any other guests in the house?'

'No.'

'Will you be there?'

'Of course.' He frowned at her. 'Do you object?'

'It's your house, Sir William. However, I will still need to inspect the place, thoroughly,' Jessica insisted. 'I don't see how I am going to fit all that in by six o'clock.'

'I'm sure you'll manage, JJ,' Adams said.

Jessica gave him a glare, and Bland decided to leave them to it. 'Well, six o'clock sharp. I assume you will be properly dressed?'

'If you mean will I be in uniform, Sir William, the answer is no. That would be self-defeating as regards protection. But I will be properly dressed.'

'Do you carry arms?'

Jessica looked at Adams, unsure how he would like her to answer that. 'Sergeant Jones is armed when on duty,' the commander said. 'And is both a first-class shot and licensed to kill, if necessary, to protect the life of her subject.'

Sir William looked Jessica up and down. 'I am sure she is very highly trained,' he agreed. 'But has she ever had to use her training? Have you, for instance, ever shot at a man, Sergeant Jones?'

'I have never shot *at* a man, Sir William,' Jessica said. 'But I have shot a man. More than one.'

Sir William looked at Adams, and received a reassuring smile. Another long look, then Sir William said, 'Stansted, six o'clock,' and left the room.

'Would I be right in recalling that he is Sir William Bland the arms dealer?' Jessica asked.

'That is correct,' Adams said.

'And wasn't he done a few years back for illegally exporting arms to Afghan terrorists?'

56

'He was charged,' the commander said carefully. 'But never convicted. The case collapsed. It all happened long before this recent business blew up.'

'And isn't he the Sir William Bland who was once charged with inflicting GBH on a prostitute?'

'He is.'

'But again, he escaped conviction.'

'That case also collapsed for lack of evidence. It was the woman's word against Sir William's, and it turned out, firstly, that she did not bring the charge until after she had discovered that Sir William was a millionaire, and secondly, that she was into S&M and permitted it from all of her clients. Do I denote a suggestion of antagonism?'

'I can't say he is one of my favourite people.'

'But you will not let that opinion interfere with your job, I hope.'

'I'd appreciate some more background, sir. I am assuming that there is an Afghan, or at least, a fundamentalist terrorist link?'

'Apparently there isn't. This appears to be an old-fashioned crime for gain.' Adams rested his elbows on his desk. 'You are probably aware that about fourteen years ago, Kharram became oil-rich, like so many of its neighbours. The preliminary test drilling was carried out by Worldoil, and as this proved positive, Worldoil did a deal with the sultan and was given a concession to drill and develop any oil found in the country for a period of twelve years. Neither side then had any idea how things were going to turn out. But of course, as you know, the deposit beneath Kharram has proved an absolute bonanza; the whole country appears to be sitting on a vast lake of oil. Now the concession comes up for grabs again this year. Everyone anticipates that the sultan will renew the Worldoil rights, but it hasn't actually happened yet, and there is an awful lot of loot at stake. So three other big oil companies have submitted competing bids. This is perfectly normal and straightforward. However, the concept of kidnapping the sultan's only daughter to influence his final choice is another matter.'

'Do we have any idea which of the three rival companies might be behind this?'

'No, we do not. On the face of it, they are all global concerns and strictly on the up and up. But in this day and age, who knows what is on the up and up and what isn't?'

'Well, do we have anything on the people who tried to carry this out? Surely the Kharrami police must have some thoughts?'

'We need to remember that it is only about ten years since Kharram has been dragged, kicking and screaming, into the twentieth century, never mind the twenty-first. Before then, it lived in rather the eighteenth. A lot of the credit for this must go to the sultana, Bland's daughter, who has had a big role in the modernising of the state. When you meet her, don't be taken in by her fluttery help-me-I'm-only-a-frightened-woman act. Our information is that she is every bit as tough as her dad, and as prepared to bend the rules – and that's saying a lot. And of course, as with all modernisers, she has trodden on quite a few toes, especially in the region of fundamentalist religion. Unfortunately, there is little evidence that she has had much effect on the Kharrami concept of law and order. This is still very fundamental. If you're caught stealing, you have your hand chopped off. If a woman is caught in adultery, she is stoned to death...'

'What happens to the man?'

'He gets a good wigging. It's still a man's world out there, I'm sorry to say.'

'And if you're caught taking a drink, you get eighty lashes, or whatever.'

'Not so, remarkably. This is one area where the sultana has had an influence. I gather she rather likes a drink herself, and so does her husband. Drinking is permitted in Kharram, as long as it is done strictly in private. We are straying from the point. Police methods. As I say, they are primitive. They don't have a special branch. I'm not even sure any of their police have received training in modern methods of detection. Certainly there has not been, up to now, any screening of visitors. However, we do have one piece of information that may be useful: the villains were not local.'

'How do we know that?'

'Because this princess was able to describe two of her kidnappers, and she said they were Caucasian. And, incidentally, they spoke English.'

'You mean they didn't drop a bag over her head, and they weren't masked? *And* they chatted her up? That sounds a bit careless.'

'It does. But we need to remember that, careless or not, they still blew up some forty people. And I have no doubt that they thought they were dealing with a cosseted eighteen-year-old princess who would collapse in sheer terror if attacked.'

'And she didn't.'

'She seems to have waded into them hip and thigh. You want to bear in mind that she is definitely what might be called feisty.'

'Mummy's girl. You'll be telling me next that, again like her mother, she likes a drink.'

'She does.'

'Shit. If you'll pardon me, sir. Don't tell me she's on the needle as well?'

'I have no information on that. But I wouldn't be too surprised if she sniffs.'

'You are making my day, sir. What do I do about that?'

'Nothing. No matter what disguise she

may be using, she is still virtually a visiting head of state. Your job is to protect the young lady's physical health. Not her morals.'

'Not even if they get in the way of her physical health?'

'She will have her mother with her, at least for a while. Perhaps you could have a heart-to-heart with her.'

'If you say so, sir. Now, this house. I assume it is large, rambling, and is in its own grounds.'

Adams pushed an envelope across his desk. 'There is a complete set of plans. There is also a full report on what happened in Kharram.'

'Plans are not half as much use as an inspection. And I am not being allowed the time for that.'

'I appreciate that. But I know you'll do the best you can.'

Jessica stood up. 'Very good, sir. I had better get on with it. Just let me get the essentials straight. The princess and her mother are coming here in secret. Can I count on that?'

'God knows. I have no idea what kind of security obtains in Kharram, but once she gets here, she's incognito.'

'Therefore we cannot be sure whether or not the people who tried to nab her in Kharram will know that she's done a bunk. Or where she's done a bunk to.'

'We must hope not. I would imagine the kidnappers, having let her slip through their fingers, almost literally, will be keeping a very low profile. I mean, if the Kharramis chop off the hand of anyone caught stealing, and stone adulterous women to death, trying to think what they might do to someone caught trying to kidnap their princess rather makes the imagination boggle.'

'It rather stimulates mine,' Jessica said. 'However, it would make my business a lot easier if I had some idea who we are dealing with.'

'*May* be dealing with,' Adams pointed out. 'We have no evidence to suggest that they will try again.'

'With respect, sir, I have never heard of any terrorist, or group of terrorists, who will blow up forty people to achieve their objective, and then, having failed to achieve that objective, will simply walk away.'

Adams stroked his chin.

'Equally, sir, the Kharramis must feel that she is still in danger, or they would not have got her out of the country so quickly.'

'That's true. But surely, by reacting so quickly and so positively, the Kharramis have spiked the opposition's guns.'

'They will not stay spiked for very long, sir. Not after forty deaths. There is too much at stake.'

'Well, I suppose you may be right, although

I sincerely hope you are not. But even if you are, I don't see what more we can do about it save watch the girl. We have absolutely nothing to go on, unless the Kharrami police turn something up, and I wouldn't hold my breath on that.'

'Again with respect, sir, I think we can do some spadework on our own. The fact that these people spoke English suggests some link with this country. And then we have their MO. I'd like to have sufficient computer time made available to see if we can turn something up. I will certainly get the princess to make up an identikit picture of the people she was close to, as soon as she arrives.'

'Well, all right. Tell Superintendent Moran to assign one of his people. You can refer him to me, if you have to.'

'Thank you, sir. One last thing: what about Summerby?'

'Well, you're off that, of course. Does he need a lot of cover?'

'Not really. Once he's in that mansion of his he's secure. We're only required when he goes out.'

Adams nodded. 'I'll have Manley put in a replacement for you. You can also use Manley for replacing the other members of your team. I'll put him in the picture. Good luck.'

Jessica had an idea she was going to need it.

She drove out to her flat, which was in Clapham. It was not ideal, and was not in an ideal location, but she and Tom had had to abandon their previous home in the Docklands when they had become too closely involved with the international terrorist organisation commanded by her old enemy Korman. That business, which had required her to join the SAS on a temporary basis and undergo that unit's horrendous but worthwhile training schedule, had been responsible for her promotion to sergeant, as she had been regarded as the principal cause of its being brought to a successful conclusion. But the success had been purchased at a high cost, not only in the life of more than one of her colleagues and the ending of the career of at least one more, but in her own psyche, not to mention her relationship with Tom.

It was Tom who had introduced her to the protection arm of the Special Branch, when she had been a disillusioned detective-constable following the ending of her marriage. After that it had seemed natural for them to become partners. They liked each other, and they were good in bed together. Or perhaps the words to use were *had been* good in bed together. But the fact was that the word 'love' was very seldom mentioned in their relationship, and although as she grew older she from time to time felt extremely broody, neither had the word 'marriage'. And she had to admit, if only to herself, that she could not see herself married to Tom. Maybe she was just unlucky with men.

But the Korman business had left its mark in more ways than she cared to admit. She was quite sure that she had not lost her nerve in the slightest degree. When she held a weapon, her hand was as steady as a rock, and if she had not had to face a life-threatening situation since Korman's death, she did not doubt that she could do so with her habitual calm. But yet, after being ambushed by Korman's people in her own home, she still hated entering the empty flat.

Slowly she climbed the stairs to the first floor. The building, in the middle of the day, was so quiet it could have been empty; she suspected most of the other residents were out to Sunday lunch or in a pub. She unlocked the door, having to do it twice, as the lock was a double; even a policeman's flat, certainly when it was not known to be a policeman's flat, was as likely to become a victim of the current crime culture as anyone else's.

She pushed the door in. With the rain still falling from a dark sky, the hall was gloomy, and terribly empty. She longed for a dog, or even a cat, to keep her company, but with both Tom and herself likely to be away for days on end, and at very short notice, the idea was quite impractical.

She closed the door behind herself, and looked at the mail she hadn't had a chance to read. There were the usual irrelevancies, mostly for Tom, but one envelope was addressed to her, in a neatly sloping hand. It was a hand she had seen before, although for the moment she couldn't place it.

Her whole body, damp and chill, was crying out for a hot tub, but she supposed it would have to wait. She sat at her desk in the small lounge and punched a telephone number, then booted her computer, while absently slitting the envelope. 'Hi, Andie. JJ. What are you on?' She listened. 'Well, I want you to call Superintendent Manley, and tell him I need you. I need Chloe as well.' She knew the two women shared a flat. 'Yes, I do know it's Sunday. Don't tell me you've been to church. And the same to you. No, I can't tell you what it's about, but I can tell you it'll take up most of the next few weeks ... You never said a truer word. Listen, you and Chloe come here at two o'clock this afternoon and I'll put you in the picture. Okay, half past. But not a minute after; we don't have any time to waste. See you.'

She replaced the phone, and found herself staring at the sheet of paper that had slipped from the envelope. *As Tuesday is your birthday, how about meeting for a drink, just for old times' sake. Call me. B.*

Jessica's first reaction was, of all the goddamned cheek! And he obviously hadn't changed a bit, the bastard. Call me! Still giving orders.

But she had a feeling that she was going to be alone on her birthday, save maybe for one or two of the girls ... supposing they could take time off their assignment. And in those circumstances, an ex-husband was better than no one. Besides, she was curious as to what he might be like now, after seven years; she had not expected ever to see him or hear from him again. Of course, if by any chance Tom were to get back in time ... but she didn't think there was too much possibility of that.

How the hell had he got her address?

She called Louise. Older than and senior to both Andrea and Chloe, Louise, always so calm and cool, at least when on duty, was the natural second-in-command for a job like this. Unfortunately, her domestic life was even more of a disaster than Jessica's had once been – at least in Jessica's opinion – and on this occasion she got the dreadful Jerry.

'How should I know where she is?' he demanded, aggressive as ever. 'You should know that better than me.'

'Well, I don't. Sorry to have bothered you.' She used Louise's mobile number instead, something she was usually reluctant to do, just in case her friend might actually be on a job at the moment. But she got through quickly enough.

'Two thirty?' Louise asked. 'Oh, good. That means I won't have time to go home for lunch.'

'Trouble?'

'Just one of his moods. See you.'

Jessica turned on the water, made it as hot as she could stand, added bath salts, and sank into it. Nothing had ever felt so good. She knew she should be thinking of how best to go about the new assignment, but could not stop herself thinking about Brian.

The divorce had been both messy and, she supposed with hindsight, unnecessary. Seven years ago she had been young enough and romantic enough to suppose that when one loved, one did so for ever and to the exclusion of all else. To come home early after a long day at the office and find Brian naked in her bed with their downstairs neighbour had caused an explosion, and by the time she had simmered down the business had got out of hand, with lawyers already involved.

The unpleasantness had arisen over the settlement, involving such things as possession of the flat. All very infantile, looked at from a perspective of seven years and a great deal of experience. And from a realisation, suddenly brought back to her by the letter, that Brian had been far more her sort in bed than Tom was. A fact of which he was undoubtedly aware, even if he was unaware of Tom's existence. Still, to see him again...

She washed her hair, dried herself and put on a dressing gown, sat with her hair dryer while she read the report Adams had given her – becoming more concerned with every page – then made herself a microwave lunch, and, while she ate it, called Superintendent Moran. 'Sergeant Jones, sir.'

'JJ!' They had always got on very well. But even if he was in his office, he felt obliged to point out, 'You do know today is Sunday?'

'Yes, sir. But it won't keep till tomorrow.'

'Problem?'

'Info, sir.'

'Tell me.'

'I'm looking for someone who may have operated in, or out of, England, and who speaks the language fluently. He will be a bomber, and an utterly ruthless destroyer, of both life and property, who may also have indulged in kidnapping for gain, but on somebody else's behalf. In fact, I would say all his work is contractual. He will employ a team. And he will have some links to big business.'

'Hm,' Moran said. 'But you are not saying that he is necessarily English.'

'No, sir. Only that, as he uses English, he

could have some links here. He may also have been in and out of the Gulf State of Kharram, probably over the past couple of years, and more especially, the past few days.'

'Now really, JJ, are you asking me to find someone going in and out of a foreign country without even a name? Do you know if this character started from here?'

'No, sir, I do not. But if you can come up with a name, or even several names, it would narrow the search, wouldn't it?'

'It is still going to take one hell of a lot of time. You're sure this is an urgent matter?'

'Commander Adams suggested you might like to call him about that, sir.'

'I see.'

'I would also hope to provide you with some identikit pictures in a day or two.'

'Of our man?'

'I don't think so. But of two of his people. You may be able to trace them.'

'You do that, Sergeant,' Moran said, his tone considerably less warm than when the conversation had started.

Jessica sighed. But she had more immediate problems of her own.

'I know this is absurdly short notice,' she said, surveying the faces in front of her in her lounge. 'But that is the nature of the beast. Obviously, it is also top secret, but as

I know you all keep up with the news, I also know you will figure it out for yourselves quickly enough. However, we are working on the premise that no one outside the immediate Kharrami palace circle will have any idea that Karen Smith is actually Princess Karina.'

'How big is this palace circle?' Chloe asked. Short and plump, with habitually scattered fair hair and vivaciously ugly features, and what many of her superiors considered far too large a bust measurement for a policewoman, she was, Jessica knew, a bundle of often unsuppressed energy.

'That is an imponderable,' Jessica replied.

'In other words...' Andrea suggested. In complete contrast to her flatmate, she was tall and slender from the top of her immaculately brushed auburn hair, which she wore long and past her shoulders when not in uniform, past her handsome, mostly immobile features, all the way down to her elegantly long legs, which were presently encased in boots.

'Quite,' Jessica agreed. 'But this is what we are going to assume, until it is proved otherwise. We have another problem; she will be staying at her grandfather's home in the country. Well, in darkest Hampshire. This is apparently built on the lines of a fortress, with both entry and exit covered by security cameras and the lot. Not to mention

71

guard dogs.'

'Sounds like a piece of cake,' Louise opined. Dark-haired and serious, with attractively plain features, she looked, as always, entirely relaxed, whatever her problems at home. 'And they need four of us?'

'One must always be on call, and there will be occasions when a back-up is necessary. The point is that while the princess may be as safe as houses when she's in the house, she is not going to stay there, and her movements are apparently unpredictable. She has a penchant for what she considers a good time, and this seems to lie in the direction of nightclubs and the like.'

'I like nightclubs,' Chloe said enthusiastically.

'I'll bear that in mind. Now ... weapons.'

The operatives were allowed to indulge their personal taste in guns, providing they were not conspicuous. Louise, predictably, took from her shoulder bag a Browning nine millimetre pistol. Many regarded this as both unnecessarily heavy and old-fashioned, but it carried a thirteen-shot magazine and had an undoubted man-stopping capability at a considerable range. Andrea preferred a Glock Model Seventeen semi-automatic, which, if lacking the range and power of the Browning, actually had a seventeen-shot magazine and the great virtue of being extremely light, owing to its mainly plastic body. Chloe used a Walther PPK. It was not a weapon of which Jessica approved, as, although it was small and light and easily concealed, it was not really a man-stopper and had only a seven-shot magazine, but she knew Chloe was very good with it. She herself preferred a Czech-made Skorpion blow-back machine pistol, which she considered combined all the best aspects of the others. Unloaded, it weighed just over a kilo, carried either a ten- or a twenty-round magazine – she usually used the ten for reasons of weight – and would stop a man at seventy-five metres.

She inspected each of the other weapons herself, making sure they were in perfect working order before moving on to the next item in her agenda. 'Buzzers.' Each wore, on her wrist next to her watch, a pager, operating over a very short range, but which would immediately alert their back-up.

'You really think we are going to need these?' Louise asked.

'It is possible. There is something I think you should know,' Jessica said. 'The characters who attempted to kidnap the princess in Kharram didn't care who got hurt. Purely to distract attention, so far as we know, and have her running for her life, they detonated a bomb in the nightclub where she happened to be, following which they invaded the premises with automatic weapons. As a

73

result of these tactics, something like forty people were killed. They are still not certain of the exact number. However, one of the dead was a member of her own party, *not* a bodyguard, while two others were policemen, who *were* the princess's security guards. They were shot at close range while they waited in their car. The evidence – the fact that their guns were still holstered and that none of the passers-by had any idea what had happened – indicates that they were murdered in the coldest of blood.'

The three women gulped.

'And seeing as how,' Jessica went on, 'in this country we are not allowed to shoot first and ask questions later, I think we need to approach this job with the greatest of care.'

'Just to kill forty people ... all for money?' Chloe asked.

'All for money,' Jessica agreed, and looked at her watch. 'Fifteen forty-five. Now, I have to get out to Stansted. Louise, I want you three to go down to Blandlock – that's the name of the house – and familiarise yourselves with the place. I mean, every nook and cranny. You'll also need to suss out the staff. They know you are coming, and Sir William assures me that they have all been with him for years and are absolutely trustworthy, but I'd like that checked out. I'll take over from you when I arrive with the official party, some time after six.'

'What about Sir William?' Andrea asked.

'He is as nasty a piece of work as you will ever meet,' Jessica said. 'But you'll have to put up with him. Try to avoid getting into a position where you have to wind up slapping his face. Anyway, for a start he'll be at the airport with me, so you won't have any problems this afternoon.'

'If he is a nasty piece of work,' Louise said, 'then...'

'We don't know that. I am informed that the princess's mother, Bland's daughter, is a very tough egg, although she does not give that impression on first sight. But she may also be a very nice person. Let's work on that theory. Right. Let's move. Louise, will you make up a roster, beginning at six this evening? We want the usual six-six-six-three-three, so we don't always work the same shift.'

'For how long?' Louise asked.

'Make it for a week. I'll organise a second squad for the next week, then it's us again. I told you, it's a long job. Now, as I said, I'll take the first watch, six until midnight. To avoid disrupting the household, my replacement will have to come in early; I shall be spending the night. I'm told they're preparing accommodation for us, Louise. Perhaps you'd check that out as well.'

Jessica closed the door behind them, then

75

packed her shoulder and overnight bags, adding a parka in view of the weather. Then she sat in front of the computer; on his letterhead Brian had included his e-mail address.

Correctly, she should just ignore the letter. But that would only lead to more letters. And the fact was...

She calculated. She was on duty from six to midnight tonight. On the basis of her instructions to Louise, her next spell would be three to six tomorrow, Monday, and noon to three on Tuesday, her birthday, following which she would be off-duty until six o'clock on Wednesday morning. That certainly gave her time to have a drink on Tuesday evening, providing she got to bed early. And alone?

Curiosity, she told herself. Just curiosity. But irresistible. Anyway, she could not afford to have anything on her mind right now.

She typed, *I'll be in the King's Head at seven Tuesday evening,* hesitated a moment, then pressed Send.

Burke replaced the phone and surveyed the four people standing before his desk. 'He is not amused,' he said. 'Neither am I. I have never heard of such a total fuck-up. You had the girl in the car with you. You were within seconds of making the transfer. There were four of you. And you let her get away.'

His tone remained quiet, unemotional, but

was the more frightening for that. He was a slender, precise man, who dressed carefully and neatly. Rosen had never seen him not wearing a suit with a carefully knotted, quiet tie. The precision extended to his features, somewhat aquiline in a long face, and his dark hair neatly parted on the left, smoothly brushed. He spoke English flawlessly, and had an Irish name, but Rosen would not have bet that either was his nationality. But he was well known in the international underworld, as a man who took on commissions, recruited a first-rate team, and carried out whatever assignment he had accepted. If he was known to be expensive, he was also known to pay very well, which is why he was served by the best. There was no record of his failing to succeed before, thus Rosen, who had worked for him on two previous occasions, did not know how he intended to react.

He glanced at Sonia, who was standing beside him. He had not worked with her before, although they had met when Burke was recruiting his team, and he did not know if she had a previous acquaintance with their employer. He had assumed she was to be a back-up, to come into the picture after the princess had been safely secured. Now he had not yet made up his mind about the way she had handled herself, the almost careless manner in which she had shot the princess's

friend. That might indicate utter ruthless-
ness, or utter panic, or simply a desire to
prove herself to the men on her team. But
that she was both good-looking and sexy
could not be argued. At the moment,
although she did not actually look frightened, she was definitely apprehensive, while
the two drivers were endeavouring to be as
anonymous as possible. They definitely intended to leave the explanations to him. 'She
took us by surprise,' he said.

'An eighteen-year-old girl.'

'That is all the information I was given, Mr
Burke,' Rosen said. 'No one told me that she
would react like a tigress.'

'What did you do to her to make her react
like that? Or say to her?'

'Nothing,' Rosen said. 'She just reacted
when she realised she was being kidnapped.'

Burke regarded him for several moments.
'A tigress,' he said at last, and looked at
Sonia. 'I was told that you can be a tigress,
Madame Solere.'

For a moment Sonia certainly looked like a
tigress. But her voice was quiet. 'We were
handicapped by your instructions, Mr
Burke.' Burke raised his eyebrows. 'You said
that she was not to be harmed, or even
tarnished, in any way,' Sonia accused. 'This
meant that we could not ... *convince* her that
she should obey us. In any event, I thought
Mr Rosen had her under control. I did not

know that he had let her go.'

The bitch, Rosen thought. He had an urgent desire to hit her. But perhaps his time would come.

Burke regarded her in turn for some moments, then he said, 'I'm afraid that you will have to share the responsibility. And the fact is that we have had a miserable, and possibly costly, failure. We have stirred up the entire country, as if it were an ants' nest we have carelessly probed with a stick. Forty people are dead, and, as everyone in this benighted land seems to be related to every-one else, we have several million grieving relatives calling for our heads.' He looked over their faces. 'Or other parts of our bodies. The only good thing about the disaster is that it does not yet appear that the media, or anyone else, have linked the bomb explosion and the deaths to the princess. Her name has not yet been mentioned. And we know that very few people knew she was in Quadrino's when it went up.'

'Perhaps she is dead,' said one of the drivers eagerly.

'If she is dead, then we are in deeper shit than ever,' Burke told him. 'But she is not dead. As she was alive when she escaped from you, we may be certain that she is still alive, and is back at the palace by now. I am awaiting confirmation of that from our people there. And the event will be traced

79

back to her soon enough. First of all because of the deaths of her two bodyguards, who were assassinated quite separately from the bombing. And secondly, because of the death of the German ambassador's son. May I ask who shot him?'

He looked at Rosen, but Rosen kept his mouth shut. If Sonia wanted to paddle her own canoe, then she would have to get on with it.

'I shot him,' Sonia said.

'Why?'

'He was between me and the princess. He deliberately stepped in front of her.'

'You had a gun in your hand. Could you not just have struck him on the head?'

'That would have meant stepping against him. He might have grappled with me.'

'And you do not like grappling with men.'

'He might have disarranged my clothing.'

'Of course.'

'In any event, how can they connect the death of one foreign tourist with the princess?' Sonia demanded.

'I would say they have already done so, as his father will have known he was attending her birthday party. I imagine the palace already knows of it. That was another botched job. The princess's other friends had accompanied her. If you were going to kill one, you should have killed them all. Now I am faced with the problem of what to do with you.'

For the first time Rosen and Sonia looked at each other, realising that they might be in some danger.

'As you made no effort to conceal yourselves,' Burke went on, 'the princess will undoubtedly be able both to describe you and identify you.'

'We were not told to conceal our faces,' Sonia said, prepared to be defiant.

'I know,' Burke conceded. 'That was my fault. Like you, I could not imagine you not succeeding. The question is, what is to be done now? Our principal, as I have said, is unhappy with the situation. He sought a termination of our contract, but as we are on a no-win, no-pay basis I talked him out of that. However, we have now only a matter of a week to complete our task, because at the end of that time the fresh concession will be signed and our principal will have lost. So will we. Unfortunately...' he gave a little sigh. 'I do not see how I can continue to employ you, if the princess, and through her the police, can identify you.'

'You must get us out of the country,' Rosen said. He hadn't told Burke about the prostitute, but there was always the chance, when her body was found, that someone had seen him, and then her, go into the alleyway ... and only him come out.

'Yes,' Burke said thoughtfully. His tele-

81

phone rang, and he picked it up. 'Yes?' He listened. 'That is very interesting. Thank you very much, Mustafa. You have done very well. Go to the usual place tomorrow morning and there will be a present for you.' He replaced the phone, carefully, while his employees held their breaths. 'That was my man in the palace,' Burke said. 'He tells me that, at dawn this morning, Princess Karina and her mother left the palace, very secretly, with none of the usual guards of honour and fanfares. You may not have succeeded in kidnapping the princess, but you certainly seem to have frightened her, or at least her father and mother.'

'Where can she have gone?' Rosen asked.

'She went to the international airport.'

'Then she is lost to us,' Sonia said. 'She could be going any place in the world. Unless you have an agent at the airport to tell us which flight she caught.'

'She will have taken her father's private jet.'

'But we still do not know her destination.'

'I think we do,' Burke said. 'The princess has left her father's palace in a great hurry, only six hours after an attempt was made to kidnap her. One could say that she has fled. She has taken with her only her mother and one of her ladies, a woman called Cerise Mahliah. The security guards who accompanied her to the airport have now returned to the palace; it is from them that Mustafa discovered what had happened. The plane took off at ten o'clock. As I have said, this bears all the earmarks of a flight, and there simply has not been time for the sultan to have arranged any kind of safe haven for her in any other country – with one exception. I would say it is absolutely certain that the princess has been taken to England, by her mother, whose home it is. In any event, I would hope to have confirmation of this very shortly.'

'How?' Sonia asked.

'Mustafa has arranged it.'

Sonia looked puzzled. If Mustafa had only just found out that the princess had left the country, and, unlike Burke, had not yet worked out where she was going, how could he have arranged for someone in England to tell him when she arrived?

Rosen was more inclined to concentrate on essentials, and looked at his watch. 'And she took off at ten? She will almost be there by now. So she is still lost to us. Great Britain is a big country.'

'Save that, as I have said, there has not been time for the sultan to have been able to arrange any secure hiding place for her, again, with one exception. She has gone with her mother. Thus they will have gone to the home of her grandfather, the arms dealer, Sir William Bland. That can have been arranged by a simple telephone call. I could say that, in panicking, the young lady has played right into our hands. A private house? What more could we ask? Thus I am prepared to give you a second chance.' He glanced from face to face. 'Both of you. All we need to do is get you out of the country.'

'How?' Sonia asked.

'You will leave by car. You will have to be concealed, but that will merely be uncomfortable, not dangerous.'

Sonia made a face.

'Once you are across the border, tomorrow morning, you will fly out to England.'

'We have no cover,' Rosen said.

'You do not need cover. No one knows who you are. You will simply fly into England as tourists. I assume you both have passports with valid English visas? Very good. Make sure that your flight goes into Heathrow. You will be met by Loman. You remember Loman?' He again looked from face to face. Both Rosen and Sonia nodded. 'Well, I can tell you that *he* is entirely reliable. I will get in touch with him and put him in the picture by the time your plane lands.'

'And?' Sonia asked.

'You regain possession of the young lady.'

'Just like that?'

'You'll be assisted. Loman will fill you in.'

'It will be difficult to get her out of the country,' Rosen said.

'You do not have to get her out of the country. Loman will organise a safe place for her to be kept. All we have to do is possess her, and make sure Yusuf knows this.'

'She will have security,' Rosen pointed out.

'Once you have reconnoitred the situation, and made your plans, you have carte blanche to deal with her security.'

'Even if they are Special Branch?'

'I shouldn't think that will be likely,' Burke said. 'But even if they are, they are only policemen. Flesh and blood. And as I said, you will have assistance, if you feel that you need it. Just tell Loman what you require. But I intend to be there myself. I do not intend to have any more fuck-ups. Make your plans, but do nothing until I join you.'

'And the princess?' Sonia inquired.

'I do not think we need worry any longer if she is harmed. We just want her long enough to make her father do as we wish,' Burke said.

'I would like a private word,' Sonia said.

Burke raised his eyebrows, but he waved the men from the room. Rosen hesitated, concerned, but then he obeyed his boss.

'Well?'

'I would like Rosen replaced.'

'He has offended you?'

'I do not like the way he looks at me.'

'Has he made advances?'

'He would not dare.'

85

'Well, then…'

'But he looks at me. He strips me naked with his eyes.'

'As long as it is only with his eyes…'

'He gives me the creeps. Would you like to have someone strip you naked with their eyes?'

'That would depend on the someone,' Burke said, suggesting that he might not object if it happened to be her.

'And he is incompetent,' Sonia said. 'He let the girl go. We had her, and he let her go. I'm not certain that it wasn't an act of treachery.'

Burke glanced at the midday newspaper lying on his desk. The entire first four pages were filled with headlines and photographs of the bomb outrage, although no one had yet apparently linked it with the princess, nor, it seemed, did anyone know that she had left the country. But on the middle page there was a very brief item concerning the discovery of the body of a woman, lying in an alley with her throat cut. She had been a prostitute, and no one seemed to have considered her death, in such a place and at such a time, to be anything more than coincidence. Burke did not believe in coincidences. The alley where the body had been found was only a stone's throw from the nightclub, and he knew of Rosen's penchant for using a knife.

Rosen had not reported the incident. He

86

was solely concerned with the job he was given, and was the more valuable for that. His deadly single-mindedness had to be an asset. While, as far as Burke was concerned, this bitch had only hearsay to recommend her.

'And I am quite sure you are wrong,' he said. 'He was careless, perhaps, but nothing more than that.'

'I still think he should be replaced. I wish him replaced.'

Burke studied her. 'How many times have you worked for me, Sonia?'

'This is the first.'

'And so far it has not turned out very well, has it?'

'Are you accusing me...?'

'I am stating a fact. Rosen has worked for me on two previous occasions, with success every time. He will not be replaced. He will, in fact, take command of this second phase.'

Sonia stared at him. Burke smiled. 'And you will work with him, and obey him. And if he wishes to get his hand into your knickers, you will smile and enjoy it.'

'And if I refuse? If I resign?'

'You cannot resign,' Burke told her. 'You are on a contract, and you know too much.'

'Are you threatening me?'

'No,' Burke said equably. 'I am warning you. You came to me with the highest credentials, Sonia. I was told you were the ideal person to handle this young woman. Well, so far I have seen nothing to convince me that you are. It is up to you to prove it to me. So you will go to England, and you will assist Rosen in getting hold of the princess. Once you have done that, you may amuse yourself with her, until her papa signs that paper.'

Sonia drew a sharp breath. 'And then?'

Burke smiled. 'Then we will reconsider the situation. I may even let you kill her. But you have to get hold of her, first. You will enjoy that, won't you, Sonia?'

Sonia's tongue came out and circled her lips.

The Fugitives

'Well,' Sir William commented, 'I really would not have recognised you, Sergeant Jones.'

'Thank you, Sir William,' Jessica said. She had left her car and travelled by train, as she assumed she would be riding shotgun, as it were, from the moment the princess touched down, and was wearing her favourite working outfit, which consisted of a dark blue trouser suit over a white shirt, with crêpe-soled black low-heeled shoes. This enabled her both to look attractive – the more so now that her hair was dried and brushed – and to be at her most mobile, if she needed to be. Her Skorpion was invisible in her shoulder bag; her overnight bag and parka waited on a chair. 'But I think you should drop the sergeant.' They were in the VIP lounge, and there were only a couple of other people near them, but she believed in being careful.

'Absolutely,' he agreed. 'So, do I call you Jessie?'

'Miss Jones will do, sir. No one calls me Jessie.'

'Point taken. And where do you keep your gun? In your knickers?'

'I don't think you want to find that out, sir,' Jessica said, realising that this was going to be an even more difficult assignment than she had feared. She gave a sigh of relief as the hostess left her desk to approach them.

'The private Kharrami jet is landing now, Sir William.'

'Excellent. Where can we meet it?'

'We will send a minibus to bring the passengers to the terminal building, sir.'

Bland looked at Jessica. 'I think we should accompany the bus,' Jessica said.

'I'm afraid that will not be possible, madam. You are not authorised to enter a prohibited area.'

Jessica felt in her inside breast pocket, and took out her card wallet, flipping it open.

The woman looked at it, and gulped. 'Is it a criminal matter?'

'Not yet,' Jessica told her.

The woman telephoned her superior, and got a clearance; he had been informed of the situation by Commander Adams. Five minutes later Jessica and Bland were being driven across various taxiways and waiting areas to park in the shade of some trees and watch the executive jet glide to a halt at the end of a subsidiary runway half a mile away.

'You handled that very well,' Sir William said. 'You could grow on me.'

'It is my business to handle things well, sir,' Jessica said, eyeballing him.

A customs van arrived, and this led the way to halt beside the aircraft. The steps were already down and a hostess wearing the smart Kharrami gear of green jacket over white pants, with a small white peaked cap, was standing in the doorway. 'Sir William Bland?' she asked in English.

Bland was already out of the bus and striding forward. 'That's me.'

Jessica followed. She supposed that at this moment her charge, and therefore herself, were as safe as they were going to be for the next couple of weeks, although she was still tensed, her gaze sweeping the perimeter fence nearly a mile away. But now she watch-ed the passengers descending the steps. The sultana came first, slightly overweight but still a very handsome woman, her size accentuated, to Jessica's surprise – she had expected a haik, or at least a kaftan – by her flowing flowered dress, worn short enough to reveal her still very good legs. Jessica reflected that Arab men were supposed to prefer a bit of weight on their women, and reminded herself of what Adams had told her – that the sultana was the most liberated of women and enjoyed proving it wherever possible.

Thus Princess Karina had a way to go, for she was very slender, in her case also accentuated by her equally surprising clothes, for she wore jeans and a shirt, and as she was also not very tall she could be described as tiny, certainly when compared with her mother. Even more to her surprise, Karina's black hair was cut short, but fluttering in the breeze it framed her heart-shaped face and her quite exquisite if heavily made-up features. The woman behind her was quite definitely an Arab. Taller than the princess, and identically dressed, her jeans and shirt indicated a full figure, and her black hair, surrounding heavy although handsome features, was long and luxurious. Again to Jessica's surprise, all three women were bare-headed.

'Daddy!' the sultana cried incongruously, throwing both arms round her father for a hug and a kiss. 'Oh, I'm so glad to be here.'

'I should think you are,' Sir William agreed, disengaging himself to greet his granddaughter. 'Great Scott, but you have grown!' Jessica had to wonder when last he had seen her. The princess accepted a hug and a kiss, although her expression revealed no great pleasure at his embrace. 'And this is...?' Sir William looked at Cerise, obviously liking what he was seeing.

'Cerise,' Karina explained. Jessica liked the sound of her voice.

Sir William threw both arms round Cerise, to her obvious embarrassment. But now Vanessa was looking at Jessica, somewhat suspiciously. 'This is Miss Jones,' Sir William explained. 'Actually, she is Detective-Sergeant Jones, of the Special Branch.'

'A policeman?' Vanessa looked alarmed.

'Police*woman*,' Sir William corrected. 'She is here to protect you. I have arranged round-the-clock protection for you.'

'She doesn't look like a policeman,' Vanessa remarked. 'She's too small. And too young.'

As if I wasn't actually here, Jessica thought, preparing to dislike her as much as she did her father, although she supposed her last remark was something of a compliment. 'I am assured that her hidden talents are prodigious,' Sir William said.

As Vanessa was showing no inclination to shake hands, Karina stepped forward, arm

92

outstretched. 'Hi,' she said. 'I'm Karina.'

Jessica squeezed the proffered fingers, noting as she did so the several very expensive rings as well as the watch. 'I think you mean Karen,' she suggested.

'Spot on,' the princess agreed. 'I must try to remember. Do I call you sergeant?'

'Her name is Jessica,' Sir William said. 'We don't want to broadcast the fact that she is a policeman.'

'But my friends call me JJ,' Jessica said.

'Great.' Karina gave Jessica's fingers another squeeze. 'This is Cerise.'

Cerise shook hands.

'Can we leave now?' Vanessa asked.

Sir William looked at Jessica, and Jessica looked at the customs officer, who had been waiting patiently. 'I assume you ladies have nothing to declare,' he said.

'Do we look as if we have?' Vanessa demanded, determined to be aggressive.

'Just a formality, Your Highness.'

He turned to his colleague. 'May I see your passports, please?' the immigration officer requested.

'Passports?' Vanessa inquired.

'These ladies are travelling under diplomatic immunity,' Sir William said. 'Were you not informed?'

'I was informed that they had diplomatic immunity, sir. Nothing was said about their not having passports.'

'Well, what do you propose to do? Send them back? Then you'll have a diplomatic crisis on your hands.'

The immigration officer looked at Jessica, who showed him her wallet. 'I think you will find this has been cleared with the Home Office,' she said. 'And of course, Sir William will take full responsibility for these ladies while they are in this country. Won't you, Sir William?'

'Well, certainly.'

'The responsibility is yours, Sergeant,' the immigration officer said, handing Jessica back her wallet. 'You may leave now.'

Vanessa snorted at the suggestion that Jessica was in command. 'What cheek,' she remarked as the officers drove off. 'I hope you intend to report him, Daddy.'

'Ah...' Sir William looked at Jessica.

'They were only doing their jobs, Highness,' Jessica said. 'We have a lot of difficulty with illegal immigrants in this country.'

'Are you suggesting that I am an illegal immigrant? Or the princess? I was born in London.'

'Then you have every right to be here. But I'm afraid, technically, this does not apply to either the princess or her lady-in-waiting. Therefore someone has to take responsibility for them. But as long as they are in the care of Sir William and myself, there should not be a problem.'

Vanessa gave another snort, but she led the way to the bus. 'We're not going home in this, I hope?' she asked.

'You'll drive us to the short-term car park,' Sir William said.

The driver glanced at Jessica, seated beside him, and she nodded. He then spoke into his radio, and received confirmation from his office. 'Big job,' he muttered.

'Just an extra five minutes,' Jessica said.

The princess was seated immediately behind her. Now she said, 'Don't you have a gun? You should have a gun.'

'Oh, she does,' her grandfather said.

'Show it to me,' Karina commanded.

'Not here,' Jessica said. She couldn't see Karina's face, but from the sudden silence she gathered the princess was not pleased. The job was growing more difficult by the moment; up till now Karina had seemed quite friendly. But a few minutes later they were at the car park, outside of which a Rolls waited. The driver was a rather typical chauffeur, heavily built and featured, and wearing a green uniform; he left the wheel to help the bus driver unload the bags and Jessica's gear and pack them into the boot. 'I assume this gentleman has been with you for some time,' Jessica said softly, standing beside Sir William.

'Five years. My God, you don't suppose—'

'It's my business to cover every possibility.'

'But five years...'

'Anyone can be suborned.'

'But no one can even know my daughter and granddaughter are here yet.'

'I wouldn't count on that, either,' Jessica told him.

The drive to Blandlock was long, owing to heavy traffic, but was thankfully uneventful. Jessica sat in front beside the driver, whose name was Parkin, and who had a pleasant manner to belie his somewhat grim exterior. There was a partition, but she yet overheard some of the conversation in the back, which dealt mainly with the horrific events of the previous night. What she heard did not make her any fonder of her clients, as there was not a word of sorrow for the forty dead victims, except for the German ambassador's son, who had apparently died heroically trying to save the princess. She also gathered that, while Karina had been educated mainly in England, she had gone to finishing school in Switzerland, and so it was three years since she had last been here.

But Blandlock was every bit as much of a proposition as she had feared it would be. Anything less like the fortress she had been promised in the specification given to her by Adams could not be imagined. Set back from the road, surrounded by trees, it was not even properly fenced; there was only a low wall. While the building itself was large and rambling, a quick glance indicated to Jessica that it probably had at least a dozen exterior doors. Even the reputedly fierce dogs, a pair of Dobermans, appeared more anxious to lick her hand than bite her.

'Actually, there are fourteen exterior doors,' Louise said, having waited for her. Once she had been introduced – she apparently matched Vanessa's concept of a policewoman far more than Jessica did – she took the team leader on a guided tour of the house. Jessica became more and more concerned with every step. Apart from the many entries and exits, which in several places gave access to clearly seldom used hallways, and which, although locked, would not hold up a competent burglar for five minutes, once inside the house she discovered a perfect rabbit warren of corridors and staircases, all softly carpeted to drown the sound of any footsteps. 'What about all these security cameras?' she asked.

'There are a few. But four of the five I've inspected don't have any film.'

'Shit!'

'An assassin's gold mine,' Louise agreed.

'Or even a kidnapper's. She can't stay here. Unless he's prepared to pay for a team of at least twenty.'

Louise wrinkled her nose. 'Even if he is, do

97

we have the manpower?'

'No. So like I said...'

They were on the second floor, and Louise opened a door. 'This is ours.'

The room was quite large, and comfortably furnished as a sitting room. A door on the far side gave access to a small bedroom and a bathroom. The bed was a single, but one of the pair on night duty would always be up. 'And the princess?' Jessica asked.

'Right below us.'

'That's not a hell of a lot of good.'

'It's the best I could do. Maybe you'll have more clout. Ah, Mrs Harley. This is Sergeant Jones, who is in charge. Mrs Harley is the housekeeper.'

Mrs Harley was looking hot and bothered; she had clearly spent the last half-hour in Vanessa's company. She was, Jessica estimated, in her middle forties, and was an extraordinarily good-looking woman, with fine features, curly red hair, and a considerable bust, amply displayed by her somewhat tight-fitting black dress – it had to be supposed that she had been handpicked for the job by Sir William, and that, until the arrival of her employer's daughter, she had ruled the domestic roost. Jessica wondered if that meant more problems for her. Mrs Harley's voice matched her appearance, neat and well modulated. 'I hope everything is to your satisfaction, Sergeant?'

'Actually, it isn't, I'm afraid.' Mrs Harley raised her eyebrows. She was clearly not used to being confronted, and to have it happen twice in the space of an hour was more than she was prepared to accept. 'To do our job properly, you see,' Jessica explained as winningly as she could, 'we need to be at least on the same floor as the princess, and preferably in an adjacent room.'

'That is not possible,' Mrs Harley said. 'The princess's bedroom is situated between that of her mother and that of Sir William. These were his instructions. I was under the impression that you would use this room simply for changing, and, ah ... It has its own bathroom.'

'And guarding the princess?'

'Well, you could sit in a chair in the corridor outside her room.'

Jessica concluded that the woman had watched too many bad Hollywood movies. 'There is also the matter of the security cameras.'

'What is the matter with them?'

'When last were they used?'

'They're switched on every night.'

'I meant, when last was their film looked at?'

'I have no idea. There has been no reason to.'

'Well, if you'd care to look now, you'll see

that most of them have no film in them.'

'Good lord!'

'So, how soon can this be rectified?'

'Well, tomorrow, I suppose. If the man can come tomorrow.'

'Then that will have to do.'

'Perhaps you would have dinner with me,' Mrs Harley suggested, seeking to defuse any incipient crisis, 'and we can discuss it.'

'That would be very nice, thank you. All right, Louise, thanks for everything. Who's my partner?'

'Andie. I thought it best if you and I were first and third.'

'What time does she report?'

'She said after dinner. Is that okay?'

Jessica nodded. 'Well, I'll see you in the funnies.'

Louise opened the door, and encountered Karina. 'Your Highness.'

'Karen,' Karina said. 'Are you one of them?'

'I prefer to think of myself as one of *us* ... Karen.'

'How many are there, of us?'

'Four.'

'Well, I guess I'll meet them all in time.' She entered the room, and looked at Mrs Harley.

'I hope nothing is wrong, Highness?'

'Miss,' Karina reminded her. 'Nothing is wrong at the moment, Harley. I just wish to have a word with the sergeant.'

'Of course.' Mrs Harley glanced at Jessica, then followed Louise out of the room.

'So...' Karina threw herself into a chair. 'You're the boss woman, right?'

'Right,' Jessica agreed. She didn't want the princess, or anyone else, to be in any doubt about that.

Karina thrust her fingers into her short hair. 'You like?'

'Ah ... very cool.'

'I think it stinks. Mummy's idea. People associate the Princess of Kharram with long hair. So now I'm disguised ... *she* thinks.'

'Every little helps. It'll grow.'

Karina snorted. 'So, tell me.'

'What would you like to know?'

'You're supposed to be protecting me, right? From those guys who tried to get me in Kharram?'

'From anyone.' Jessica sat beside her. 'But they would appear to head the list.'

'You know what they did?'

'I'd like to hear it from your lips.'

'Shit! They blew up a whole nightclub. Just to get at me.'

'That must have been terrifying.'

Just for a moment, Karina looked puzzled. 'You know, it wasn't. I don't remember being afraid. I wanted to take the bastards on.' She grinned. 'And I did.'

'So I've heard. Very successfully. But the

101

next time – if there *is* a next time – they'll know you're not the type to lie down. Then the going may really get rough.'

'They wanted me alive.'

Jessica nodded. 'That does make it a bit easier. We don't have to consider things like a bullet from a distance.'

'It's just a job to you, eh?'

'That's how it has to be, Princess. But it's a job I know how to do. And incidentally, if it's any relief to you, it's a job in which I'm required to lay my life on the line to protect yours.'

Karina studied her for several seconds. 'How do you feel about that?'

'Simply that it's my business to make sure that neither of us gets hurt.'

'You reckon? Do you know how many guys were involved?'

'Do you?'

'No. But there must have been a hell of a lot. And one woman. Now *she* frightened me.'

'Why her, in particular?'

'Well, I saw her shoot a man, one of my best friends, just like that. Absolutely in cold blood.'

'Sounds nasty.'

'But more than that. There was something about her ... ugh.'

'I'd like to get one of our experts down here tomorrow, and have you do an identikit picture of her. And of the bloke.'

'Is that relevant? They don't know where I am.'

'I have an idea that they may be able to find out.'

'Shit! I thought I was safe here.'

'It's our business to make sure that you are. But I'd like a few adjustments.'

'Shoot.'

'It is quite impossible to make a place like this safe unless we employ the Brigade of Guards. The house is too easy to get into, too impossible to patrol. The grounds are totally exposed.'

'So?'

'I'd like you to move out, to one of our safe houses, where we can take proper care of you.'

'Say, I'd like that.' Her face fell. 'Mummy would never agree.'

'I'll have to persuade her.'

Karina shook her head. 'You'll never do that. She doesn't like you.'

'She doesn't know me.'

'Makes no difference. She forms instant opinions about people, and they never change.'

'Hm. Well then, you'll have to do it. I'll have a go at your grandad.'

Karina continued to look sceptical. Then she brightened. 'Show me your gun.'

It was important to keep this young

woman on her side. Jessica got up, opened her shoulder bag, and took out the Skorpion.

'Let me see.'

Jessica made sure the safety catch was on, and handed her the weapon.

'It's so light,' Karina said. 'Will it kill somebody?'

'Yes.'

'How many shots does it have?'

'It has ten in the box. But when necessary I carry a spare box.'

'And you can extend the butt...' said Karina, doing so.

'That gives you extra accuracy,' Jessica said.

'What sort of range?'

'Effectively, say seventy-five metres.'

'That doesn't sound very far.'

'It's for defence, not attack.'

'Have you ever fired it?'

'Of course.'

'I meant, in anger.'

'We don't ever fire in anger, Your Highness. But I have fired it in the line of duty.'

'I wish *I* had one of these. Don't you think I should have one?'

'No,' Jessica said, and took the gun back.

Karina stood up. 'Will you be coming with me tomorrow?'

'Tomorrow?'

'When I go shopping.'

'You wish to go shopping tomorrow?'

'Of course. As I am in England, I wish to go shopping. I wish to go to Harrods, for a start. And then Cartier.'

'Won't it keep? Until next week?'

'Why should it keep until next week?'

'Well, as I told you, Your Highness, I'm not altogether happy with the situation here. I think we should sort that out first, before you start doing the rounds.'

'But if you don't think I'm safe here, won't I be safer in London?' There was certainly some logic to that. 'You'll be telling me next,' Karina said, 'that I can't go to a nightclub.'

'A nightclub?'

'That's what I like to do, go to nightclubs.'

'Ah! But to do that, you need an escort.'

'I'll get Grandpa to arrange that. And one for Cerise. And one for you, if you like.'

'How nice of you. When were you planning to do this?'

'As soon as Grandpa can fix me up with a date. Tomorrow night.'

'The best night to go to a nightclub is Saturday,' Jessica said, desperately attempting to buy time.

'That's six days away.'

'You'll be surprised how quickly time passes.'

'Hm. We'll have to talk about it. But you

will be with me tomorrow morning?'

'No. I'll be off duty. If you do intend to go shopping tomorrow you'll have Louise. That's the woman you met just now.'

Karina's insistence on shopping created another problem: if this girl went up to town tomorrow, she would probably want to stay out for lunch, which meant there would have to be a switch.

'Oh, yes. Is she as good as you?'

'You don't know how good I am,' Jessica said absently.

'That's true. I have to dress for dinner. Seems we wear long frocks. Have you got one?'

'Not with me,' Jessica said. 'But I'm dining with the staff.'

Actually, it was only Mrs Harley, although the small dining room was well furnished, and the cutlery was silver. 'How long have you been with Sir William?' Jessica asked. She was not just making conversation.

'Oh, six years,' Mrs Harley said. 'Ever since Lady Bland died. But do call me Barbara. And you are...?'

'Jessica. But please call me JJ. What's he like to work for?'

Barbara raised her eyebrows at the directness of the question. 'I find him very congenial.' Jessica tried to remember if either of the court cases had been less than six years ago; she couldn't be sure. 'How long are *you* going to be working for him?' Barbara countered. 'Wine?'

'No, thanks – I'm on duty. I'm not working for Sir William. I am working for the Government, and by secondment, I suppose, for the Government of Kharram. You do know why I'm here?'

'Someone tried to bump off the princess.'

'Close. It was a kidnapping attempt. But they blew away a lot of people trying to get to her. How many of your staff know about it?'

'Sir William said it had to be a secret, so I haven't told anyone.'

'Good. What's the arrangement with the dogs?'

'They're locked up at night. Otherwise they bark and keep everybody awake.'

'Aren't you double-glazed?'

'Yes. But they're loud dogs.'

'Still, I'd like that reversed. They're probably the best protection we have, if only because of the noise they'll make.'

Barbara drank some wine. 'I'll have to ask Sir William.'

'I'd like you to do that.'

'Tonight?'

Jessica considered. It was already past nine, and she supposed this was the safest night of all; no one outside the family circle could possibly know as yet that the princess was in residence. 'Tomorrow will do. I assume you have a gardening staff?'

'Four.'

'Well, I wonder if you could ask them to report anything unusual, either in the grounds or just outside them. I'm thinking especially about footprints which shouldn't be there, or people who shouldn't be there either.'

'They'll wonder why.'

'Tell them it's been reported by the police that there have been several burglaries in this area, and you're just being careful.'

'All right. But ... do you really think those Kharrami thugs will dare follow the princess here?'

'Our information is that they weren't Kharramis,' Jessica said. 'And I think they may well be able to track her down to this house, given enough time.' She didn't add that, before they could have enough time, she proposed to have Karina out of here and into a proper safe house.

'So how much time are we talking about?' Barbara inquired.

'From your point of view, just as long as the princess chooses to remain here.'

Barbara drank some more wine.

Jessica visited the drawing room after dinner, after she was sure that the family had also finished their meal. They were seated to either side of a roaring fire, drinking brandy. Sir William wore black tie, and the women were in evening gowns and dripped jewellery. 'JJ!' Karina shouted. 'Come in and have a drink.'

Her mother snorted, but Sir William gestured towards the decanter on the sideboard.

'Thank you, but I won't.'

'On duty, eh?' Sir William said.

'That is absolutely right, Sir William. I wonder if I might have a word.'

'Any time,' he said expansively.

'In private, sir?' She wondered if she was wasting her time, in view of the amount he had obviously had to drink already. But she felt that he might actually be more amenable when in a relaxed mood, and there was no real indication that he was drunk.

'Why not?' He heaved himself to his feet. The sultana gave another sniff. Jessica followed Sir William through a door on the far side of the drawing room, across a hallway which she had not yet encountered – she wondered how many of these there were in this house – and into a book-lined study.

'Sure you won't change your mind?' He gestured at another sideboard, where there was another brandy decanter and several balloon glasses.

'No, sir.'

'Well, I hope you won't mind if I do. Sit.' Jessica chose a rather straight-backed small settee to one side of the desk. To her dismay, Sir William sat beside her. 'Problem?'

'Several.'

'So?'

'This place is indefensible.'

'You think so? What about my Dobermans?'

'They happen to be locked up.'

'Ah. Good thinking. You want me to let them out?'

'Tomorrow will do.'

'Right. That make you happy?'

'Not enough. Even with your dogs loose, this house is too easy to get into. I think we should get the princess out of here.'

'To go where?'

'A safe house of our own, where we can more properly look after her.'

'Her mother will never agree.'

'She's your daughter. Can't you insist?'

'You got any children, JJ?'

'No, sir.'

He peered at her. 'You ever been married?'

'I have been married.'

'And it didn't work out, eh? The fellow must have been mad. Anyway, I can tell you, in this modern day and age, insisting on anything with one's children is counter productive. Especially when she happens to be a queen.'

'Thank you.' Jessica stood up. 'Well, Sir William, if you won't co-operate, I feel obliged to inform my superiors that I cannot guarantee the safety of your granddaughter. Or anyone near her. That includes you.'

'They'll kick your ass. You can't walk away from a job like this.'

'Whatever I do depends on what I am told to do. But I must paint the picture as I see it. I cannot expose my team to a hiding for nothing.'

'You're a bumptious little bitch, aren't you? Your team, are they all as good-looking as you?'

'I've never thought about it. I'll say good-night.' She stooped to pick up her shoulder bag, but Sir William seized her wrist, pulling her down so that she fell, on her stomach, across his lap. It happened so suddenly, and with so little warning, that for a moment she didn't react; she was in any event winded. And she was across his knees. Before she could move, his hand was releasing the waistband of her pants and pulling them down her thighs, and at the same time digging his fingers into the elastic of her briefs to pull them down as well.

'What you need,' he said, 'is a good spanking. I've wanted to do this since the moment I saw you.'

Jessica did not waste the time cursing at him. She was still holding her shoulder bag, and this she swung over her head. The Skorpion might be lightweight as regards firearms, but inside the bag it still made an effective cosh. Sir William gasped as it landed on his forehead, and Jessica was able to roll away from his hands and his lap and land on the floor.

'You bitch!' he said. 'You attacked me.'

Jessica got to her knees and pulled up her briefs and pants, then reached her feet, straightening her jacket and getting her breathing under control. 'And I will attack you again, if you ever try something like that again.'

'I shall report this.'

'Snap.' She went to the door.

'Where are you going?'

'To resume my duties of guarding your granddaughter, Sir William.'

'You going to tell her about this?'

'Not unless I have to,' Jessica said, and closed the door behind herself.

Now she really did feel like a drink. Instead she went up to the apartment she had been allotted and sat there, seething, for some time. She didn't suppose she would report Sir William's assault. Those misfortunes went with the job, and had to be dealt with on a personal level. But she certainly did intend to report that, if the people who had carelessly blown up a nightclub in Kharram tried their luck at Blandlock, she didn't think she could stop them, not unless she could

112

have all her team on duty at once, and that would mean a huge back-up ... which the department didn't have. The commander would simply have to give Sir William – and, if necessary, the sultana – an ultimatum: if you want the princess protected, you must play it our way. That would also remove herself, and the others, from any risk of being assaulted by this dirty old man.

She gave a start of alarm when there was a knock on her door. If that bastard had followed her up here ... But it was Andrea, looking as casually elegant as always, even when wearing a shirt and jeans with her inevitable knee-length boots, and carrying an overnight bag. 'You look as if you've seen a ghost.'

'Sorry. You gave me a start. I never heard the car.'

'It's blowing a bit. Some pile.' She prowled around the room. 'Not too bad. Mind if I turn in?'

Jessica looked at her watch; it was just gone ten. But Andrea, she knew, could fall asleep at the snap of a finger. 'Help yourself. I'm going to have a look around.'

She left the apartment and walked the corridors. The family had gone to bed; she presumed the women, at least, were dog-tired after their ordeal of the previous night. In the kitchen the staff was putting away the last of the crockery and cutlery. They seemed happy enough to see her, even if they obviously didn't know what she was doing there, although they correctly assumed that she was some kind of security guard employed by the princess. They would have to be put in the picture soon enough; as she gathered that they all slept in, when they came down tomorrow morning they would find a new face in their midst.

She was still hoping to have things sorted out by tomorrow evening, but she was becoming less and less satisfied with her current situation. 'Did you see the young lady who just arrived?' she asked at large.

'I let her in,' one of the footmen said.

'Why?'

'Well, she rang the back doorbell.'

'So you let her in. Do you always admit anyone who rings the bell?'

'She said she was one of your lot.'

'Did you ask to see her credentials?'

'Never thought of it. *Isn't* she one of your lot?'

'Yes. But she might not have been.'

Jessica went in search of the housekeeper, but Barbara was not to be seen; she had apparently gone to bed.

She unlocked one of the side doors and went outside. It was a splendid night, but equally a bad one from a security point of view. As Andrea had said, there was a fresh breeze blowing, which not only had the trees whipping to and fro with quite a noise, but was also scudding the clouds across the sky and the moon, alternating areas of brightness with others of extreme darkness. From the pen she could hear the dogs barking, but she didn't think that could have any significance at the moment.

Her muscles tensed as she suddenly saw a light, but then she realised that it was a car's headlights; the road was apparently closer than she had thought.

She watched the lights until they were out of sight, then went back inside and up the stairs to the third floor, disturbed by her agitation, which had nothing to do with Sir William's behaviour. If she had been on umpteen protection assignments before, they had always been properly organised, with time to suss out the surroundings, to arrange things, to take control. Here the control was lacking; she had been pitchforked into an uncontrollable situation. Well, that had to be put right – tomorrow.

At the top of the stairs she encountered Barbara, wearing a dressing gown and with her hair in a plait. 'Oh,' the housekeeper said, embarrassed. 'I didn't know you'd still be about.'

'I'm not here to sleep,' Jessica pointed out.

'Oh. Yes, I suppose not. Well...'

'You may find that he is in a bad mood,' Jessica said.

Barbara, just starting to go down the stairs, checked and turned, cheeks pink. 'I have no idea what you are talking about.'

'Just thought you'd like to know.' Jessica looked at her watch; it was half past eleven. 'By the way, what time do you surface?'

'About seven, as a rule.'

'There'll be a replacement coming in at six.'

'Oh. The gates will still be locked.'

'Who's in charge of them?'

'Parkin, the chauffeur.'

One of the few members of this household she actually liked. 'And what time does he wake up?'

'I'm afraid I have no idea.'

'Then we'll just have to *get* him up. I assume he lives on the premises?'

'He has a flat over the garages. Do you want me—'

'I'll do it. I'll only call you if I have to. Where will you be?'

'What do you mean?'

'I mean, will you be in your own bed?'

'Well!' Barbara said. 'I think you need to remember that you're just the hired help.'

'Just as you need to remember that I was not hired by you,' Jessica pointed out. 'And that I am here to do a job of work. Now tell me, where can I reach you, say at a quarter to six tomorrow morning, if I need you?'

'I shall be in my bed.'

'Your own bed. Thank you. Have a nice night.' She didn't suppose she would, though.

Predictably, Andrea, a sheer delight in a satin and lace nightgown, was sleeping like a baby. But it was ten to twelve. Jessica shook her awake, then departed for the bathroom. Andrea joined her, toothbrush in hand. 'All well?'

'Nothing in this bloody place is well,' Jessica said.

'Tell me.'

'You should be all right until tomorrow morning. Just remember that no one in the house, save you and me, has the least concept of security. And if you happen to run into Sir William, walk the other way. Rapidly.' Andrea was very close to being a beautiful woman, which made her the more vulnerable.

'Don't tell me he's had a go at you? Already?'

'He's a fast worker.'

'Shit! What did you do?'

'I hit him. But that's not to say he won't try again, if he thinks he may have found a softer target.'

'Am I allowed to hit him too?'

'Be my guest. Just remember to do it

defensively. It would be bad form to break the arm of our employer.'

'How about his prospects?'

'I'm afraid they have to stay intact. Nighty-night.'

Unlike Andrea, she slept in the nude and it took her some time to fall asleep – only to awake, it seemed, seconds later, when the buzzer on her wrist pierced her consciousness.

The Traitor

Jessica rolled out of bed so violently she landed on her hands and knees. She pulled on her shirt and pants, whipped her pistol from her shoulder bag, and went to the door, only then looking at her watch; it was just after three.

As she opened the door she heard a scream, but it definitely was not Andrea, who both by training and temperament was not the screaming type. The hall was dark, but there was a light switch by the door, and this she flipped.

Now there was sound from downstairs, including voices, and she hurried along the hall and down to the next floor, where she found several people – Sir William, in a brocade dressing gown; the sultana, equally in a dressing gown, as was Barbara Harley; Karina, wearing a short nightie with panty bottoms – all emerging from their various bedrooms together, and all talking at each other; no one appeared to have noticed that Barbara and Sir William had emerged from the same doorway.

They gave a chorus of oohs as they saw Jessica's gun, then she was past them and running down the next flight of stairs, to discover Cerise lying on the floor of the downstairs hall; she also was wearing a nightgown, a long one, but was looking distinctly dishevelled and revealing a lot of leg. Kneeling beside the lady-in-waiting was Andrea, looking as calm as ever, but holding Cerise in place with a shoulder lock.

'What happened?' Jessica asked, aware that the rest of the household was coming down the stairs behind her.

'This person attacked me!' Cerise wailed.

'Arrest her!' Sir William commanded.

'She happens to be my assistant,' Jessica said. 'What happened?' This time she addressed Andrea.

'She jumped me,' Andrea explained.

'That's what *she* says,' Vanessa snapped.

'Well, let's hear what Cerise says,' Jessica suggested, and glanced at Karina. But the princess was preferring not to say anything at the moment. 'Let her up, Andie.'

Andrea released the lock. Cerise sat up, straightened her nightgown, and pushed her hair from her eyes. 'I heard this noise,' she said. 'So I went to investigate. And this person attacked me.'

'She says you attacked her.'

'Of course she didn't,' Vanessa declared. 'Cerise wouldn't attack anyone.'

'I see. But I am sure you will agree, Your Highness, that if my colleague attacked Cerise, she must have had a reason for doing so.'

'I'm sure she did. You will have to ask her.'

'Whatever the reason, Your Highness, we may assume that if Andrea attacked her, it was in order to do her an injury. Are you injured, Cerise?'

'Well...' Cerise flushed. 'I am bruised from being thrown to the floor.'

'Quite. Would it surprise you to know that if my colleague had attacked you, her training in unarmed combat would have enabled her to lay you out, or break one of your arms, or, indeed, kill you in a matter of seconds, not just lay you gently on the floor.'

Cerise gulped. 'I didn't know who she was. I saw this figure, and I reacted.'

'And you left your room after hearing a noise, and came downstairs.'

'You are behaving as if Cerise was guilty of some crime,' Vanessa protested.

'I am merely trying to find out what exactly happened, Your Highness. Did you hear a noise, Cerise?'

'Yes. I said that. I heard a noise.'

'And you sleep with your bedroom door shut?'

'Well, of course I do.'

'Thus you have very keen hearing.'

'Well...'

Jessica looked over the angrily watching faces; Karina remained impassive. 'Did anyone else hear a noise?'

'We were asleep,' Vanessa said.

'But you were awake, Cerise.'

She grabbed at the straw. 'Yes. I was awake.'

'Well,' Jessica said, 'whatever happened, Andrea was within her rights, and performing her duty, by making the rounds, as she was within her rights both to defend herself against any attacker, or to accost anyone she found wandering about the house who could not immediately account for her, or his, movements. That is why we are here.'

'I shall report this incident to your superiors,' Sir William said.

'Please do that,' Jessica said. 'Now I suggest we all go back to bed.'

There was a great deal she still needed to ask and find out, especially from Karina, but to do that she needed to get the princess alone.

* * *

'You know I did not attack that woman,' Andrea said when they had regained their bedroom.

'Of course I do,' Jessica said.

'You didn't ask her what she was actually doing out of her room.'

'I didn't think she would tell me. What *was* she actually doing out of her room?'

'She was making a telephone call.'

Jessica raised her eyebrows. 'At three o'clock in the morning?'

'Yes.'

'Where was she calling from?'

'The phone in the downstairs hall.'

'Do you know who she was calling?'

Andrea shook her head. 'I heard her talking, and tried to get closer, but she heard me, hung up, and attacked me.'

'Interesting.'

'Sinister, if you ask me.'

'You could be right. I'll chase it up in the morning. You okay?'

'Oh, sure,' Andrea said.

Jessica undressed and got back into bed. 'Wake me at five forty-five,' she said.

Once again she slept soundly, following her preferred practice of not thinking about the job when she was not actually on it. Andrea awoke her just before six, and she dressed herself, adding her parka because of the

122

drizzle, and left the house. She crossed the courtyard to the garages, and climbed the stairs to the apartment above.

She had to knock several times before the door swung in. 'What the shit...?'

'Perhaps you'd like to rephrase that,' Jessica suggested.

Parkin wore pyjama bottoms – hastily donned, she estimated – and looked extremely embarrassed, the more so when a woman asked from the bedroom, 'Who is it, Peepee?'

'Ah...'

'I'm broadminded,' Jessica assured him. 'Peepee, was it?'

'What's the matter?' he asked. 'What's happened?'

'Nothing, yet. I just want you to open the gates for me.'

'Why?'

'Because I have asked you to. And I wish it done now. I'll wait for you to get dressed.'

He gazed at her for several seconds – he was about twice her size – then decided against challenging her further. 'I can release the gates from here.'

'Then do so.'

She went back to the courtyard just in time to watch the gates swing in to admit Louise, who drove her Vauxhall up to her, scattering water left and right. 'You look as if you have problems.'

'Yes,' Jessica told her, and outlined the events of the night.

Louise whistled. 'You actually slugged the bastard?'

'Actually.'

'Doesn't he have a lot of clout? Suppose he goes upstairs?'

'With his record I don't think he'll get very far. But I strongly recommend that you do not find yourself alone with him.'

'Point taken.'

'It's the other matter – Cerise and her phone call – that's important.'

'What do you want done?'

'I'm going to work on the boss for a change of location,' Jessica said. 'It's up to you to follow up on what Cerise was up to. You'll have to go softly-softly; we didn't get too much of a response from the princess last night, but all the other responses were definitely hostile. However, we need to know who Cerise was calling and why, why she was using one of the house phones instead of a mobile – presuming she has a mobile – and why she used one of the downstairs phones rather than the one in her bedroom.'

'Consider it done.'

Louise, Jessica reflected, had never been short of confidence, at least when working. 'I will. Now, Karina wants to go shopping this morning, in town...'

'Is that a good idea?'

'It's probably a better idea than hanging about here. She's probably going to take this Cerise with her, but, if you get the opportunity, you might at least be able to find out if Karina knew she was making that phone call. We also need to know how long Cerise has been in the princess's employ, and how close they are.'

'Will do,' Louise said.

'She'll also probably want to stay out for lunch.' By now they had been joined by Andrea, who was ready to leave. 'Andie, will you put Chloe in the picture, and tell her to expect a call from Louise at about eleven-thirty, telling her where to report. It'll be somewhere in town. Lou, do try to have our girl keep as low a profile as possible; I don't think it would be a good idea to lunch at the Savoy Grill, just for starters. It would also help if she dressed down a little. She doesn't seem to go in for designer clothes, but she walks around with half of Cartier on her fingers, which might give people ideas that Karen Smith is a bit out of the ordinary.'

Louise nodded. 'And you?'

'I'll wait for a call from Chloe to tell me what's happening at three. Meantime I have a lot to do.'

She and Andrea drove into town in Andrea's Clio. 'Shall I pick you up, say just after two?' Andrea asked. 'No use using two cars.'

'You don't have to. You're not on again till six.'

'I'd like to. I'm not going to be doing anything else save sleep.'

Jessica felt the same way after her badly broken night, although she didn't reckon she could spare more than a couple of hours.

It was seven by the time she got into the flat, and there was an e-mail waiting in her computer. It consisted of only two words: *Communicate. Moran.*

It would have to wait until her brain was clear. She made herself some breakfast, then went to bed, awoke at ten, showered, dressed, and went to the Yard feeling thoroughly depressed, and not just about her present job – although she was still seething over Bland's utter male chauvinism, the way he had actually laid hands on her! And touched her naked bottom!

The main cause of her current depression, however, was that there was still no message from Tom. And right now, with that silly date for tomorrow evening looming, she desperately needed some reassurance that he really was the man for her. Besides, Tom, being in the same line of business, was about the only person with whom she could discuss the current mess. The girls were simply splendid, but she was very well aware that to them she was a living legend, who had been in the front line of more shoot-outs and

126

murder attempts than all of them put together. They reckoned she knew it all, and could cope with it all, thus they tended to agree with anything she proposed, any theory she might put forward; right now she needed analysis, not blind faith.

Adams was in a meeting, so she told Mrs Norton to hold the next slot for her, then reported to Moran. The superintendent was a little man with a somewhat grim face but a very relaxed manner. 'Sit,' he suggested. Jessica did so. 'Burke,' he said. 'Mean anything to you?'

'Not a thing.'

'I didn't suppose he would. He's never operated in this country.' He opened the dossier on his desk which contained the computer printout. 'Anthony Burke. Born Stanislav Tarnowski, Kiev, 1954. Educated University of Kiev, majored in languages. Left the Ukraine in 1982, just in front of the KGB. Wanted in Russia for blackmail and extortion, backed by threats of – and, in more than one case, implementation of – explosions. Considered to have at least one murder to his credit. Whereabouts over the next few years unknown, but it would appear that he travelled about Western Europe and the States, presumably making contacts, and changing his name. Now has an Irish passport.'

'Links to the IRA?'

'None that we can discover.'

'How did we get to know of him at all?'

'People like Burke do leave their mark. We were contacted five years ago by the FBI, asking if we knew anything about him. They gave us the Russian background. Seems they would like to interview him regarding a couple of explosions in the States. Both of these were connected with blackmail attempts. Not by Burke, though. The extortionists in each case sought business concessions, and, when these were refused, indicated that something nasty would happen, and it did.'

'Sounds familiar. Why wasn't he arrested?'

'They had no proof. Apparently there was a tip-off, but that was in the name he was then using – Bartlett. However, as they managed to discover that this Bartlett had been seen in the vicinity of both explosions, as I say, they felt that a chat might turn something up. Unfortunately, Bartlett had already left the country, for England. Using his Bartlett passport, he certainly landed here, but then he disappeared, having, as we now know, changed his name to Burke. The Americans, meanwhile, had been hunting around, and they came up with the Russian background I have already given you. With all of that info, we did finally relate Burke to Bartlett to Tarnowski.'

'But still he wasn't arrested.'

'Again, no proof. The Russians, what with the upheavals of the past fifteen years, had lost interest, and our legal people had to advise the Yanks that they simply did not have sufficient evidence to apply for extradition – a couple of dubious sightings close to a crime does not make a man a criminal, even if he could be identified as a criminal in another country. So, for the past five years he has been living quietly and comfortably in Wiltshire, scrupulously keeping his nose clean.'

'Couldn't you do him for his forged passport?'

'His Burke passport is genuine. Issued in Ireland. Somehow he has obtained Irish nationality.'

'He seems to have covered all the angles. So how do you link him to us?'

'Two things. Although, as I have said, Burke has been very careful not to even get a parking ticket in this country, we have a pretty good idea that he has been working abroad. Again, there is no proof, simply the fact that where there have been extortion-linked explosions or killings in various parts of the world, they are all parts of the world which Burke had visited just prior to the events.'

'And still no proof.'

'Nothing that would stand up in court, especially as the people on the spot have

129

never made the slightest attempt to correlate their knowledge with anyone else's, and in fact when we have offered assistance it has invariably been refused. You know that most of these emergent countries have a built-in suspicion of the British.'

'Are you telling me, sir, that Burke was in Kharram these past few days?'

'Our best hope of ever nailing him is that, like most successful criminals, he becomes more and more overconfident with every success. I don't know what name he used on this trip, but, as you know, you need a visa to get into Kharram. Well, we've been in touch with the Kharrami Embassy. They were most co-operative. Now, there is no record of a Burke applying for such a visa. But four visa applications over the past couple of years, all in different names and submitting different passports, have been returned to the same address – Burke's address. Apparently no one thought anything of this coincidence – admittedly, each application was several months apart – until you raised the matter. However, we can now be fairly certain that Burke has spent a good deal of time in Kharram over the past two years, which fits with your estimate of the time needed to set up this job.'

'Thank you, sir. But am I any further ahead? This man Burke certainly seems a likely suspect, but, as you say, we have no proof of anything with which we could arrest him, and I assume we have no MO.' She paused to look at her superior.

'Apart from the fact that it nearly always involves blowing somebody up, no. However, these are early days, JJ. It would seem pretty certain that he operates a team. There is no way he could carry out these affairs on his own. We are now working on identifying and if possible locating any associates, and we may well get a lead from there. We are also, again in view of your request, applying for permission both to put his house under surveillance and for a wire tap. This will, of course, take time...'

'Which is the one commodity I lack, sir.'

'Well, stick with it, and we'll continue our research. Will a photograph of Burke be any help?'

'Could be. Although if, as you say, he employs others to do his dirty work...'

'Take it anyway.' He pushed it across his desk. 'It's not a very good one, I'm afraid, but it's all we have. He's the fourth from the right, circled.'

Jessica studied the print. It was, as the superintendent had suggested, not very distinct, but it did indicate that Burke was the sort of man one would never look at twice, at least not without reason. 'And the others?'

'Nothing on any of them. Now, Sergeant,

I'm sure you have a lot to do...'

'There's just one more thing, sir.'

Moran raised his eyes to heaven. 'Yes?'

'I have a name for you to check out, if you can. Cerise Mahliah. She is lady-in-waiting to the princess.'

'And you don't trust her,' Moran remarked sceptically.

'As a matter of fact, I don't. She claims never to have been in England before, yet in the small hours of this morning she was telephoning someone.'

'She could have been calling Kharram.'

'I don't think she was. When Detective-Constable Hutchins, who happened to be on watch, approached her, she attacked her.'

'Could be a typical Arab reaction to being accosted.'

Jessica gave him an old-fashioned look. 'I'd like that call traced, sir.'

'Well, I'll have to get an order for that as well,' he said.

'I think you'll find the commander will be useful there, sir.'

'All right,' Moran said, somewhat wearily. 'One would suppose this was a top-priority murder case.'

'It already is, in Kharram. I am trying to prevent it becoming one here, sir.'

'All right, keep your shirt on. I'll chase up that call, and I'll have the name fed into the computer, but the odds are a million to one on our turning anything up. However, if she's on the spot, why don't you let us have a photo? That might help.'

'I will get you a photo,' Jessica said.

'Good girl. By the way, you were also going to let me have identikit portraits of the two people your princess could describe.'

'I'm going to get those this afternoon.'

Moran nodded, and closed the Kharram file. 'Keep in touch.'

There was not a lot more joy to be had upstairs. 'I've had a telephone call from Bland,' Adams said. 'He's not happy with you and your lot.'

'In a word, sir, snap.'

'As he, or certainly Kharram, is picking up this tab, you simply have to regard him as your employer.'

'If I were to regard him as my employer, sir, I would quit right now, and then charge him with sexual harassment.'

'You're not serious.'

'I am very serious.'

'Tell me.' Jessica gave him a blow-by-blow description of what had happened. 'Good heavens,' he commented when she had finished. 'Are you making an official complaint?'

'No, sir, I am not. I wouldn't have brought it up if he hadn't done so.'

'Well, of course, he didn't mention that

incident at all. Just that you and your people were stepping on everyone's toes. I mean this business of Detective-Constable Hutchins virtually laying out the princess's lady-in-waiting...'

'Hutchins was acting in self-defence, sir.'

'That's not what they say.'

'I happen to believe Hutchins, sir.'

Adams regarded her for several seconds. Then he said, 'All right. You say that you are not complaining, or would not have if they had not raised the matter first, but you did request this meeting. So tell me what you want to talk about.' Jessica did so. Adams listened carefully, but was shaking his head long before she had finished. 'They'll never go for it.'

'We don't know they won't until we put it to them,' Jessica argued.

'If everything you have told me is true, JJ, I don't think it would be tactful to put it to them right this minute. Bland would certainly assume that you are more interested in avoiding any further contact with him than in protecting his granddaughter. You may regard the house as indefensible, but the point is that no one knows Karina is there. Nor do I see how they can find out.'

'I would say they already have, if Cerise is a rotten apple.'

'But you don't know that she is. I suggest that finding out the truth about her is your first priority – after protecting the princess, of course. If you can turn up something on this woman, then we will have a concrete reason for moving Karina. Personalities won't come into it.'

Jessica sighed. 'Yes, sir.'

She spent the next half-hour with Manley, trying to sort out a relief team for the following week. As she wanted her present team to have the week off – she reckoned that by then they were going to need it – that didn't increase her popularity. 'Putting four of you on this job is causing a strain anyway. To put four more...'

'You'll have to take it up with the boss, sir. I am only carrying out my instructions.'

He snorted.

She then arranged for an identikit expert to meet her at Blandlock at four, and to bring a camera. It was half past twelve before she got home, to find Louise sitting in her car outside the apartment block. 'Now you have problems,' she suggested.

'I just thought it might be nice if you offered to give me lunch.'

'Consider it done, as long as you're in the microwave mode.'

'A sandwich will do.'

'You have to keep your strength up.' Jessica led the way upstairs. 'What's on your mind?' she asked over her shoulder. She tried not to

135

become involved with her team's personal lives; her own was too complicated to bear investigation. Thus she did not really know the true relationship between Andie and Chloe; they had certainly been partners for some time, which, as far as she was concerned, only made them better at their jobs, certainly when working together. Louise was altogether more fragile domestically, because her partner was somewhat fragile, at least mentally.

'It all went off rather well,' Louise said.

'Did she have a satisfactory day?'

'And how. She had a gold credit card and didn't spare it.'

'Must have been fun. Did you make any progress on the points I mentioned?'

'I didn't make much headway with Cerise, except that she's been with Karina for yonks. Just about ever since the princess can remember; they were playmates as kids. It would appear that Karina trusts her absolutely.'

Jessica unlocked the door of the flat and led the way in. 'And the phone call?'

'I'm afraid it wasn't mentioned. I couldn't get rid of Cerise, even for a moment, and I didn't want to raise it in front of her.'

'Point taken. I'll see what I can do this afternoon.'

'Anyway,' Louise said, 'I handed over to Chloe at twelve. They're lunching at the Star of something or other. Seems the princess has a passion for Indian food, and there's not a lot of it available in Kharram.'

'That's neat.' Jessica hunted in her fridge. 'Pizza?'

'Great. Anything I can do to help?'

'Just pour yourself a drink, sit down, and tell me why you're here.'

Louise took a sherry and sat down, one leg thrown across the other. 'I need congenial company.'

'Jerry being difficult?'

'He sure didn't like my going out at five this morning.'

'Surely he knows that goes with the job?'

'He's gone off the job as well. Wants me to give it up.'

Jessica laid the table. 'Are you going to?'

'I don't want to. I enjoy it.'

'And you can't tell him to bugger off?'

Louise sat at the table and played with her fork. 'I love the guy. Well, sort of.'

'You mean his bed manners suit yours,' Jessica said, thinking *lucky for some*.

'Well, that's important, don't you think?'

'Very. So, when were you thinking of going home?'

'Well, I'm on again at midnight. He's going to make the most frightful stink.'

'Didn't you consider this when you made up the roster?'

'I didn't, actually. You told me what you

wanted, and I just filled it in.'

'Well, I suppose it can be changed. Listen, why don't you take my three-to-six slot this afternoon, and I'll do the midnight-to-dawn spell.' Which would mean kaput on her being in the pub at seven tomorrow, she thought, as on that schedule she'd be back on duty at six tomorrow evening. But she was not altogether sorry to drop that silly caper.

'Oh, I couldn't do that,' Louise protested. 'That would bugger everyone up. I just thought that if I didn't go home until tomorrow morning, well, it might make him think a bit.'

Jessica sighed. 'Okay, you're welcome to stay here if you feel it would be best. There's just one thing: there's no chance of him barging in here looking for you and raising the roof? Because if that does happen, I'm going to charge him with disturbing the peace, and lock him up.'

'He doesn't even know your address,' Louise said. 'And he certainly doesn't have any idea I'd come to you.'

'I'll hold you to that,' Jessica said.

'You,' Loman said, 'look like something the cat dragged in.'

Loman was a large, fat man, with florid cheeks and ebullient good humour. But Sonia did not find him amusing at the moment. 'I *feel* like something the cat dragged in,' she said. 'I want a hot bath.'

Loman escorted them to the exit. 'Rough?' He addressed the question to Rosen, as being the more likely to give him an un-emotional response.

'Tedious,' Rosen said.

'Have you any idea?' Sonia inquired. 'Eight hours lying in the back of a truck beneath all kinds of garbage. With *him*!'

Loman raised his eyebrows. He had only met them on one previous occasion, when they had come to his house for their inter-views, and, as the interviews had been con-ducted by Burke himself, he had not really had anything more to do than help Ruby serve coffee.

Rosen grinned. 'I just felt I should reassure her from time to time,' he said.

'He makes my skin crawl,' Sonia said. 'And when we finally got to the airport, our flight was out in an hour. We didn't even have time to clean our teeth.'

'You shall have your hot bath,' Loman promised, leading them to where his car was parked. 'And clean your teeth. But...' He looked at his watch. 'We do not really have too much time to waste. Tony was most insistent about this. He is coming in tomor-row morning, and wishes to have the job completed within forty-eight hours. From now.'

'That is providing we know where the

139

young lady is,' Rosen said.

'Oh, we know that.' Loman got behind the wheel. Rosen sat beside him in the front; Sonia got into the back. 'She is just where Burke supposed she would be – at her grandfather's country home.'

'Is that fact?' Rosen asked. 'Or wishful thinking?'

'Fact, confirmed last night.'

'How? You have been there?'

'I did not have to go there. We have an agent inside.'

'Who will assist us when the time comes?' Sonia asked.

Loman drove out of the car park and turned on to the road for London. 'If she can, without revealing her identity.'

'A woman?' Sonia's tone was disparaging.

'You are a woman, Madame Solere,' Loman pointed out. 'But there is a downside to the information she gave us: there is a Special Branch protection unit in place.'

'Shit!' Rosen commented. 'Burke said there wouldn't be.'

'Well, even Burke can't be right all the time. It would appear that this Bland guy has more clout with the Home Office than we supposed. However, look on the bright side. This is a female squad.'

'Come again?'

'Women police, Rosen. Just up your street. I suppose they felt this was necessary

140

because they are dealing with a Kharrami princess.'

'How many women?' Sonia asked.

'She's not certain. She thinks four. The important thing is that they are not all there all the time. Usually there is one, or perhaps two. On the other hand, they are Special Branch. That is, they will be highly trained and competent markswomen. Does this present a problem?'

'No,' Sonia said. 'You say he wants it wrapped up in two days?'

'That is correct. You have today and tonight to reconnoitre and make your recommendations; the mission will be completed tomorrow night.'

'Are we allowed to contact our insider?' Rosen asked.

'No. She has carried out her part of the business, fingering the princess. She will inform us if there are any important changes in the security procedure.'

'But ... are we to use the same methods as in Kharram?'

'Yes.'

'But, if we do that...'

'People will be killed. That cannot be helped, any more than it could be helped in Kharram.'

'The insider...'

'Has served her purpose.'

Rosen gulped. Although he was quite

141

capable of cold-blooded murder, he did not like to think of their own people being killed.

'And afterwards?' Sonia asked. 'What do we do with the princess?'

'It is essential that she is taken alive, and if possible unhurt; we will need her to contact her father. But Burke will be here to oversee that. What he wants, tomorrow, is a full report on the grounds and the best way to go about it.'

'There are certain things we will need.'

'They are waiting for you at my house.' Loman grinned. 'With that hot bath.'

As promised, Andrea arrived at five past two, wearing a dress and high heels and looking spic and span and soignée. Jessica gathered that she had spent the entire day, so far, in bed; certainly it was impossible to tell that she had had a virtually sleepless night.

She raised her eyebrows at the sight of Louise lounging in her underwear, but did not comment. It had actually been a very pleasant if slightly disturbing hour since lunch. Jessica had never been into women intimates, or even close friends. Now she was beginning to understand what an emotional blanket such a relationship could be. In this instance she supposed she had been the blanket, as Louise had wanted to do the talking, and she had been happy to let her, finding it incredible how someone who appeared so calmly in control of her life could actually be in such a mess, living with an MCP who on occasion even knocked her about, but with whom she was at least sexually in love, although Jessica was beginning to wonder if it was actually love or mere habit. Better the devil you know...

She felt that talking about it had helped Louise, but it had also created problems for her. It had been suggested by Manley, her immediate superior, that Louise was in line for promotion, and that she, Jessica, might like to give an opinion on her capabilities. Well, she had no doubt as to Louise's capabilities as regards her work, but now she had doubts as to her ability to withstand any additional stress.

'There's no problem, is there?' Andrea asked, obviously curious as to why her two superior officers had spent the afternoon together.

'No,' Jessica said shortly, and Andrea, who had worked with her before on several occasions, knew better than to pursue the matter.

The rain had stopped, the sun was out, and it was a remarkably warm day for April. Chloe was sunning herself on a lounger on the front terrace. She had her shoulder bag beside her, and was undoubtedly armed, but Jessica could not help feeling that she was unnecessarily exposed – and not only to any would-be sniper lurking in the trees only a couple of hundred yards away. 'All well?'

Chloe sat up, leaving the bra top of her bikini behind. 'Quiet as a mouse.'

'Well, it's unlikely to stay that way while you're undressed. Where is Sir William?'

'Haven't a clue. He spent the day in town. I haven't seen him at all. We came home in the Rolls after lunch, and then the sultana went back up, again in the Rolls. They sure do work that Parkin; I gather the sultana and Sir William will be coming back together.' She put on her top to follow Jessica and Andrea into the house. 'Everyone else is asleep.'

Jessica listened to splashes coming from the pool, which was at the rear of the building. 'Not everyone. You go and get yourself dressed and take off.'

'Oh. Right.' Chloe would obviously have been quite content to stay.

'Do you need me?' Andrea asked.

Jessica shook her head. 'You're not on duty until six.'

'Well, I'll just run Chloe up to town and come right back.'

'Do that.'

Jessica walked through the silent house – presumably the staff was also indulging in a siesta – and emerged through the glass door on to the pool apron. And felt distinctly relieved that Andrea had not accompanied her. The woman in the pool was Cerise, and she had gone a stage further than Chloe.

Cerise didn't notice Jessica for a few minutes, then, tossing her wet hair from her forehead, she swam towards the side. 'Enjoying the view?' she inquired aggressively.

'There's a lot of it,' Jessica agreed. 'You do know that you are overlooked by the staff windows upstairs.'

'Give them a thrill,' Cerise said, and came up the steps.

There was no towel in sight, and no clothes either; she must have walked down from her bedroom naked.

'Is the princess resting?' Jessica asked politely.

Cerise stood with her back to her, holding up both arms to the afternoon sun, now drooping towards the west. Definitely a sun worshipper, Jessica thought.

'Yes, she is resting,' Cerise said.

'Well, I wonder if you could wake her up, say at half past three.'

'She does not usually rise at that time.'

'Tell her that I have someone coming to help her make up an identikit portrait of the two people in the car with her.'

Cerise lowered her arms and turned to face her. 'I do not think she will be able to help you. It was dark, and she only saw them for a few minutes.'

'She says she can remember them,' Jessica insisted. 'So, if you would be so kind…'

Cerise snorted and went into the house, throwing her long, brown legs in front of her, large hams sliding wetly against each other. Jessica sat down on a wooden deckchair. The things I do for England, she thought, or at least the Metropolitan Police Commissioner. She only hoped that Cerise would put something on before Moriarty arrived to take her photograph.

But Karina was pleased to co-operate, once she was up and showered and dressed. By then a van had arrived, filled with all her morning purchases, and the various boxes had to be opened and admired – most of it was of good quality but of very little relevance to the business of living, in Jessica's opinion. Shoes figured prominently – why she had no idea, as the princess seemed continuously to wear thongs – nor did the extensive range of lingerie seem relevant, as it was very obvious that Karina did not indulge in bras, and Jessica suspected that she also wore thongs beneath her jeans.

But she was in excellent humour, and when Sergeant Moriarty arrived she settled down to a long session with him, being fascinated by the way he could change eyes or noses on his laptop at the touch of a button. He was finished at five, apparently well satisfied. 'I'll have something for you tomorrow morning,' he said.

Jessica looked at Karina. 'Oh, I'll be here,' Karina promised.

'Just before you go...' Jessica said. They had been joined by Cerise, fortunately dressed. 'I'd like you to take a photograph of this young lady, if you would, Sergeant.'

'Happy to oblige, Sergeant.'

'A photograph? Of me?' Cerise demanded. 'I do not wish a photograph taken of me. Highness...' She looked at the princess.

'Our women do not like being photographed,' Karina explained.

'I think you are speaking of your peasant women, Highness,' Jessica suggested. 'Not a sophisticate like Cerise. It really is most necessary.'

'Well...'

'I most strongly object, Highness,' Cerise said.

'Let the sergeant take the photograph,' Karina said.

Cerise hissed her annoyance, but allowed herself to be posed while Moriarty flashed his bulb.

Jessica saw him out. 'Some dame,' he commented.

'She knows that,' Jessica agreed. 'When you have developed that print, would you give it to Superintendent Moran?'

'Will do. Have fun.'

'You have got to be joking,' she said, and returned upstairs.

'We're going for a spin,' Karina announced. 'To look at the countryside. I suppose you want to come along.'

'I suppose I'll have to. May I ask when you decided to do this, Your Highness?'

'Five minutes ago. You're not going to say I can't. You can't expect me to stay cooped up in this mausoleum.'

'Of course I do not.' Jessica reflected that such an impromptu decision could not be known to anyone else save for Cerise. But it was Cerise she wanted to get rid of for a while. 'Which car were you going to use?'

'I don't know. One of the cars from the garage. The Rolls, if it's there.'

'The Rolls has gone up to London to pick up Sir William,' Cerise said. 'And the sultana.'

'That means the chauffeur has gone up as well,' Jessica said, and looked out of the window at Andrea's Clio coming down the drive. 'But you can use ours. It comes complete with driver.'

Karina moved to the window to look out. 'It's terribly small.'

'There's room for two.'

'Two?'

'Well, there's no need for Cerise to come too.'

'But I want to come,' Cerise said. 'I want to

148

look at England.'

'Some other time.'

Cerise looked at the princess.

'Why should Cerise not accompany us? I am sure there is room for three, even in that little car,' Karina said.

'There is something I urgently need to discuss with you, in private,' Jessica said.

'Well...'

'It is to do with last night,' Cerise snapped. 'If it concerns me, I should be present.'

'Well...' Karina said again.

'Have it your own way,' Jessica said, realising she was going to have to take the bull by the horns. 'Has Cerise told you, Your Highness, what she was doing last night when she encountered Detective-Constable Hutchins?'

'She could not sleep, and was going to the library for a book.'

'That is what she told you?'

'Yes. That is what happened.'

'She was using the telephone, Highness.'

Karina looked at Cerise.

'Well...' Cerise said.

'You did not tell me this,' Karina said.

'I did not think it was important.'

'I think it is very important,' Jessica said. '*How* important depends on who you were calling.'

'Cerise?' Karina's voice was deceptively quiet.

'Well...'

'Tell me the truth. Or I will have you whipped.'

Jessica's jaw dropped. This was England, in the twenty-first century. Then she remembered what Adams had told her of Kharrami law. At the same time, glancing rapidly from one to the other, she was sure they had exchanged looks, as if to indicate that this was merely make-believe. The idea that the two of them were ganging up on her, if only unspokenly, irritated her. But Cerise appeared to take the threat seriously. 'I was told to do it, Highness. Just to call that number, and give my name. That is all.'

'What number?'

'I cannot remember. It was written on a piece of paper.'

'Where is this paper?'

'I threw it away.'

'You say you were told to do this. By whom?'

Cerise licked her lips. 'Mustafa.'

Karina frowned. 'Mustafa? You mean my father's equerry?'

'Yes, Highness.'

'Why did he wish you to do this?'

'He did not say.'

'And you just agreed to do it?'

'Well...' Cerise blushed.

'You took money from him!'

'Well...' Another circle of the lips.

Karina snapped her fingers. 'He is your lover. You have taken a lover!' This time Cerise did not speak, but merely hung her head. Karina looked at Jessica. 'Do you wish to ask her anything?'

'I would be interested to know why she used the downstairs phone instead of her mobile or the one in her bedroom.'

'I can answer that. We left Kharram in such a hurry she forgot the mobiles. As for the bedroom phones, there is something the matter with the circuit, and when one of the upstairs phones is used, all the others go *ping*.'

'Which means she was determined that no one should know of the call,' Jessica said.

'Yes,' Karina said. 'Who do you think she was calling?'

'I don't know. But whoever it was, someone out there now knows that Your Highness is in residence here. You have simply got to get out.'

Karina stared at Cerise, who was now trembling. 'I will telephone my father,' the princess said, 'and have Mustafa arrested and put to the question. As for you...'

Cerise fell to her knees. 'Please, Highness!'

'Excuse me,' Jessica said. 'When you say, "put to the question"...'

'Oh, they will burn his balls a little. That always makes them confess.'

'Shit!' Jessica muttered.

151

'As for this one...' Karina said.

'Ah ... I'm afraid burning people's balls, or any other part of them, is not legal in this country.'

'She is my servant.'

'Certainly. But as long as she is in England, she comes under English law.'

Karina looked quite put out. 'Very well. I will send her back to Kharram for questioning. In the meantime, lock her up.'

Cerise gave a moan of terror.

'On what charge?' Jessica asked.

'Oh, for heaven's sake, Sergeant...'

'You see, Your Highness, she has committed no crime.'

'She has betrayed me.'

'She has been indiscreet. But I'm afraid there is no magistrate in this country who would issue a warrant for her arrest on the grounds of one telephone call. We would have to prove that the call was made to someone who intended to harm Your Highness.'

'Who needs a warrant? She is my servant, and I wish her arrested. Is that not sufficient?'

'I'm afraid not. The fact that she is your servant gives you no rights over her other than to sack her, and even that may be disputable in law.'

'My God! What a country. Very well. Cerise, you are sacked. Pack your bag and get out.'

'But...' Cerise looked at Jessica, discerning her as the closest thing to a friend that she had at the moment. 'I have no money. Nowhere to go.'

'That is your business,' Karina said.

'I think it may be a good idea for her to remain here,' Jessica suggested.

'I do not wish to see her again.'

'Well, you need not. This is a big house. Do you still wish to go for a drive?'

'Yes. I need the fresh air. More than ever, now.'

'Right. The first thing we must do is settle Cerise.'

She rang the bell and used her alarm, which brought both Barbara and Andrea. Jessica outlined the situation, which did not appear to surprise Andrea, but left Barbara gasping and looking to Karina for confirmation.

'You will take your instructions from Sergeant Jones,' Karina said.

Barbara looked at Jessica.

'I wish Cerise to be given a room away from the main part of the house,' Jessica said. 'One which does not have a telephone. She will be fed her meals in her room. And you will remain there, Cerise, until we can sort something out. You had better lock the door, Mrs Harley.'

'You mean I am to be kept a prisoner,'

153

Cerise said. 'You just said you have no right to do this.'

'I have no right to arrest you,' Jessica agreed. 'And I am not arresting you. I am simply providing you with food and accommodation until, as I say, we can sort something out. The alternative is to send you back to Kharram. On the first available flight.'

Cerise drew a sharp breath. 'You cannot do that.'

'I can, and I will. You have entered the country without a passport as a member of the princess's entourage. When you cease to be a member of the princess's entourage you immediately become an illegal immigrant, subject to deportation.'

Cerise swallowed, and looked at the princess.

'That is ideal,' Karina said. 'Have her deported. Then we can let Colonel Bartruf take care of her.'

'No!' Cerise cried. 'You cannot. He would...' She bit her lip.

'Then behave yourself,' Jessica said. 'And it may be possible for you to apply for political asylum. Andrea, we would like to borrow your car. I'll leave you to keep an eye on things here.'

'Will do.' Andrea and Barbara ushered the trembling Cerise from the room.

'You are not seriously going to allow her to

claim political asylum?' Karina asked as they got into the little car and drove out of the grounds.

'Let's sort out *your* problems first, Your Highness. Where would you like to go?'

'Anywhere. Somewhere with lots of trees. We do not have trees in Kharram. Only date palms. Daddy keeps planting proper trees, and they keep dying. They say there is too much salt in the soil.'

Jessica swung left along the lane to join the main road; they weren't all that far from the New Forest. She thought that the lane was unusually busy this afternoon; there was a telephone van parked about a hundred yards from the Blandlock gates, apparently making repairs to the overhead cable, and a small green Ford driving slowly past the gates. This braked as they came out, and they drove past it. Jessica made a mental note to have the workmen checked out when she returned.

'Do you think she was telling the truth?' Karina asked.

'About the phone call? I think she was, basically. But I also think she knew who she was calling.'

'But you would not make her tell us.'

'As I said, we don't go in for that sort of thing, physically, in this country. But there are ways of putting pressure on people. As for instance, by letting Cerise consider her

155

situation for the rest of today and tonight, and then having a chat with her tomorrow and suggesting that her chances of obtaining political asylum would be that much greater if she co-operated with us.'

'I have always heard that the British are a devious people,' Karina commented. But there was admiration in her tone.

They were now driving down the A3 towards Portsmouth in quite heavy traffic, and Jessica was studying the cars behind them in her rear-view mirror as well as those which from time to time overtook them; she was not driving very fast. This was instinctive owing to her training, and it was important not to overreact without sufficient proof of a problem. However... 'I understand that you and Cerise have been friends for a long time,' she remarked.

'Oh, yes. Since I was a little girl. You know how it is. It was decided that I had to have a playmate, and she was chosen. She comes from a very good Kharrami family. Up till the telephone business I trusted her absolutely.'

'She has never given any indication of jealousy, or perhaps republican or fundamentalist sympathies?' Jessica continued to study her mirror.

'No, no. Well, not that I have noticed.'

Not, Jessica supposed, that the princess would have noticed very much in the behaviour of her employees. 'Where does she live? I mean, when you are in Kharram?'

'She has rooms in the palace.'

'But she has time to herself? I mean, she can leave the palace and go off on her own?'

'Yes.'

'And therefore, perhaps, meet up with people of whom you know nothing?'

'I suppose so. But she seems to have formed an attachment to my father's equerry. Can you believe it? Without telling me.'

She was clearly very put out, although Jessica couldn't be sure whether it was the fact of the affair or of Cerise not having confided it that was annoying her.

'Are you really going to have this man Mustafa arrested?'

'Of course I am.'

'And tortured?'

'That will be up to Colonel Bartruf. But he has the right to do so, by law.'

'I must study your laws,' Jessica said, and took another look in her mirror. 'Princess Karina, I have to tell you that we are being followed.'

The Indiscretion

Sonia took off her yellow hard hat and fluffed out her hair. 'Did you see that?'

'Did I see what?' Like her, Rosen wore blue overalls and a hard hat.

'That car.'

'I saw it come out of the gates. But it is not the sort of car that belongs to a millionaire. It was a tradesman.'

'It was the princess.'

'What? You are crazy.'

'It was the princess, being driven by some blonde woman.'

'My God! Did she see you?'

'I don't think so. They were talking.'

'Well, that is a lucky escape.'

'I think we should go after them.'

'Why?'

'For God's sake, Rosen. We'll never have a better opportunity. We were sent here to get the princess. We were told we would have to blast our way in past the Special Branch, and here she is falling into our lap.'

'To go after her, now, would be too risky,' Rosen objected. 'And it would be against orders.'

'Risky? She's alone with one other woman.'

Rosen considered. He was, as always, unhappy with the way Burke did things, the total secrecy in which he operated, never letting any of his people know anything more than he considered essential for the job in hand. He blamed the disaster in Kharram on the fact that he had been told nothing of the overall plan, had merely been directed from moment to moment by his mobile. Now again he had no idea what the overall plan was. But he was flattered by the fact that Burke, who had recruited a very large team to carry out the kidnapping, had been prepared to let him – albeit with the assistance of this detestable woman – finish the job on his own, and he was quite sure that for them to disrupt Burke's plans or disobey his precise instructions in any way would mean curtains for them both; Burke did not forgive twice. 'We don't know what arrangements have been made. They may be on their way to a rendezvous with some police people. Anyway, that green car is following them. He is clearly an escort. I say we stick to our orders, and our plan. We have a pretty complete picture of the daytime comings and goings. We will remain here the night, and make up a full schedule for Burke tomorrow. Then it is up to him to give us our orders.'

'You intend to remain here the night?'

'Yes.'

'You don't think someone may find it suspicious, that a telephone repair van should be parked here all night?'

'Why should they? No one has queried us so far. If anyone does, we simply drive away.'

Sonia pulled her nose.

'Don't turn your head,' Jessica said as Karina started. 'He can see us.'

'What are you going to do?'

'I'd like to take him out, if that's okay with you.'

'Won't that be dangerous?'

'I don't think so. There's only one of him.'

'And of course you have your gun. You do, don't you?'

'Yes,' Jessica said. 'I have my gun. But there is always the chance that it is pure coincidence that he should be there, a couple of cars back, and staying there, when most of the traffic is overtaking us. It can't do any harm to find out, and it might do us a bit of good. I must ask you, though, not to do anything unless I tell you to, and when I do tell you to do something, to do it without question or hesitation. Will you promise me that?'

Karina hesitated a moment. Then she said, 'You are asking me to place my life in your hands.'

'Your life is already in my hands, Highness.'

Karina grinned. 'Why, so it is. I promise.'

'Well, then...' They were approaching a side road. Jessica signalled and then swung to her left, leaving the traffic behind. The road was deserted. But the green car behind them turned off as well. Jessica drove for a hundred yards along the road, then stopped without signalling. The green car had stayed some thirty yards back, but even so it had to brake violently to avoid running into the Clio. As it stopped, Jessica was out of her door, her right hand buried in her shoulder bag, fingers curled round the butt of her Skorpion, caressing the trigger. 'Stay put,' she told Karina.

The door of the other car was open, and a young man was getting out. 'Whew!' he remarked. 'That was sudden.'

Jessica studied him. He was very well-dressed as well as good-looking, and wore a little moustache, but he spoke with a foreign accent.

'Why were you following us?' she asked.

'I wanted to speak with the princess.'

'You—'

But Jessica was interrupted by Karina, who disobeyed her instructions and got out of the car. 'Henri!' she shouted. 'Oh, Henri!' She ran past Jessica to throw herself into the man's arms. 'They told me you were in hospital. I didn't know how badly hurt you were.'

161

'I wasn't hurt at all, really,' Henri said. 'Just a bump on the head. But you ... I didn't know what had happened to you.'

'Oh, they tried to kidnap me, but I got away.'

'To come here.' He looked past her at Jessica.

'Oh,' Karina said. 'This is Sergeant Jones. My bodyguard.'

'Bodyguard?' Henri was as surprised as most people when informed that the delicate little blonde was a policewoman.

'Oh, she's very good.' Karina's voice was a trifle doubtful, as she had never seen Jessica perform. 'And she has a gun,' she said more positively. 'Show him your gun, JJ.'

'When we get to know one another,' Jessica suggested.

'Oh,' Karina said. 'I'm sorry. You haven't been introduced. This is Henri Ferrière. He is a very dear friend. He was with me at the nightclub, Quadrino's.'

'Ah,' Jessica said. 'And now you are here, Mr Ferrière. How did you know to come here?'

'When I was released from hospital, I went to the palace to find out how the princess was. They told me she had come to England to stay with her grandfather.'

Jessica resisted the temptation to throw up her hands in despair. 'You saw the sultan?'

'No, no. The sultan is not seeing anybody.

I spoke to one of the servants.'

'I see. Would this have been a man named Mustafa?'

'No, no, it wasn't Mustafa. It was somebody else. I don't know his name.'

'I see,' Jessica said again. 'Your Highness, your grandfather gave me to understand that both your departure from Kharram and your destination were being kept a close secret.'

'Well, it was. But you know how people are.'

'I'm learning every day,' Jessica said. 'So, we have a situation where it seems everyone in the palace, and, I suspect, everyone in Kharram, knows exactly where you are.'

'Well, I suppose they do.'

'Right. Tell me, Mr Ferrière, why did you follow us instead of coming to the house?'

'I was trying to do that. I only landed a couple of hours ago. So I hired a car and drove down here. I had been given the address, but I wasn't sure which house it was, and while I was looking, I saw you drive out of the grounds.'

As had happened with Cerise, Jessica noted a quick exchange of understanding glances between Karina and the man; there was something going on she did not yet know, but if that continued to irritate her, it delineated her own way the more clearly. 'I think you and I need to have a chat,' she said. 'But right now our first priority has to

163

be to get back to Blandlock. You can follow us. Come along, Your Highness.'

'Aren't we going for a drive? You said we were going for a drive.'

'There's been a change of plan.' She virtually bundled Karina into the car, did a four-point turn, and headed back for Liphook. The green car did the same, taking somewhat longer over the turn.

'What's the panic?' Karina asked. 'Because Henri turned up? He's quite harmless.'

'I'm sure he is. But don't you see, Your Highness, that if he could find out where you are so easily, so can anyone else? Including your would-be kidnappers. We simply have to get you away from Blandlock, even if I have to kidnap you myself.'

'Oh,' Karina said. 'I see what you mean. But they'll never agree.'

'I don't intend to give them the chance to disagree. You say this man is harmless. Just who is he, anyway?'

'A friend.'

Jessica glanced at her; Karina's cheeks were pink. 'To use tabloid-speak, a close friend?'

'Well, he'd like to be. But I'm a princess, and he...'

'Yes?'

'Well, he comes from a good family, and has lots of money ... but there's the religious business too.'

164

'Do you pray to Mecca every morning, afternoon and evening?'

Karina grinned. 'When I remember. But Mummy and Daddy could never allow me to marry Henri.'

'Would you like to marry him?'

'I think it might be fun. But the man I marry will be the next Sultan of Kharram. That means he has to be an Arab of royal blood, and at least pretend to be a devout Muslim.'

'And those who might fill the bill are thin on the ground.'

'If you throw in sexual attractiveness, very.'

'Tough. You say Henri has lots of money. What does he do for a living?'

'I don't think he does anything.'

'It's not possible to do nothing and have lots of money.'

'I think his parents finance him. To keep him out of France.'

'What we call a remittance man. Do you know this for a fact, or is this what he has told you?'

'He told me.'

'I see. And how long have you known him?'

'About six months.'

'Where did you meet?'

'At a party in Kharram. You're not suspicious of Henri? I told you—'

'That he's harmless. It's my business to be suspicious. Now, are you going to co-operate

165

with me one hundred per cent?'

'Of course.'

'In that case there is going to be a further change of plan. You are going to come home with me and stay put for a day or so while I sort things out.'

'There'll be the mother and father of a row. Won't you lose your job?'

'Not if you tell everyone it was your idea. We'll just stop and pick up some things ... Shit!' They had reached the turn-off to the Blandlock Lane, and just in front of them, approaching from the other direction, was a Rolls.

'That's Mummy and Grandpa,' Karina said.

'Yes. So ... *another* change of plan. If we go home now, they'll want to keep you there. So we'll skip that bit.'

'Oh. Right. What about Henri?'

Jessica drove past the turn-off for about a mile, then pulled into a lay-by and signalled Henri to do the same. He came to her window. 'The princess and I need to disappear for a while,' Jessica told him. 'Where are you staying?'

'I'm not staying anywhere at the moment. I told you, I only got in this afternoon, and I went straight down to Liphook. I thought I might be able to stay there.'

'You can try it, if you like, although under no circumstances must you let on that you met us. I would recommend an hotel.' She gave him one of her cards. 'That is my mobile number. Call me on that when you are settled somewhere, and we'll arrange a meeting. And please, Henri, do not attempt to follow us, otherwise I shall have you arrested.'

Henri looked past her at Karina.

'Trust her,' the princess said. 'I do.'

'Won't he be able to trace your address from the phone number?' Karina asked as they rejoined the traffic.

'That's why I gave him the mobile number. If he does manage to track it down, he'll find it's registered at Scotland Yard.'

'Gosh. I feel quite excited. As if it's all happening.'

'Hopefully, it's not going to happen at all. Weren't you excited the other night in Kharram?'

Karina considered. 'I was more exhilarated.'

'You could've been killed.'

'But I wasn't.'

'True.' The green car had disappeared. Jessica called Andrea on her mobile. 'How are things?'

'Not too good. His nibs and the sultana are home.'

'And?'

'Well, firstly, they're all uptight about the

princess not being here...'

Jessica looked at Karina, who waggled her eyebrows.

'And secondly, they refuse to believe anything bad of Cerise.'

'So?'

'They've let her out.'

'Well, she's their problem.'

'Well, I'll feel a whole lot happier when you're back. When *are* you coming back?'

'I'm not.'

'Not?!' Andrea's voice rose an octave.

'Listen. Something else has come up, and I am now certain that it is too dangerous for the princess to remain at Blandlock for a moment longer. So I am taking her somewhere safe.'

'Your place?'

'Andie, you are just too quick for your own good. I'll forget you said that, and you'll forget it too.'

'They won't like it.'

'So handle it the best way you can. Louise will be down at six, and she'll back you up. She'll be bringing your car.'

'Thanks. But if the princess is no longer here, why do we need to be here?'

'Let's say it'll confuse the enemy. I'll be in touch.'

She did feel it was necessary to obtain some kind of authority for what she was doing,

168

however, and, having reached her flat at five and brought Louise up to date with the situation – still lounging in her underwear, Louise was taken aback at the sudden appearance of the princess, and hastily borrowed one of Jessica's dressing gowns – she telephoned the Yard.

'Hello, Mrs Norton. Is the boss in?'

'He's just leaving.'

'Well, will you ask him if I can have a word? It's urgent.'

'Yes?' Adams asked, a moment later.

'I have a problem and would like clearance, sir.'

'Tell me about it.' Jessica did so. 'Hell,' he commented. 'You're sure you're not overreacting?'

'I am trying to do my job, sir,' Jessica said. 'Of protecting the princess. I cannot do so, with the staff and facilities at my disposal, if she has become an open target.'

'Hm,' Adams agreed. 'Where is she now?'

'At my flat. I would like that to stay confidential.'

'Quite. Is she happy about this?'

'At the moment, yes.'

'And you wish to keep her there?'

'No, sir. This is not a very large flat. I would like to have her in one of our safe houses.'

'Hm. But you're happy for her to stay the night.'

169

'One night, yes, sir.'

'Very good. Leave it with me, and I'll see what can be sorted out. You do realise that I will have to put the sultana in the picture. I mean to say, the princess *is* her daughter.'

'I do understand, sir. But I would appreciate it if you would not tell the sultana where the princess is spending the night.'

'Oh, come now, JJ. Are you suggesting...?'

'No, sir. I have two things on my mind. One is that, on the evidence of what I have seen and heard, the moment you tell the sultana where Princess Karina is, the whole world will know of it. The second is that I wouldn't put it past the sultana to turn up here, loudly.'

Adams sighed. 'You do put me in some difficult positions, JJ. I'll see what I can do. I'll get back to you.'

'Try to make it before ten, sir. Or tomorrow morning.'

'Why before ten?' Karina asked when Jessica had replaced the phone.

'I go to bed at ten when I'm not on duty.'

'Oh. Can't we go out?'

'You're not dressed for it.'

Karina looked down at her jeans, and apparently took stock of the situation. 'I don't have any nightclothes.' Then she gave one of her grins. 'You can lend me some of yours. We're about the same size.'

'I can't lend you any of mine,' Jessica said.

'Because I don't have any.'

'Oh!' Karina looked into the bedroom. 'There's only one bed!'

'We'll work something out.' She had herself not taken in all the ramifications of having someone spend the night – someone who was not Tom and who was in addition a princess.

'What do you want me to do?' Louise asked.

'I wonder if you could go down early, and give Andie some back-up.'

Louise nodded. 'I'll just get dressed. Attitude?'

'You're as foxed as everyone else is. I have just taken off with the princess, and you don't know where.'

'They'll be after you with both barrels.'

'Hopefully, the boss will straighten them out.'

'Okay. Well...' She went into the bedroom. Jessica followed her. She had been so preoccupied when she had come in that she had not immediately noticed that Louise was looking distinctly stressed. And angry.

She closed the door. 'Tell me.'

'Oh ... I was a fool, I suppose.'

'In what way?'

'I called Jerry. Well, I wanted to make it up.'

'You didn't tell him where you were?'

'Of course I didn't. I just wanted to chat, tell him I'd be home tomorrow.'

'And he wasn't happy.'

'Happy? He cursed and swore, used every obscenity in the book, called me every name he could think of ... God, the bastard. If he was to walk in that door right this minute I'd shoot him in the balls.'

Jessica gazed at her. It was a strong temptation to pull her out and take her watch herself. But she had Karina on her hands. 'You okay for tonight?'

'Oh, sure.' She gave a twisted grin. 'I'll get over it. You know what I'd like? For those kidnapping bastards to start something tonight. I'd blow the whole lot away.'

'Just make sure they're the right bastards,' Jessica said, and left her to it.

'Is she your lover?' Karina asked.

'My...?'

'Oh, you call them partners over here, don't you?'

'Louise is neither my lover nor my partner, except in a strictly professional sense. We each have a partner – male.'

'I didn't mean to offend you. It's just that her being here, in her undies...'

'She happens to be in the middle of a tiff with her partner, and was taking shelter.'

'Oh. Well...'

Louise re-emerged, fully dressed. 'I'll see you tomorrow. Have a nice night, Princess. You say I'm to use Andie's car and leave mine here?'

172

Jessica nodded.

Karina watched the door close. 'What about my things?'

'I'm going to sort that out now.' Jessica called Andrea. 'How is it?'

'Fairly hysterical.'

'Has Adams called?'

'Not yet.'

'Par for the course. And Cerise?'

'She's fairly hysterical too.'

'Well, Louise should be with you in an hour. She's fully briefed. And the boss is going to try to sort things out. Now listen. I want you to get into the princess's bedroom and collect her nightdress, her toothbrush and paste, her hairbrush...' She turned to Karina. 'Anything else?'

'My spray.'

'And her deodorant. When Louise gets there, leave her in charge and bring those things up to my flat. We'll expect you.'

Karina prowled around the flat. 'Very neat. And you live here all alone?'

'No. I told you, I have a partner. But he's away right now.'

'Oh. You're into men, then?'

'Aren't you?' Jessica began to feel a little uneasy.

'I've never had the chance to find out. May I watch your television? It's years since I've watched English television. Daddy won't

173

have a dish.'

'Help yourself. I'll get a meal together.'

It was only just after six, but she suspected it might be a long evening, even if her apprehensions were entirely wrong. For the moment, however, Karina was totally absorbed; the apartment block had a satellite aerial, and there were some sixty channels available. Karina surfed back and forth.

Andrea arrived just on seven. 'Am I glad to be out of there,' she said. 'If only for a couple of hours. With respect, Your Highness.'

'Going wild, eh?' Karina asked.

'That has to be the understatement of the year.' She laughed. 'It was all I could do to stop them calling the police. I know they called the Home Office.'

'Didn't the commander get on to them?'

'He hadn't when I left. And the fuss when I collected this stuff!' She began taking things out of her shoulder bag. 'They figured, quite correctly, that I know where you are, Your Highness. I really thought I might have to shoot my way out. Your grandfather – again with respect, Your Highness – suggested that we go into his office for a private chat.'

'What was wrong about that?'

'Well...' Andrea looked at Jessica, eyebrows arched.

'I'm sorry to have to tell you, Your Highness,' Jessica said, 'but your grandfather

174

cannot keep his hands off anything with boobs.'

'Good heavens! How do you know that?'

'Because he had a go at me last night.'

'And you never said anything?'

'We have to take all sorts. But there is no reason we have to accept it.'

Karina looked at Andrea. 'And did he...?'

'I declined his invitation. I have a feeling he might have pressed his point, but fortunately Louise turned up at that moment.'

'Louise!' Jessica said. She had forgotten that summoning Andrea up to town would mean that Louise would be on her own for a couple of hours.

'She can take care of herself,' Andrea said. 'Can't she?'

In her fragile mental state? Jessica wondered. 'I suppose so.' It certainly was not the time to start acting like a mother hen, except as regards the princess. 'Well, thanks a million, Andie. You'll put Chloe in the picture when she comes in tomorrow morning?'

'You bet. See you. And you, Princess.'

Jessica served supper. 'Plain fare, I'm afraid. The wine's not too bad, though. Ooops. Would you rather have water?'

'I'd prefer wine.'

'Then wine it shall be.' She poured. 'You don't approve.'

'In my business, one approves of everything one's client does or wishes to do. With-in reason,' she hastily added. 'And anyway, didn't old Omar Khayyam have a word for it?'

'A loaf of bread, a jug of wine, and thou,' Karina said, 'is paradise enow.'

'I think you left out the bit about the wilderness,' Jessica said. 'But the point is, he was a good Muslim, wasn't he?'

'He couldn't have been a good Muslim if he liked wine,' Karina pointed out, and giggled. 'Like me. You are a good cook.'

'One picks things up.'

Karina finished her meal and then her wine. She stood. 'Are we going to make love?'

Jessica nearly choked on her wine.

'I have upset you again,' Karina said.

'Ah ... you surprised me.'

'You do not wish to make love? I know you have a partner. But as he is not here, and we have the whole evening in front of us...'

Jessica desperately wished she hadn't had anything to drink. She certainly didn't want to upset the girl, but... 'We are forbidden to make love with our clients.' Which she supposed was absolutely correct, even if she had never had it spelled out for her.

'You do not like me,' Karina said.

'I like you very much, Highness. But as I said...'

'You would rather I was a man.'

'Not at all,' Jessica lied. 'But rules are rules.'

'But if we are going to share a bed...'

'It's a very big bed,' Jessica pointed out. But all manner of thoughts were rushing about her brain. 'If I may ask, do you ... Are you and Cerise...?' Which might explain the meaningful glances. Although the princess had certainly seemed very angry with her maid. And she had exchanged an equally meaningful glance with Henri.

'Sometimes,' Karina admitted. 'Quite often. Whenever I get the urge. But you...'

'I'm as square as they come,' Jessica said. 'I got into men very early on, and have stayed there ever since, in a manner of speaking. The thing is, this job doesn't really give me much spare time, as you may have gathered.'

'When you have finished with me, you will immediately belong to someone else?'

'Let's rephrase that,' Jessica suggested. 'When my superiors come to the conclusion that you are safe, or when you return to Kharram, yes, I will be assigned to someone else.'

'I would like to keep you,' Karina said.

'I think you need to rephrase that as well.'

'I would employ you as my permanent bodyguard,' Karina explained.

'In Kharram.'

'Oh, yes. It is much better there. Except for trees. You will like it there. Listen, I will even

177

provide you with a man.'

'That sounds entrancing. The problem is, I have a home, here, I have a job, here, and I have a man, here.'

'I would pay you very well. Tax-free.'

'And I don't see myself gelling with your police methods. So, thanks, but no thanks.'

'Ah well...' Karina returned to the dining table, sat down, took a small box from the pocket of her jeans, opened it, and with a very small spatula lifted the white powder to her nostrils.

'Just what are you doing?' Jessica inquired.

'Having a sniff. I always sniff when I'm stressed.'

Jessica whipped both the box and the spatula away from her and took them into the bathroom. She emptied the cocaine down the toilet and flushed it.

Karina stood in the doorway. 'What the fuck...?'

'Sniffing is out, on these premises.'

'You had no right ... You said you were required to go along with anything I might wish to do.'

'I also said, within reason. Cocaine is an illegal substance in this country.'

'I am not subject to your laws.'

'But I am. If cocaine were to be found in my flat I'd lose my job. Let's go to bed. Tomorrow could be a long day. And Princess, remember, as long as you are here, I am on duty, even when I'm sleeping.'

Karina sighed. 'I think we could have great sex together.'

Thankfully, the phone rang. Jessica answered it.

'It is Henri,' the voice said.

'Oh, right. Where are you?'

'I am in an hotel.'

'Where?'

'It is somewhere in South London.'

'Ah.' That sounded rather close.

'Is Princess Karina still with you?'

'Yes, she is.'

'May I speak with her?'

Jessica gave Karina the phone, and waited.

Karina listened, spoke a few words in a language Jessica did not understand – presumably Arabic – and then looked at her. 'He wishes to come and see me.'

'Not tonight.'

'Why not?' Karina pouted.

'Because it would be an additional complication. When we get you sorted out, we'll see about Henri.'

Karina spoke into the phone again, then raised her head again. 'He is very upset. He says he has travelled all this way to be with me, to protect me.'

'Tell him the protection business is *my* business. Tell him to be patient, and he will have all that he wants. Or at least, all that you are prepared to give him.'

★ ★ ★

Jessica lay awake for some time. There was a great deal to be considered, quite apart from the girl lying beside her. At least the princess had dropped right off to sleep, on her own side of the bed, even if she also had decided not to wear her nightie. The important question was what might happen next – and she wasn't thinking of her relations with Karina. She had meant to have the telephone van checked out, and had quite forgotten about it, what with everything else. That was something to be done first thing tomorrow morning. But ... had she overreacted? The fact that everyone in Kharram might know where the princess was did not mean her would-be kidnappers did. On the other hand, there was absolutely no point in maintaining the princess in a secret location, surrounded by bodyguards, if it was no longer a secret. And in any event, Cerise had clearly been instructed to let the villains know that the princess had arrived.

Cerise! She sat bolt upright. What other instructions had she been given? And she was now free.

Jessica got out of bed, and tiptoed into the lounge, closing the bedroom door behind her. The time was eleven fifteen; Andrea would still be on duty. She punched the numbers. 'How is it?'

'Quiet as the grave.'

'Did Adams call?'

'Yes, thank God. He spoke with Sir William. And seemed to straighten things out. The sultana isn't happy; well, she's lost her daughter, at least pro tem.'

'We'll get it all straight tomorrow. Have you been visited by a man?'

'Chance would be a fine thing. What man?'

'A sexy French hunk named Henri Ferrière.'

'Not that I know of. What do I do with him when I've got him?'

'I'm sure you'll think of something. Just remember that as far as we currently know he's on our side. Now listen. Cerise. What is she doing?'

'She's gone to bed. They've all gone to bed.'

'By bed, I assume you mean in her old room.'

'Yes.'

'And where are you at this moment?'

'In our apartment.'

'And Louise?'

'At the moment, sleeping like a baby.'

'What do you mean, at the moment?'

'Well, she seemed rather uptight when she arrived.'

'She is rather uptight. She has man trouble.'

'Ugh! Is there anything I should do?'

'Just be soothing. And keep her away from

181

Bland. In her present mood she might just shoot him.'

'I'll see what I can do. But at least she's not likely to run into him in the middle of the night.'

'Right. Now I have an idea that Cerise may make another telephone call tonight. So you'd better keep an eye on her. Tell Louise.'

'Attitude?'

'Just see that she doesn't use a phone.'

'Suppose she chances the ping of the phone in her room?'

'Find the control panel and unplug it, then cover the downstairs phone.'

'There'll be hell to pay if his nibs or the sultana tries to make a call from their bedrooms.'

'That also is hardly likely in the middle of the night. If it crops up, tell them you are acting on my orders.'

'Will do. May I call you if there is a rumpus?'

'Of course. But try to keep it until tomorrow morning. Have fun.'

She went back to bed. Karina was still asleep, on her back, snoring slightly. Jessica lay beside her, and was asleep in seconds. To awake, it seemed, seconds later, as her phone buzzed.

'Will she call tonight?' Sonia asked.

They sat in the cab of the telephone van,

drinking coffee after their sandwich dinner. This had been brought to them by Loman. It was nearly midnight, and they could see the lights of Blandlock House glowing through the trees.

'There is no reason for her to do so,' Loman said. 'Unless there has been some change in the arrangements. And if she does, she will wait for the family to go to bed. It won't be till after midnight.'

'Will it not be risky to signal at all? What about these policewomen?'

'After midnight, everyone will be asleep. Except for Cerise.'

'She knows where we are?'

'Oh, yes. I told her how we would be handling things.' He grinned. 'I did not tell her how you mean to go in.'

'But she knows where we are. Are you sure she is reliable?'

'She has proved so, thus far,' Loman said.

'Where did you find her?'

'We did not have to find her. She came with Mustafa. But she has been the princess's playmate for years. They were friends as children.'

'And she and her friend Mustafa are in this for the money?'

'There is politics involved as well. Kharram has virtually been supported by Worldoil for the past dozen years. If Worldoil now loses its franchise, Yusuf will find its replacement –

our principals – much more difficult to deal with, and there is a strong chance it will destabilise the regime.'

'And who are our principals?'

'I do not know. And if I did, I would not be at liberty to tell you. I only know what Burke has told me.'

'What I was thinking was that if the regime is destabilised, and Yusuf is deposed, isn't there a possibility that the resulting civil strife would interfere with the profits our principals must be looking for?'

'That is a risk they are apparently prepared to take. As I said, there is more than profit involved here, at every level.' He stretched. 'Well, I am for bed. I look forward to hearing your report.'

'Lucky for some,' Sonia commented as he disappeared into the gloom. His car was parked a quarter of a mile away. 'But I think I will follow his example.' She left the cab, and went to the back of the van.

Rosen had been studying the house through his binoculars. Now he put these away and came back to sit on one of the bunks and watch her taking off her shoes and overalls. 'She's asleep. Reliable! Ha.'

'Do you mind?' she asked.

'You should not ask so many questions of Loman.'

'Why not? I am interested in what I do. In the reasons for it.'

'You should not be. People like you and me – mercenaries – should certainly be interested in our allotted task. But only that. Seeking to find out why we have been given the task is counter-productive and distracting. It can also be dangerous. And Burke will not like it.'

'Are you my schoolmaster or something?'

'I am your commander.'

She snorted. 'Who believes in doing everything by the book? Had we gone after the princess this afternoon, the business would be done by now.'

'Or we would be in prison, if not dead.'

'Dead?'

'If the police were involved, as I am quite sure they were.'

'The police do not shoot people in England.'

'You are out of touch,' Rosen commented. 'And you are also out of order. You will be disciplined.'

Sonia glared at him. 'You would not dare.'

'I have been told, by Burke, to conduct this operation as I see fit, until he arrives to take over.'

Sonia licked her lips, remembering her last conversation with their employer. 'So,' Rosen said, 'undress.'

'Why?'

'You came back here to go to bed, didn't you?'

'We are working. I did not intend to undress.'

'We have done all we can for today, unless this woman telephones. So you may undress.' He grinned. 'I give you permission.'

'And you are going to undress also?'

'Certainly.'

'I do not—'

'Like men,' he finished for her. 'That will be part of your punishment.'

'If you touch me...'

'You will submit. Because I am your commander, and because if you attempt to resist me I will hurt you, very badly.' Sonia stared at him for several seconds, then slowly unbuttoned her blouse. Rosen watched her, his eyes glowing. 'Release your hair,' he said. 'I want to see your hair.' Sonia obeyed, still staring at him. 'I like that,' he said. 'Continue.' She took off her blouse, dropped her trousers, and turned her back on him. 'Face me,' he said. 'I can look at your ass afterwards.'

Sonia took off her brassiere and laid it across a chair. 'I shall make a full report of this unnecessary and obscene behaviour to Mr Burke,' she said.

'He'll enjoy that.'

Sonia let her panties slip down her thighs and stepped out of them. 'Satisfied?'

'Getting there.' He stood up and against her, cupping her breasts, sliding his hands

186

down her sides to caress her pubes before going behind to grasp her buttocks. 'Now lie on the bed, on your face.'

'God, no!' she protested.

'I am going to beat you,' he explained. The phone buzzed. 'Shit!' he muttered. But he picked it up.

'One of them has left the house,' Cerise said.

'Is that important?'

'She is on foot, and she is walking up the drive.'

Rosen frowned. 'Why?'

'She must have seen your van and become suspicious.'

'In the middle of the night? We were told they would be asleep.'

'Well, she must have been awake.'

'Shit,' Rosen said again. 'Is she armed?'

'They are always armed.'

'All right. How many more are in the house?'

'Only one. But I think she is asleep.'

'And the princess is also asleep?'

'The princess is not here.'

'What? What do you mean?'

'She went out this afternoon with the head one, the one called Sergeant Jones. And she has not come back. She is staying with Sergeant Jones.'

'Shit!' Rosen said a third time. 'The sultana has permitted this?'

'There was a big fuss, but she has agreed. Listen, I must go. Someone may come.'

'Not so fast. When are the princess and this Jones coming back?'

'I do not know. Nobody knows.'

'Jesus! All right, where has this Jones taken the princess?'

'I do not know that either.'

'You,' Rosen said, 'are as much use as a lump of shit.' He switched off the phone.

Sonia had been listening. 'You see, I was right about this afternoon. If we had taken advantage of the situation...'

'Shut up,' Rosen said. 'And get dressed.'

'What are you going to do?'

'It is what *we* are going to do.'

'I will take no responsibility for this fuck-up. Let's get the hell out of here.'

'It is not going to be a fuck-up, and we are not going anywhere. Do you not suppose this woman knows where her sergeant has taken the princess?'

'It is likely.'

'So, we will wait for her to come to us, and then persuade her to tell us. This will make our task even easier, because, having removed the princess from the care of her mother and grandfather to a secret address, they will feel that she is utterly secure.'

'You are going to snatch an English policewoman? You must be mad.'

'She is the one who is mad, coming out

188

here on her own. She is like an overripe apple, falling from its tree into our arms. What is so important about an English policewoman? She is flesh and blood, tits and ass, like any other woman. All we have to do is prevent her using either her gun or her mobile telephone.' He grinned. 'There will be something in it for both of us.'

The Catastrophe

Sleepily Jessica reached for the phone. 'Yes?'

'Andie.'

Jessica tried to get her brain working while she checked the time. Twelve thirty in the morning. Louise's watch; Andie should be in bed. 'Tell me.'

'I don't know. Something ... I was awakened fifteen minutes ago by my buzzer.'

'Louise?'

'Had to be.'

'Cerise telephoning again?'

'I don't know. I got up, and went downstairs. Nothing.'

'Then what alarmed Louise?'

'That's what I mean.' Andrea's normally calm voice rose an octave. 'I can't find her. I'll swear she's not in the house.'

189

'Shit!' Jessica muttered. 'Have you buzzed her back?'

'Yes. But there was no reply.'

'And her mobile?'

'Yes. Again, no reply. Listen, I heard a car engine just now.'

'In the yard?'

'On the road, I think.'

'*Shit!* Listen, when you drove in and out this evening, was there a telephone repair van parked in the lane?'

'Ah ... yes.'

'Did Louise mention it to you?'

'No. Should she have?'

'Yes, she should have.'

'Well, like I told you, she seemed sort of preoccupied this evening.'

She shouldn't have been on duty at all, Jessica thought savagely.

'Do you want me to see if that van is still there, and check it out?' Andrea asked.

Jessica came to a quick decision. Obviously that was what Louise had done, throwing all of her training – and, indeed, common sense – overboard in her desire, as she had herself said, to blow the bastards away. As for what had happened to her... 'No,' she said. 'Sit tight. I am coming right down.'

Karina was awake. 'What's happening?'

'I don't know, but I have to find out. Listen, you promised to do exactly as I said. Right?'

190

'Ye-es.' Karina's tone was doubtful.

'Well, I have to go out. What I want you to do is stay right where you are. If I'm not back by morning, make yourself some breakfast, but do not, under any circumstances, leave the flat. I will call you as soon as I can, so you can answer the phone, but you must not, again under any circumstances, identify yourself to any caller except me. If they ask, tell them you're the daily help. Understand?'

'You *are* coming back?'

'Of course I'm coming back.' She dressed herself, checked out her pistol, and put a spare magazine in her bag, just in case. Like Louise, she felt in a killing mood.

She drove as fast as was compatible with only just breaking the law, but even so it was nearly two before she swung into the lane. This was empty, but she stopped by the telephone pole where she had seen the van the previous afternoon, got out, and shone her torch on the ground. The tyre marks made by the van were clearly visible. She sent the torch beam roaming through the trees and bushes on either side. There were one or two broken twigs, but that could have happened at any time. It was still far too dark to make a proper search. She got back into the Land Rover, punched Andrea's number.

'She hasn't come back. Oh, JJ, what are we to do?'

191

'Mother's here,' Jessica told her. 'Have Parkin open the gates.'

'He'll be asleep.'

'So, wake him up.' She swung the Land Rover into the driveway, and braked, staring at the iron gates illuminated in her headlamps. She didn't want to think, but she had to, not only because there were hard facts to be faced, but because she had to determine how far to carry this. She had to accept that one of her team was either dead or kidnapped. The thought made her blood boil. The point was that it would make most other people's blood boil as well, especially the media. Once they got hold of the story any chance of the princess retaining her anonymity was done.

The gates swung in, and she drove on to the forecourt, deliberately gunning her engine and slamming her door as she got out. The dogs surrounded her, barking and snarling. 'Bugger off,' she told them, and there was so much menace in her tone they slunk off into the gloom.

The front door was open, and Andrea was waiting for her, fully dressed, while above her head lights were starting to come on. 'The van has gone,' Jessica told her.

'You think...?'

'Yes. Or she would have come back here.'

'Then...' Andrea licked her lips.

'We don't know that. Not that the alternative is any better. These people are after Karina. They'll have to suppose Louise knows where she is.'

'But...'

'Yes,' Jessica said grimly. She had no idea how Louise would stand up to torture, especially in her present mental condition. But the very thought had her blood boiling all over again. But worse than that, if Louise were to crack, quickly...

They went to the foot of the main staircase, and faced Sir William. 'What the devil is the reason for all this racket?' he demanded, as aggressive as ever. 'Do you know the time?'

'The time is two fifteen, Sir William. And there is an emergency.'

'An emergency? Where is my grand-daughter? What has happened to her?'

The sultana had appeared behind him. 'My poor darling!'

'The princess is perfectly safe,' Jessica said, praying that she was telling the truth. 'But there has been suspicious activity outside of this estate. One of my officers went to investigate, and has not returned.'

They stared at her, unable to comprehend. But now they had been joined by Cerise; Barbara was apparently keeping discreetly out of sight.

'There will have to be an investigation of what has happened,' Jessica said. 'This means that, very shortly, there will be a considerable police presence here. Perhaps you'd like to go back to bed, while you can.'

'Let me get this straight,' Sir William said. 'One of your women, a member of what I was told is a top-class security unit, has wandered off into the darkness all by herself and gone astray? Wasn't that a bit careless of her?'

'Yes,' Jessica agreed, resisting with an effort the temptation to hit him.

'And you think something has happened to her? She's probably trodden in a rabbit hole and twisted her ankle.'

'That is unlikely,' Jessica said. 'She has an alarm call with her, as well as a mobile phone, both of which she would use were she not either unconscious or under restraint.'

'Or dead, eh?'

'Yes, Sir William,' Jessica said through gritted teeth. 'Or dead. Now go back to bed.' She deliberately omitted the 'please'. 'Not you,' she added, pointing at Cerise. 'I want to have a word with you.'

'You're not starting that all over again,' Vanessa protested.

'I'm continuing from where I left off,' Jessica told her. 'Now, if you'll excuse us.' She pushed through them, Andrea behind her, and reached Cerise. Cerise looked as if she would like to have taken to her heels, but apparently decided against it. 'Upstairs,' Jessica told her. The three women went up to the policewomen's apartment. 'Lock the door,' Jessica said. 'And you, lie on the bed.'

The two women obeyed her, both looking distinctly apprehensive, Cerise no doubt because she was familiar with Kharrami police methods, Andrea because she had never seen her boss in such a mood, and had no idea what she might be meaning to do. Cerise lay on her back, nightdress neatly arranged down to her ankles, hands folded on her chest, clearly anticipating the very worst; her breasts rose and fell as she breathed. 'First things first,' Jessica said. 'Andie, call Chloe, tell her she's on duty as of now. Tell her to get dressed and get round to my flat. She will find the princess there, and she is to stay with her until I return. No one except you or me is to be admitted. Warn her that there is a possibility someone, or some-*ones*, may try to get in. Right?'

Andrea nodded, and used her mobile. Jessica used her own, firstly to call Karina. 'Hello?' Her voice was tremulous.

'Me. Are you all right?'

'I'm scared stiff.'

'Any callers?'

'No. When are you coming back?'

'Soon. Listen, Chloe will be with you in half an hour. She will identify herself. Let her in and then take her instructions until I can get back to you.'

'What's happening?'

'Everything. Be a good girl and sit tight.' She switched off and looked at Andrea.

'Chloe's on her way.'

'Right. Keep an eye on our girl.' Andrea sat on the bed beside Cerise, obviously trying to look as fierce as possible. Jessica thumbed her mobile. 'Duty officer, please.'

'Rogan.'

'Good morning, sir. Detective-Sergeant Jones.'

'Yes?' Inspector Rogan's tone was watchful; he knew Jessica was Special Branch, and he also knew she was in a special protection unit. Jessica outlined the events of the past twelve hours. 'You are telling me that Detective-Constable Pleyell went out to investigate this strange van, by herself, in the middle of the night?'

'I'm afraid so, sir.'

'Should you have had someone that inexperienced in such a position?'

'Detective-Constable Pleyell has been on the force for eight years, and in the Special Branch for four. She is one of our most experienced operatives.'

'Then what in the name of God was she doing?'

'I'm afraid she was under some stress, sir. I will make a report.'

'Thank you, Sergeant. Now, what about

this van? You say you spotted it at five o'clock yesterday afternoon, but you did nothing about it. Why?'

'Things got extremely fraught about then, sir. I was having to take steps to protect my principal from what I assumed was some danger from another source. I meant to have the van investigated, but it slipped my mind.'

'That will have to go in your report.'

'I understand that, sir.'

'Very good. You did get the number?' Jessica gave it to him. 'That's something. Tell me how you wish this handled.'

'At the moment it is simply a disappearance, sir. But it could be more serious. The difficulty is that this operation is top secret. That is why I have come direct to you instead of the local police.'

'They will have to be informed, or they're liable to be unhappy.'

'I appreciate that, sir. This is rather urgent, as I have to assume that Detective-Constable Pleyell's life may be in danger. If you could set the wheels in motion, I will be making a full report to Commander Adams as soon as he is likely to be out of bed, and discover from him how it should be handled media-wise.'

'If what you have been telling me is accurate, Sergeant, I think this is one occasion when you should wake the commander from his beauty sleep and suffer his comments. I will get things moving, in so far as I can. That is, I shall trace that number and start looking for sightings, and I will send a forensic team down to look over the ground. I can't offer more than that without using television coverage. Is there anyone you feel should be informed of the situation? Has Pleyell a partner, husband, immediate family?'

'There is a partner, sir. But I think he can keep for a few hours. He knows she's on an assignment, and he won't be expecting her back until well into the day. I will handle it.' She could only hope she was right.

'Very good. Now, your principal: you are absolutely sure she is safe?'

'Yes, sir.' Again, a silent prayer.

'Very good. You come back to me as soon as you have clearance on how public I can go. Remember that within an hour of my people starting work the local police will have to be put in the picture.'

Jessica put down the phone and gazed at it for several seconds. 'Problems?' Andrea asked.

'Nothing I didn't expect.'

'Can I go back to bed now?' Cerise asked.

'No.'

'I will have the law on you.'

'That is absolutely correct. You are going to have the law on you, very heavily, just as soon as I have made another phone call.'

'You touch me, and I will scream.'

'If she makes any noise at all, Andie, you have my permission to break her arm.' Andrea licked her lips; Jessica couldn't be sure whether it was in anticipation or apprehension. But Cerise decided to keep quiet. Jessica punched the numbers, waited: she was certainly apprehensive.

'Yes?' A woman's voice.

'May I speak with Commander Adams, please?'

'At this hour?'

Jessica had never met the commander's wife, but she had to assume she was dealing with a matchingly formidable personality. 'It is very urgent.'

'And who may you be?'

'Detective-Sergeant Jones, ma'am.'

Presumably Adams had been lying beside his wife, close enough to hear the voice on the phone, judging by the way he apparently snatched it from her hand. 'JJ? What's happened?'

'Far too much, sir.' Jessica went rapidly through what she had told Rogan.

'Hell's bells,' he commented. 'Isn't that girl experienced?'

'Very, sir. But she was – *is*, I hope – undergoing some domestic problems.'

'You should have taken her off the squad.'

'I know that, sir – now. I'm afraid I did not consider it serious enough at the time. She

199

has always been one of my most reliable colleagues.'

'And what do you think has happened to her? Do you think she is dead?'

'I don't think she was killed at the site, sir. Hopefully Inspector Rogan's forensic people will be able to confirm that. But I believe she was snatched when she tried to investigate that van.'

'Why would they wish to do that? Take such a risk?'

'I believe they are aware that the princess is no longer at Blandlock.'

'How could they possibly know that?'

Jessica looked at Cerise, who was staring at her. 'I think I am in a position to find that out, sir. I will come back to you on that. However, assuming I am right, I would say that these people feel that Detective-Constable Pleyell knows where we are holding our principal.'

'Does she?'

'I'm afraid so, yes.'

'And you think they may ... My God!'

'Yes, sir.'

'But I mean, can they? I mean, would they?'

'Judging by their behaviour in Kharram, sir, I believe they both can and would.'

'Good God! And do you think, well, that Pleyell might succumb?'

'It is a fairly well-established fact, sir, that

200

anyone will succumb to sufficient pressure.'

'She must be found! Quickly!'

'Yes, sir.'

'But it's not your concern, JJ. Your concern is the princess. She must be moved.'

'With respect, sir, I believe our best chance of nailing these people is if they come after her at my place.'

'You think you can cope? You said you wanted her moved.'

'Yes, sir. Have you a safe house arranged?'

'Not yet. I intend to fix that in the morning.'

'Then I consider that I am more able to protect her in my flat than anywhere else until the new place is ready.'

'Do you wish a back-up?'

'I would like to bring the squad back up to strength, sir. And just in case they come in numbers, I'd like a back-up squad available, yes. But they should stay at the Yard until called.'

'I'll arrange it. What about the other people in the building? You will remember that these people used a bomb in Kharram.'

'I do remember that, sir. But they want the princess alive. When they bombed the front of the nightclub in Kharram, they knew where she was, that she would not be affected by the blast, and that she would be flushed into the open. All this means that they believe in careful reconnoitring before undertaking any action. I believe we can cope with this. Will you give me carte blanche?'

'Oh, yes. Well, please be sure that if you do shoot anybody it is one of them.'

'I will, sir. And the rest of it?'

'I will handle that. As for you, just make sure you don't leave the princess's side for a moment,' he ordered, and replaced the receiver.

'He sounds agitated,' Andrea remarked.

'Wouldn't you be? Suppose they'd got Chloe?'

'Shit!'

'Don't you start. Now, our business is to get back up to town. If Lou is giving in, it'll be about now, I imagine.' She punched numbers. 'Thank God you're there,' she said. 'Everything all right?'

'Seems so,' Chloe said. 'Her nibs is agitated.'

'So am I. We'll be with you in an hour.'

'What about her?' Andrea thumbed at Cerise.

'I think we'll take her with us. I imagine the princess is better at asking her important questions than we could possibly be.' Breath hissed through Cerise's nostrils, and the nightdress was heaving again. 'Unless you'd like to answer a few questions now. Who are these people?'

'I do not know. I have said this.'

202

'And I am not convinced. Right. We don't have any time to waste. Handcuffs, Andie.'

Andrea took the cuffs from her bag. Cerise gave a gasp of discomfort as Jessica grasped her thighs and rolled her on to her face, while Andrea pulled her arms behind her back and secured her wrists. 'You cannot do this.'

'Watch us.' Jessica rolled her on to her back again.

'You must allow me to get dressed.'

'You gave me the impression that modesty was not one of your virtues.' Jessica took a roll of tape from her bag. 'You'll be more comfortable with your mouth shut.'

'This is kidnapping!'

'You know, you're absolutely right.' Jessica slapped the tape over Cerise's mouth, and Andrea produced a pair of nail scissors to cut it free and then smoothed it down on her cheeks. They collected their gear, left the room, and went down the stairs, marching Cerise between them. The house had reverted to quiet, although there were still lights on in various bedrooms.

'How do you suppose they'll react to waking up to discover that this one has also gone missing?' Andrea whispered.

'We'll telephone from the flat to tell them that she's under arrest,' Jessica said. They opened the door and were surrounded by leaping and barking dogs. Cerise was now

203

shivering in the dawn breeze. 'I told you to bugger off,' Jessica reminded the animals. 'Do you mind leaving your car here?' she asked Andrea. 'I need you to keep an eye on her.'

Andrea nodded, grim-faced. Her Clio was her pride and joy. They forced Cerise into the back seat, and Andrea sat beside her. Jessica drove out of the yard. In her rear-view mirror she saw one of the upstairs windows open, but she could not identify which one.

It was still dark when they reached London, which, at this time of the morning, was a world of milk floats and delivery vans. Jessica parked the Land Rover and got out, looking up and down the street. At the moment there was no one in sight. She opened the back door, grasped Cerise's arms, and pulled while Andrea pushed. Cerise, making sounds at the back of her throat like an angry cat, came out with a rush, and they half carried her into the hallway and up the stairs. 'It's us,' Jessica said.

Chloe unlocked the door. 'Am I glad to see you.' She gazed at Cerise.

'She wants to talk to us,' Jessica explained. 'Tell us things.' They pushed Cerise into the room, and Andrea closed and locked the door. She and Chloe exchanged glances of mutual appreciation.

Karina emerged from the bedroom, dressed. 'What has happened?'

'I don't know for sure,' Jessica said. 'But I would say that your would-be kidnappers, having been informed where you were to be found,' – she looked at Cerise – 'staked Blandlock out in order to work out their plan of campaign. I believe they were those bogus telephone repairmen we saw yesterday afternoon. Unfortunately, what with one thing and another, I didn't follow that up. Nor did I mention it to Louise. Again, I had so much on my mind I didn't take Louise's state of mind into consideration when allowing her to go on duty. She must have spotted the van when she arrived at six, but did not mention it to Andie. She seems to have been feeling very gung-ho, and, on taking over the watch at midnight and spotting that the van was still there, she went off on her own to investigate, thus breaking just about every rule in the book. She did call for assistance, but then just disappeared.'

'You mean they have taken her?'

'It looks like it.'

'But why?'

'Because she knows where you are to be found.'

'How can they know I am not at Blandlock?'

'That is one of the several things I am

205

expecting Cerise to tell us.'

'Mmmm!' Cerise commented.

'Oh, yes,' Karina said. 'She will tell us.'

'Right,' Jessica said. 'But we need to get organised. Chloe, will you prepare breakfast? Then we are going to set up a watch system. There will be a replacement for Louise here in a little while. We are going to station one of us outside this building, to report any suspicious activities.'

'You think they will come here?' the princess asked.

'Just as soon as Louise gives them the address.'

'You think she would do that?'

'Yes. Not willingly. But they will get to her.'

Karina looked at Cerise, who swallowed.

'Grub up.' Chloe had been frying vigorously; now she served. But no one was very hungry.

'Right,' Jessica said. 'Chloe, will you take first watch? Poor Andie has hardly had any sleep.'

'I haven't had all that much either,' Chloe pointed out. But she blew her partner a kiss.

'You'll be relieved as soon as our back-up gets here.'

'Right.' Chloe picked up her bag. 'Can I sit in my car?'

'Just as long as it's not parked right outside the door. Now don't forget: keep in constant touch.'

'Will do.' Chloe looked at Cerise, who still had the tape across her mouth and had not been offered any breakfast. 'Have fun.'

'You'd better have a lie-down,' Jessica suggested to Andrea, whose eyes were drooping.

'Give me a shout if you need me.' Andrea went into the bedroom and closed the door.

'Now let's have a chat,' Jessica said, and tore the tape from Cerise's mouth.

'Ow!' Cerise exclaimed in pain.

'Tell us what happened,' Jessica said.

Cerise looked at Karina, who took a knife from the kitchen drawer and thumbed its edge. 'You wouldn't dare!'

'Are *you*, a traitor to your country and your future sultana, going to tell *me* what I can dare?' Cerise licked her lips. 'And no matter what I do to you,' Karina told her, 'if you do not co-operate, you are going back to Kharram to be interrogated by Colonel Bartruf. Do you know what he will do to you?' Cerise gasped.

'You must tell me some time,' Jessica said to Karina. 'Now, Cerise, you have admitted that you were instructed to inform your people when the princess was in residence. You did this the night before last. Did you call them again last night?' Cerise hesitated. 'Sit down,' Jessica invited.

Cerise's knees seemed to give way, and she sat on the settee. Karina sat beside her, knife in hand. 'You were saying?'

'Yes,' Cerise said. 'I called them last night. I was supposed to give them details of your watch-keeping arrangements. But I also had to tell them that you were no longer there, Your Highness. But just before I was ready to use the phone, I saw the policewoman leave the house and walk up the drive. I had to warn them. I thought they would simply go away, and come back later. But they waited for her.'

'Didn't you guess that they intended to either kill her or kidnap her?' Jessica asked.

'I didn't want to think about it. I went back to bed.'

'And you still swear you don't know who these people are? Or where they might have taken Louise?'

'No. I swear it. You will have to ask Mustafa.'

'I think that would be a very good idea,' Jessica said.

'Yes,' Karina agreed. 'Is it all right to use your phone to telephone Kharram?'

'Sure. Who are you calling?'

'Daddy, first.'

'Then go ahead.'

'I would like to go to the bathroom,' Cerise said.

'Come along then. Just remember that if you try anything I will break your neck.' Cerise looked her up and down. 'I've been trained to do it,' Jessica told her, and unlocked the handcuffs. They went through the bedroom – where Andrea, predictably, was fast asleep, sprawled across the bed wearing only her thongs – and into the bathroom. Jessica leaned against the wall.

'What is going to happen to me?' Cerise asked. 'You said you would help me.'

'If you behaved yourself and co-operated. I don't consider allowing one of my women to be kidnapped as co-operating.'

'Have you any idea what they will do to me if I am sent back to Kharram? That Bartruf—'

'Your best hope is that Louise comes back safe and sound,' Jessica said. 'Come along now.' She extended the handcuffs.

'I would like to get dressed.'

'That will have to wait. You don't have any gear.'

'Then I would like a drink of water.'

'No harm in that.' She escorted her through to the kitchenette. Karina was still speaking on the phone, very animatedly. And now Jessica's mobile buzzed. 'Yes?'

'Lowe is on her way up,' Chloe said. 'Is she supposed to relieve me?'

'After I've put her in the picture. Any other activity?'

'People going to work.'

'Keep in touch.' Jessica switched off the phone as Karina hung up. 'Okay?'

'Mustafa will be arrested today.'

'I'd like to know anything they find out.'

The princess nodded. 'I told Daddy to keep me informed. He is very upset.'

'I can imagine.'

'Mummy has been on the phone, telling him all sorts of things.'

'I can imagine that too.' The doorbell rang, and she asked who it was.

'Here I am,' Priscilla Lowe announced. Jessica let her in. She was a large, jolly black woman, with matching features. 'What's it all about?'

Jessica closed the door. 'Sit down and I'll tell you. This is Princess Karina of Kharram.'

Karina shook hands, and Priscilla looked at Jessica. 'Do I curtsey?'

'She's incognito. Have you breakfasted?'

'Some. I'd love a cup of coffee, though.'

'So sit down.' Jessica made the coffee, and brought her up to date.

'Shit!' Priscilla commented, and looked at Cerise. 'And this is one of them? You think they're going to come here?'

'I think it's entirely possible. Would you like to take a two-hour exterior watch?'

'Right.' Priscilla finished her coffee and stood up. 'Brief?'

'Call if anyone enters the building. Or any two. If more than two, call me first and then call the Yard. There's a back-up standing by.'

210

Priscilla nodded. 'And after that?'

'You back us up, here. Are you armed?'

Another nod. 'You reckon it may come to that? Do we have the authority?'

'We do. Just so long as we don't hit the wrong guys.'

'I reckon this building must be just about empty,' Chloe said when she came upstairs. 'People have been leaving in a steady stream.'

'That figures,' Jessica agreed. 'Makes it easier for us.'

'And for them. I'm for bed. Okay?'

Jessica felt very much like going to bed herself, but she knew it would have to wait. Her mobile rang. 'Good morning, JJ,' Inspector Moran said. 'Many happy returns.'

'Many ... Good God!'

'You sound stressed. Fancy forgetting your own birthday.'

'I am stressed, sir. Do we have progress?'

'Your man is one Jaime Sanchez, Spanish national but has several aliases – and passports to match them. Professional hit man. Has never operated in the UK, at least not to our knowledge. Kills with the knife, which means he gets up close and personal. Present whereabouts unknown, but we are putting a trace on Kharram. The woman is Sonia Maquardie, alias Solere. French national, wanted for several crimes over there, including murder; she used a gun. Again, professional and contractual. Again, present whereabouts unknown, but we are tracing.'

Karina had said that her friend Manfred had been shot by a woman. 'Brilliant, sir.'

'Thank you. There is a downside.'

'Yes?'

'There is no record of Sanchez and Maquardie ever working together, or even knowing each other.'

'But, as they are both professionals, there is every possibility that they may both be employed by Burke,' Jessica suggested.

'That's true. Now, about that other woman, Cerise Mahliah. I'm afraid we have nothing on her, save that she is of a good Kharrami family and has been in the employ of the royal family for a dozen years.'

'Um,' Jessica said. She already knew that.

'There is one item. It doesn't sound important to me, but you may be able to use it.'

'Sir?'

'This woman apparently dabbles in amateur theatricals. Any good?'

'Ah ... yes,' Jessica said. 'That might be quite useful.'

'Good. Now, finally, the vehicle. We have traced the number. It belongs on a car, not a van. And was stolen on Sunday morning. So, they've obviously just switched plates.'

'On to a telecomms van? That must also have been stolen.'

'Hm. I'll check and see if any thefts have been reported. But they could just have used an ordinary van, and redecorated it.'

'Only if they were prescient, sir. The English half of the operation could not have known they were going to be used until Sunday morning, when their boss discovered that the princess had not been snatched after all. So then they stole a car for fresh plates. But the van was in position yesterday afternoon. That would have had to be a very quick paint job.'

'Point taken. We'll chase it up.'

'Thank you, sir.'

'Always happy to help. Have a nice birthday.'

'Thank you, sir. I'll try.' She put down the phone. How on earth had she forgotten her birthday? And this evening she had a date with Brian! As if either of those mattered beside what might have happened to Louise – and this Sanchez killed with a knife. That made her skin crawl.

'Do I gather we are making progress?' Karina asked. 'Your police are very efficient.'

'They try.' Jessica looked at Cerise. 'Sanchez. Maquardie. Solere.' Cerise stared at her, blankly. There was no flicker from her eyes.

213

'Are those the names of the people?' Karina asked.

'They would appear to be the names of the people who attempted to kidnap you.'

'And your police have traced them? But that is excellent. Have they been arrested?'

'No. We don't know where they are, or even if they are in this country. This might be an entirely new team.' Cerise licked her lips.

'Speak,' Jessica commanded.

'If I tell you, do you promise not to send me back to Kharram?'

'That depends on what you tell us. You're not in a position to bargain.'

Another circle of the lips. 'The man I spoke to on the phone last night, and the man who kidnapped Her Highness in Kharram, was the same.'

'How do you know that?'

'I recognised his voice. He has a very harsh voice.'

'Rosen!' Karina said.

'Come again?'

'In the car, the woman called him Rosen.'

'Well, there's a step forward.' She called Moran back. 'I have just received information that Sanchez is in the country, sir, probably using the name Rosen, and that he is involved, certainly in the attempt to snatch the princess, and probably also with the disappearance of DC Pleyell.'

'Leave it with me. I'm going to have those

214

identikits blown up and shown anyway. A policewoman has been kidnapped. This is all systems go.'

'Thank God for that.' Jessica turned to Karina. 'Your cover is probably about to be blown. But I don't think it matters. We are going all out to get the people who snatched Louise, and, as they are certainly the same people who attempted to snatch you, we will wrap the whole thing up at once.'

'Can you? Will you find them?'

'We'll find them,' Jessica asserted, more confidently than she actually felt. Her mobile rang. 'I can see this is going to be one of our busy days. Yes?'

'Sergeant Jones? It is I, Henri.'

Just about the last person she wanted to hear from. 'Good morning, Henri.'

'You said I could see Princess Karina today.'

'Did I? That was careless of me. I'm afraid it won't be possible today. Maybe tomorrow.'

'You are giving me – how do you say – the run-around.'

'I am just telling you that the princess is not available today. Where are you staying?'

'It is an hotel in Croydon.'

'Oh, yes, you told me last night. Sounds tremendous. Well, have a nice day, and call us tomorrow.' She put the phone down.

'Poor Henri,' Karina said. 'He only wants to help.'

'You can make it up to him when this little spat is over.' She booted her computer and sent an e-mail to Brian, telling him that she couldn't make tonight. That would drive him up the wall.

Waiting, Jessica reflected, was always the worst part of her job. This applied even to routine matters; it was far worse where a colleague who was also a good friend was involved. When she took Priscilla's place in Chloe's car – she wouldn't use the Land Rover because she suspected the kidnappers had identified that as hers – she was almost hoping that they would try something. Like Louise, she wanted to shoot somebody. But, she reminded herself over and over again, that was not her scene, and it was not the department's scene either. If she had to shoot someone, it had to be done coolly and with utter dispassion, and only to save life. Which posed an unanswerable question: it was accepted by everyone that these people only wanted to kidnap the princess, not kill her. So, could it ever be justifiable to kill one of them to stop Karina from being kidnapped? Especially as, while it seemed very obvious that they had committed murder in Kharram, she did not yet know if they had done so in England.

She had just been replaced by Andrea and returned upstairs when her phone buzzed.

She thumbed it almost feverishly. 'Yes?'

'I would like to speak with Detective-Sergeant Jones.'

Breath rushed through Jessica's nostrils; she recognised the voice, even if it wasn't one she wanted to hear right this minute. 'I am she, Jerry.'

'JJ? What the hell is going on?'

'If you'd tell me what you are referring to, I might be able to answer you.'

'You know what I am referring to. Where is Louise?'

'Working.'

'She called me yesterday to say she was coming home at dawn.'

'And you cursed her out. She's probably decided not to come home at all.'

'Now you listen to me, you shit—'

'No, no,' Jessica said. 'You listen to *me*, you shit. Get off my phone and stay off it, or I'll do you for harassment.'

She switched off the phone and looked at the princess. 'Was that a friend?' Karina asked.

'Only by remote control.' She found herself pacing the room, made herself sit down. It was well into the morning now. Louise had been snatched just after midnight. Ten hours! And no one hostile had approached the flat. If they had intended to torture her, there was no possibility of her holding out that long. So what were they doing?

She switched on the television, found a news programme. Louise was still a minor item. 'Concern is being felt for the where-abouts of Detective-Constable Louise Ple-yell,' the newsreader said, 'who has been missing overnight, and who may have been abducted. In this regard, the police would like to hear from the owner of a yellow van, marked as a telephone repair vehicle.' She went on to give the van number and a telephone number to call. They were clearly intent on keeping the Kharrami royal family out of it for as long as possible.

Predictably, that brought Jerry back on the phone a few minutes later. 'You bitch!' he bawled. 'You knew. You bitch!'

'We're doing all we can to find her,' Jessica said. 'Now get lost.'

'Nothing?' she asked Andrea when she returned from her watch just before lunch.

'Not a sausage. Shall I cook?'

'Help yourself.' Jessica did not in the least feel like eating. The phone rang, and they all jumped. 'If it's that bastard Jerry again...' Jessica said as she picked it up. 'Yes?'

'What's with you?' Brian asked. 'Hot, and then cold?'

'I was never hot,' Jessica said. 'Not for you.' Which wasn't altogether true. 'And something has come up.'

'Tell me about it.'

'It's a business matter.'

'You mean one of your clients has gone AWOL. Hey, it's not to do with this missing woman?'

'I'm not going to talk about it. Listen, I'll call you as soon as I have some time to myself.'

'Is that a promise?'

'Yes,' she said, not sure if it was or not.

'You are a popular person,' Karina remarked.

'With all the wrong people.'

'When are you going to let me go?' Cerise asked plaintively. 'I have helped you all I can. You said you would let me go.'

'I *will* let you go,' Jessica said, 'just as soon as we find Louise, and supposing she is alive and well. If anything has happened to her, you are an accessory before the fact. You wanted to stay in England, and you may well have to do so – in gaol.'

Cerise gulped.

'Grub up,' Andrea announced.

The only one of them who really appeared to be hungry was Cerise; before Jessica could make up her mind as to whether she wanted to eat or not, the phone was ringing again. 'JJ,' the commander said. 'Is all well?'

'Quiet as a mouse. I'm bothered.'

'We are all bothered, and none more than Sir William and the sultana. They are really raising a stink. I've had the Home Office on my back. They agree with us that the princess can't return to Blandlock, but they-'re not prepared to take the responsibility of leaving her at your place either. We're arranging that safe house for her now, with maximum security. I'll come back to you on this. We'll make the switch this afternoon.'

'Yes, sir. Am I and my people continuing?'

'Ah ... that depends on if the princess still has confidence in you. But you will be backed up by a male squad.'

'Does that mean *you* no longer have confidence in us, sir?'

'Not at all,' he lied. 'I am merely carrying out Home Office instructions. As I say, I'll be in touch with exact arrangements.'

'One more thing, sir. Will the new location be kept secret from Sir William?'

'I'm afraid not, JJ. Part of the stink they have been raising is over not knowing where the princess is, the conditions in which she is being kept, et cetera. The Home Office says they have to be humoured.'

'So the sultana will also be informed.'

'Well, of course, JJ. She *is* the girl's mother.'

Jessica sighed. 'Yes, Commander. We'll wait for your call.' She replaced the phone, surveying the anxious faces around her. 'You are to be moved, Your Highness. This after-noon.'

'Why? Am I not safe here?'

'I would have said you are safer here than anywhere else in the world at the moment.

But your ma doesn't see it that way.'

Karina blew a raspberry. 'But you will stay with me? All of you?' She looked at Andrea and Chloe; Priscilla was back on exterior watch.

'If you would like us to. You will have to tell the commander that.'

'And her?' She looked at Cerise.

'Well, I suppose once you are established in a new place, she cannot harm us any more.'

'You can't mean to just let her go?'

'I have explained, Highness, that we have to have a legitimate reason for holding her.'

'I will sue you,' Cerise said. 'I have read of this. In this country, people who are wrongly arrested have the right to sue the Government. I will receive millions in compensation.'

Her hobby is acting, Jessica reflected, and she's good enough for it to be difficult to tell when she is and when she isn't. 'It's worth a try,' she agreed. 'But you'll have to do it from a distance. As soon as we get the princess re-established, and have found Louise, I am going to have you deported as an illegal immigrant.'

'You cannot do that!'

'I can and I will. You will have the right to appeal, of course, but I doubt if you will succeed in the long run.'

'And when you get back to Kharram, I will

have Colonel Bartruf waiting for you,' Karina said. Cerise burst into tears, while Jessica wondered how much acting the princess had also done in her short life. It was something she was going to have to find out.

The phone rang. Jessica picked it up. 'What now?'

'JJ?'

'Oh! I beg your pardon, sir. Yes?'

'JJ...' The Commander hesitated. 'They've found Louise.'

The Strike

'JJ?' Adams asked. 'Are you there?'

Jessica drew a deep breath. 'Yes, sir. May I ask...?'

'Yes,' he said.

'Is it bad?'

'I have been told that it is very bad.'

'I would like to see her.'

'I'm not sure that would be a good idea. She was ... Well, she had been interrogated, rather brutally.'

'She was a member of my team, sir. And she was my friend.'

'Yes. Quite. Her body is in the police morgue. We don't have any record of next of kin...'

'She has none, sir. Only a partner. I will let him know.'

'Right. Well, when will you go to the morgue?'

'Now. My girls can take care of the situation here for the time being. May I ask where the body was found?'

'In the Regent Canal. Floating.'

'At what time?'

'Just after dawn.'

'Dawn? But it's nearly one.'

'Yes. The local police did not make an immediate identification. There were no ... Well, the body was naked.'

Jessica drew a deep breath and forced herself to concentrate. 'Is there any idea of when she died?'

'The preliminary inspection indicated that she had been dead for at least two hours when found.'

'That means she would have died at about four. So, as they snatched her just after midnight, they had her in their possession for four hours. And as she was floating, she couldn't have been in the water very long, which means they must have had to drive some distance to the canal. If she had given any information, they would surely have acted on it by now.'

'Ah. Yes. Good thinking. So you think...'

'I am certain of it.' Oh, my poor Louise, she thought.

'They are absolute fiends,' the commander said. 'If we catch them...'

'Oh, we are going to do that, sir,' Jessica said. 'But you understand that, as Louise obviously did not vouchsafe any information, the princess is as safe here as anywhere.'

'Oh, quite. You may leave her for an hour. But she will still have to be moved. This afternoon.'

'Yes, sir. Has the van been located?'

'Not yet. They're still looking.'

'Thank you, sir.' Jessica replaced the phone, wishing the world would operate on logic rather than emotion, just for a while.

Andrea and Chloe were gazing at her with wide eyes. 'Louise?'

'Yes.'

'Oh, my God!' Chloe looked ready to burst into tears; Andrea squeezed her hand.

'Bastards!' she commented. 'We are going to get them, aren't we, JJ?'

'That is my intention,' Jessica said.

'She was your friend,' Karina said. 'I am most terribly sorry.'

'She was also my colleague,' Jessica said.

'I understand. Will these people be executed?'

'Sadly, not in England. Maybe you could have them extradited to Kharram. But I suppose the hordes of do-gooders in this country and Europe, who have never had anyone close to them tortured to death, would raise a huge stink if we attempted to send them to a country where there *is* a death penalty. I'm going out for an hour. You're in charge, Andie. Nothing has changed as regards security.' She picked up her shoulder bag.

'Who's going to tell Jerry?' Andrea asked.

'I will,' Jessica said. 'But I want to see Louise first.'

'Let me get this absolutely straight,' Burke said. Although he had only arrived on a flight from the Middle East two hours previously, he looked as spic and span as ever, hair neatly brushed, tie neatly knotted. His eyes were invisible behind his dark glasses, but his expression was sufficiently grim to have both Rosen and Sonia sitting bolt upright in Loman's lounge. Loman and Ruby had wisely left them to it. 'You kidnapped a British police officer?'

'Well,' Rosen said. 'She just walked up to us.'

'You could have driven away.'

'That's what I said we should do,' Sonia claimed.

'Had we done that, she would still have been able to take our number and to describe the vehicle,' Rosen explained.

'In the middle of the night? That would only have been possible if you allowed her to come very close.'

'He wanted her to,' Sonia said.

'I had another reason,' Rosen said, ignoring her. 'I had just been informed, by the woman Cerise, that Princess Karina is no longer at Blandlock.'

'Then where is she?'

'That is it. We do not know.'

'We could know,' Sonia said. 'We could have her sitting right here, now.'

'Explain.'

Sonia told him about seeing Karina and a blonde woman driving out of the Blandlock grounds the previous afternoon. Burke looked at Rosen.

'To have followed and attempted to snatch the princess there, on the high road, would have been both highly risky and against our orders. The orders *you* gave us, Mr Burke. There was no reason to suggest that she was not going to return to the house, no indication from Cerise. It must have been a spur-of-the-moment decision. And then, while I was considering the matter, I saw this policewoman coming towards us. I realised immediately that she would know where the princess was, and acted accordingly.'

'*If* she was a policewoman. Was she in uniform?'

'No, sir. But she was a policewoman. When we searched her, we found an automatic pistol, her identification wallet, and a panic alarm strapped to her wrist. That is why we left immediately. We had to assume that when we attacked her she would have pressed the button, and we did not know what back-up she might have.'

'And was there a back-up?'

'I don't know. As I said, I thought it best to leave immediately.'

'You said she had a gun. Didn't she attempt to use it?'

'I think she was going to. The gun was in her shoulder bag, and her hand was in the bag. But she was distracted by Sonia, who was in front of her. She didn't know I was behind her. I hit her.'

'He hit her with a tyre iron,' Sonia said. 'There was so much blood. I am surprised her head wasn't split open.'

'Well, I had to hit her hard.'

'Is that why you obtained nothing from her?' Burke asked.

'No, no. When we had driven to an isolated place, we revived her.'

'I still think she was dazed,' Sonia said.

'She wasn't that dazed,' Rosen protested. 'She knew who we were.'

'But she wouldn't answer your questions.'

'She had courage,' Sonia said.

'You had her in your possession for four hours, and you could not persuade her to tell you where the princess is being kept? I am ashamed of you. What method did you use?'

'Well,' Sonia said, 'he raped her, for a start.'

'She was very good-looking,' Rosen said. 'It would have been senseless to destroy her without, well...' He glanced at Sonia. 'And I was sexed up.'

'He is a sadistic satyr,' Sonia declared.

'I hope you did not suppose that raping her would persuade her to tell us where the princess is,' Burke commented.

'No, no,' Rosen said. 'We used wire. Well, there was a lot of it in the van.'

'Did she not make a noise when you hurt her?'

'We gagged her while we used the wire, and took the gag off when we stopped so that she could speak to us.'

'But she didn't,' Burke observed. 'Are you sure you hurt her enough?'

'We hurt her enough.'

'And then she died. How did she die?'

'She choked on the gag.'

'So you drove to the canal and threw her body in. How long did that take?'

'An hour. We were in the country. But at that time of night there was little traffic.'

'What did you do with her clothes?'

'They are in the van.'

'And the van?'

'Is in Loman's garage.'

'Are you serious?'

'There is no danger. The only danger is if it were to be found by the police. As long as it

228

is in Loman's garage it is safe. We will spray it a different colour and change the number plates, just in case someone noticed it. But I should think that is very unlikely.'

Burke looked from face to face. 'And neither of you understand that you have just about botched the operation?'

'The operation was botched from the moment *he* was placed in command,' Sonia remarked.

'This woman has been a pain in the ass from the beginning,' Rosen said. 'So the operation has been botched. This is not my fault. I had no knowledge that the princess was about to be moved. I consider that we have been let down by the woman Cerise. And I took what I considered appropriate steps to retrieve the situation. It is just bad luck that the policewoman died on us.'

'It was not bad luck. It was incompetence. Inflicting severe pain upon someone with a gag in her mouth is tantamount to blowing out her brains. Now we have the entire British police force on our necks, and we have lost sight of the princess.' Burke paused, staring at the wall, while Rosen and Sonia waited apprehensively. 'And the pressure must be applied on Yusuf by tomorrow,' he mused. And then suddenly smiled, for the first time that day. 'But per-haps we do not have a disaster after all. Would you say that, with the princess, the

229

protection squad would also have been withdrawn from Blandlock?'

'I should think so,' Rosen said. 'They were there to protect the princess, nobody else.'

'Well, then, we have a way ahead. Kidnapping the princess was proposed in the first instance because it was felt that she, being the only child as well as the heir to the sultan, would be the person in all the world he would be most anxious to protect. Besides, it was considered too difficult to get hold of the sultana, who seldom left the palace, and when she did so, was always surrounded by armed guards, whereas the princess's wild habits are well known. But here we have a situation where the sultana is away from any guards, waiting for us in a country house.'

'And you think this Yusuf is still sufficiently in love with his wife to virtually surrender his kingdom to get her back?' Sonia asked.

'I very much doubt it,' Burke agreed. 'But once we have the sultana, the princess is again accessible. The sultana will tell us where she is, and we will simply do a swop.' He looked at the sceptical faces in front of him. 'They will have to play it our way, believe me. They dare not have the sultana's life on their hands.'

'You're sure you want to do this, Sergeant?' asked the morgue attendant.

230

'Yes,' Jessica said, beginning to control her breathing. She had been in here often enough before, but she always found the smell of disinfectant overwhelming; she didn't know how Willcock, the attendant presently on duty, or any of his colleagues, who had to spend hours down here, stood it – quite apart from the company they were forced to keep.

'Number thirty-one,' Willcock said, pulling out the drawer. 'It's best to think of them as numbers.'

Because they no longer have any meaning, Jessica thought. But Louise could never cease to have meaning for her, just as even her number was going to have meaning to whoever did this to her. She intended to see to that. Willcock waited, face impassive, while she looked at the naked body. Louise's expression had relaxed after death and before rigor mortis had set in, and she looked quite peaceful. 'How did she die? That bruise on the head?'

'No. It was probably strangulation. There'll be a post mortem this afternoon, but if they don't find water in her lungs, well ... You see these marks round her mouth? There are others on the back of her head, under her hair. She was gagged, quite tightly.'

'And that killed her?'

'Well, she was being tortured, Sergeant. While gagged. That means she was probably

231

trying to shriek her guts out, and the gag got in the way.'

'How was she tortured? There are no marks.'

'They used wire.'

'Explain.'

'If you really want me to. You take a length of thin wire, and you put it between the legs, and you saw it back and forth, always exerting the pressure upwards. It doesn't take long to start eating into the flesh, and, of course, that is a sensitive area of the body.'

Jessica felt physically sick. 'The man who could do this...'

Willcock raised a finger. 'Or the woman, Sergeant. Of course, I doubt she would ever have been able to live a normal life, even if she hadn't died. But I would say whoever did this intended to kill her anyway, once they got what they wanted.'

'They didn't get what they wanted,' Jessica said. 'They didn't get anything, except her life.'

'Then she was one brave lady.'

'Yes,' Jessica agreed. 'One very brave lady.'

She drove back to the flat. Don't think, she kept telling herself. Don't think. But that was a dream. She kept seeing Louise's body, and if she simply couldn't imagine it being tortured, she kept imagining what must have been going through Louise's mind while it

232

was happening. Oh, Louise!

Chloe was on watch, but they weren't in any event supposed to recognise each other. Jessica went upstairs and straight to her sideboard, poured herself half a tumbler of neat gin, and drank it. Andrea and Priscilla, Karina and Cerise, watched her with wide eyes. Priscilla licked her lips. 'Was it...?'

'Yes,' Jessica said.

'I wish to say that I am sorry,' Cerise said.

'You bitch!' Jessica swung her hand, slashing its edge into the side of Cerise's head. Cerise gasped and screamed at the same time as she tumbled out of her chair and fell to the carpet. When she tried to get up, Jessica hit her once more, again with the edge of her hand but this time on the cheek, splitting the skin and bringing a rush of blood into Cerise's mouth and down her chin. Jessica felt an awful temptation to really give her a beating.

'Help me!' Cerise screamed. Although she was about twice Jessica's size, she knew she was out of her class when it came to un-armed combat.

'JJ,' Andrea muttered, although she made no move to restrain her.

But already the outburst of killing anger, so totally foreign to Jessica's nature, was passing. 'Put something on her cheek,' she said.

'You've hardly had any sleep,' Priscilla

said. 'We can look after things. Why don't you go and lie down.'

Jessica hesitated, but she knew that if she didn't get some sleep she'd be good for nothing – if she wasn't already good for nothing.

'We'll wake you if anything crops up,' Andrea promised, kneeling beside the weeping Cerise with the first-aid box.

Jessica looked at Karina, whose expression was indecipherable, as it so often was. She went into the bedroom, stripped off her sweat-wet clothes, and turned as the door opened. 'Is there anything I can do?' the princess asked.

'Not a thing.' Jessica went into the shower.

When she came out, towelling herself, the princess was still standing there, her shirt unbuttoned. 'I mean, anything,' she said.

'Your Highness, in my present mood, if I were to lay a finger on you I would undoubtedly throttle you.'

'I know,' Karina said. 'But I have caused all this—'

'You didn't cause it,' Jessica said, getting into bed and drawing the covers to her throat. 'Except by being born.'

Karina looked as if she would have replied to that statement, but then left the room.

'The commander is here,' Andrea said. Jessica opened her eyes, for a moment unsure of where she was; the room wasn't quite steady. Andrea smiled. 'That was quite a tot you took. Shall I tell him you're unavailable?'

'Nobody tells Adams they're unavailable,' Jessica said, and swung her legs out of bed. 'And the last thing I want is him in here with me. Tell him I'll be right out.' She staggered into the bathroom, splashed cold water on to her face, debated about make-up and decided against it – if she looked as if she had seen a ghost that was not an inaccurate description.

She put on clean clothes – another of her dark blue trouser suits over a white shirt – and went into the lounge, which seemed filled with people. In addition to her own squad, all of whom were assembled, and Karina and Cerise – Cerise wearing a strip of plaster on her swollen face – there were four plainclothes officers, all of whom she knew, and the commander, as well as Inspector Manley.

'Ah, JJ,' Adams said. 'Been having a little nap, eh?'

'Sergeant Jones had no sleep last night, sir,' Andrea said.

'Oh, quite. Absolutely. Well, you'll be able to sleep well tonight, eh? You deserve it.'

'Sir?'

'I have been making the acquaintance of Her Highness here,' Adams said. 'Bringing her up to date, eh? Now she's all ready to accompany us to her new home for the next few days. Isn't that right, Princess?'

'Yes,' Karina said.

Jessica tried to catch her eye, but she avoided meeting her gaze.

Lumps of lead started to gather in Jessica's stomach, but she wouldn't accept it. 'Well, then, I'll just get my bag...'

'That won't be necessary, JJ,' Adams said. 'You are relieved of this assignment.' His gaze circled the room. 'All of you. There is no criticism involved in this. We merely feel that, owing to circumstances beyond your control, you have become too personally involved – and that, as you know, is against department procedure.'

'May I have a word, sir?' Jessica asked.

Adams gave Manley a nervous glance, then said, 'Of course.'

Jessica opened the bedroom door and ushered him after all into the somewhat tousled room in which various feminine garments, including underclothing, were scattered about the place. 'I apologise for the mess, sir. As I told you last night, it's a little small to be shared by five people.'

'Absolutely. You'll be glad to see the back of them.'

'Yes, sir. May I ask, sir: are we being permanently replaced?'

'Yes.'

'By a male squad? This is an Arab princess.'

'No one is going to invade the princess's privacy, JJ. The guard will be strictly external. We have cleared the matter with the sultana. She intends to come up to town tomorrow to be with her daughter.'

'She knows where to go?'

'We have not yet given her the address. She will be driven to it, tomorrow morning.'

'And then?'

'Presumably she will move in.'

'And will promptly tell the world where she, and her daughter, are to be found.'

'Oh, come now.'

'Commander, that woman, and those around her, do not know the meaning of the word confidence.'

'As I said, JJ, you have allowed yourself to become too personally involved in this business. I'm not blaming you. But I'm sure you'll agree that it is clouding your judgement. And now, poor Pleyell ... I know you must be very bitter about that. I am prepared to second you to the detective squad investigating that tragedy. How about that?' he asked brightly.

Jessica continued to concentrate on essentials. 'But the princess will be alone in her new home for tonight.'

'Good lord, no! There are servants, and in any event she'll have her lady-in-waiting.

That is her out there, isn't it? The one with the bruised face?'

'That is her, sir. Or rather, that *was* her.'

'What do you mean?'

'The princess has dismissed her from her service, because we discovered that she is working for the kidnappers.'

'Good lord! How do you know that?'

'She has been telephoning from Blandlock in the middle of the night, and she has confessed she was calling a man who she has identified, by his voice, as being the one behind the kidnapping in Kharram.'

'Good lord!' Adams said again. 'Why isn't she under arrest?'

'What would the charge have been, sir? Whoever she was calling, he had committed no crime in this country before this morning.'

'But now he is guilty of murder!'

'He could be. He has yet to be caught, and the charge proven. Cerise will deny that she knew anything of what he intended. She claims she was acting on the instructions of her lover in Kharram, and her duty was simply to keep this man informed of the princess's whereabouts and plans. That is why I have her here, so that she cannot spill any more beans. But I know that the princess has no wish to have her around any more.' Which, of course, she didn't know at all. But she certainly intended to keep them separ-

238

ated. All the vague and as yet uncertain suspicions that were roaming about her mind were based on the relationship between the pair.

'Hm. What a mess. You say you brought her here. Did she come willingly?'

'Ah ... no, sir. We managed to persuade her.'

'JJ, you are stretching your neck.'

'I took the action I considered appropriate, sir.'

'Does she have any idea you may have overstepped your remit?'

'I'm afraid she does. But we do have a weapon; the princess is threatening to have her sent back to Kharram, where there is apparently no remit for a policeman to overstep.'

'But if she doesn't want to go...'

'Technically, since being fired by the princess she is an illegal immigrant, unless Sir William, who has responsibility for the entire Kharrami party, is willing to vouch for her.'

'Hm. Well, this has got to be your baby, JJ. I would suggest that you take this woman back to Blandlock and have a chat with Sir William.'

'Me, sir?'

'You, sir. We certainly don't want her suing us for illegal arrest. For that reason, any pressure brought on her to keep her mouth shut must be very delicately applied, and this may well best be done by Sir William and the sultana.'

'I assume you understand that I am not their favourite person right this minute, sir?'

'A situation you rather created yourself. I am not apportioning blame; I am merely requiring you to sort it out. However, if you are apprehensive, you may take one of your women with you.'

'I am not concerned about a physical assault, Commander. I can handle that.'

'I'm sure you can, and would be pleased to do so. Your back-up will be there to act as a witness to anything that is said, and hopefully to prevent you from doing, or saying, anything you might regret. This may be very important to your career, JJ. Now, we must be off.'

He bustled into the other room. 'If you are ready, Your Highness?'

'I have no clothes, other than these and some toiletries.'

'We have a suitcase of your clothes,' Adams explained. 'Packed by your mother. Now, if you'll collect your other things...'

'I'll fetch them,' Andrea volunteered.

'And I have only this nightdress,' Cerise said.

'Ah ... you are staying here.'

'You cannot do this. I am the princess's lady-in-waiting. I must go with her.'

'I understand that you have been sacked. Is

that correct, Highness?'

Everyone looked at Karina. 'Yes,' the princess said. 'You have been sacked.'

'But you cannot leave me here. With these women. They beat me up. Look at my face.'

Adams did so. 'You do have a bruise. However did—'

'She fell over a chair,' Chloe said before he could finish his question.

'That was careless.'

'I did not fall over a chair,' Cerise shouted. 'She hit me.' She pointed at Jessica. 'Tell them, Princess.'

'You fell over a chair,' Karina said. 'I saw it.'

'Well, I am sure the swelling will go down. Ah, Hutchins. Got everything?'

Andrea held up the valise. 'Yes, sir.' One of the policemen took it.

'Well, then ... Princess?'

Karina grasped both of Jessica's hands. 'Will I see you again?'

Jessica smiled. 'If you're unlucky.'

'I want you to know that I am, and always will be, very grateful to you for what you have done. And I will bear the scar of Louise's death for the rest of my life.'

'It went with the job.'

'Nevertheless...' She pulled Jessica against her and kissed her on the mouth. 'You will remember my offer,' she whispered.

'Ahem,' Adams commented. 'We really

should be going.' Karina shook hands with the three policewomen, and followed him through the open door.

Manley was last to leave. 'I'm sorry it went sour, JJ. In my book you're due for a commendation.'

'Thank you, sir. Is there anything on the van as yet?'

'Nothing, I'm afraid. It's in a garage somewhere, and until it comes out again – if it ever does, at least looking the same – we're not going to get any help from it.'

'The commander said I could be assigned to the CID squad.'

'I'd think about that, JJ. They are as professional at their job as you are at yours. I'm not sure you'd be welcome. Why don't you sleep on it and come to see me in the morning.' He looked at the other three. 'You're now off duty. Report in tomorrow morning for reassignment.' The door closed.

'Well,' Chloe said, 'I feel kind of flat. You guys feel like the pub? Hell, it's your birthday, JJ. Let's tie one on.'

'What about this one?'

'Ah!'

'If you lay a finger on me...' Cerise said.

'You'll never speak to me again. I'll bear it. I'm to return you to Blandlock.'

'If you think that will stop me bringing an action against you...'

242

'I wouldn't even think of it, if I were you, until you've been back there. Now, I shall need a volunteer to give me a hand, just in case she acts up on the drive.'

'Me,' Chloe said.

'I'll come,' Priscilla said.

'How about me?' Andrea said. 'I can pick up my car at the same time.'

'Good thinking.' She smiled at the others. 'If you don't mind, I'll take Andie. Apart from the car, she knows the ropes better than either of you.'

'Then you'll come back and join us in the pub,' Chloe said, and looked at her watch. 'It's only just gone five. You can be there and back by seven thirty. We'll expect you.'

'We'll be there,' Jessica said. 'I do feel like getting drunk. But first...' She punched Louise's number, bracing herself.

'Yes?'

'Jerry?'

'Who is this? Jessica?'

'Yes.'

'Have you found her yet? When is she coming home?'

'Louise isn't coming home, Jerry.'

'What? What do you mean?'

'I mean that she is in a drawer at our morgue. If you want to see her, I imagine they'll let you in. But I don't recommend it.'

'You ... you mean...'

'She's dead, Jerry.'

There was a moment's silence. Then he asked, his voice trembling, 'How?'

'She died in the line of duty. There'll be an official report, in due course, and I'll let you have a copy.' She listened to a peculiar sound at the other end of the line, only slowly realising what it was. 'Jerry?' The phone went dead.

'Took it rough, eh?' Priscilla suggested.

'He's crying.'

'Shit!' Chloe commented.

'I know he was a bastard,' Jessica said. 'But ... could be he really did love her. Come on, let's go.'

'Seven thirty,' Chloe reminded her. 'The Wessex Arms. We'll drink to Louise.'

There didn't seem to be much point in tidying up the flat. Jessica wrapped an old raincoat round Cerise, and they took her downstairs and put her in the back of the Land Rover. Andrea sat beside her. 'If you don't want to be cuffed again, just behave yourself,' she told her.

There were quite a few people about, and Jessica anticipated some comment, but, although several of them were clearly curious, no one attempted to interfere or question what they were doing, while Cerise seemed to have decided that returning to Blandlock *was* her best option, at least in the short term, and was remarkably quiescent.

244

'Now remember,' Jessica told Andrea, 'in addition to helping me cope with this creature, you are charged with the responsibility of preventing me from shooting or hitting anybody, or even cursing anybody out. Those are orders from Adams.' Andrea smoothed her hair. Like Cerise, she had no desire ever to take Jessica on physically. Besides, she worshipped the ground on which her sergeant walked. Both of which Jessica was well aware. She squeezed Andrea's hand. 'I do promise to behave.'

It was not yet six, and there was heavy traffic. It took Jessica twenty minutes to get on to the A3, and even then progress remained slow. Not that she minded; she had a lot to think about. But she still hadn't got her mind in order when her mobile buzzed. 'Not more problems,' she muttered as she flicked it on.

'Happy birthday to you, happy birthday to you, happy birthday dear JJ, happy birthday to you.'

'For God's sake,' she shouted. 'Tom!'

'Thought I'd forgotten you, didn't you.'

'Of course I didn't.' She hadn't actually had the time to think about it. 'Where are you calling from?'

'The flat.'

'Eh? You mean you're home?'

'Arrived ten minutes ago.'

Shit, she thought. We only just missed each

245

other.

'I see you've already been having a party,' he said.

'Eh?'

'This place looks as if a herd of elephants has just been through it.'

'Ah,' she said. 'Yes. I'll explain it all later.'

'How much later? When are you coming home?'

'Actually, I'm not. I'm completing a job, then the girls and I are meeting up in the Wessex Arms for a drink.' And a wake, she thought, but trying to explain that over the phone would take too long. 'I should be there at about seven thirty.'

'I'll be there,' he said. 'So long as you promise to make it an early night.'

'You bet,' she agreed.

'There's a lucky break,' Andrea commented when Jessica had rung off.

'I knew he was due back sometime around now,' Jessica said. 'But I agree, it is a lucky break.'

'So who was the other bloke, the one on the phone earlier?' Andrea asked. 'Or shouldn't I ask that?'

'You're welcome. The other bloke was my husband.'

'Your...?'

'Ex.'

'But he still hankers? I didn't even know you were married.'

246

'As I said, ex. And I believe he does still hanker. But he's water under the bridge.' Suddenly she was happy, or at least happier than she had been for the past three days. The great cloud of gloom about Louise's death still loomed, and she would have liked to see the Karina business through – for all her quirks and her own suspicions that the princess was following a private agenda, she had developed quite a liking for the girl – and she was certainly not looking forward to her reception at Blandlock. But these were transients. Tom was permanent. He might not be the greatest lover in the world, and in some ways he was just as much an MCP as Jerry. But he was as solid as a rock and as dependable as one too. And he was all hers.

The traffic remained heavy, and it was nearly half past six by the time they turned down the Blandlock Lane; they were going to be late getting back to the pub, although going in to town would be quicker than coming out. The lane was deserted, to Jessica's relief; she thought that if she had seen a yellow telecommunications van she'd have started shooting right away. The gates were shut and locked, predictably. Jessica braked and called Parkin on her mobile. 'Your name, please?' Parkin answered.

'Sergeant Jones, Parkin,' Jessica said. 'Open up.'

'Ah ... is Princess Karina with you?'

'No, she is not.'

'Then is Sir William expecting you?'

'No, he is not. But I wish to have a word with him. If you don't open this bloody gate right now, I am going to be very angry.' The gates clicked open and swung wide.

'What do you reckon?' Andrea asked. 'Are we now *personae non gratae?*'

'It looks like it.' Jessica drove down to the forecourt; because of the low cloud and intermittent drizzle it was already just about dark. 'We'll just have to change his mind about that.'

'Shit!' Rosen muttered, watching the Land Rover drive through the gate. He and Sonia were crouching in the bushes on the near side of the lane; each had a pair of binoculars. 'There were three people in it,' he commented.

'So they have guests,' Sonia said. 'Who do you suppose they are, police?' Her tone was contemptuous. 'Some people are just born unlucky. But we are in luck this time. Look! The gates are not shutting again.'

'You're right,' Rosen said. 'They want to make it easy for us. Go tell Burke. It is time to move – now.'

The Dobermans frisked around the car, having been joined by Parkin. 'Good evening, miss,' he said, and looked past Jessica. 'Miss Mahliah?' His gaze drifted down the raincoat to the obvious nightdress she was wearing beneath as she stepped down from the back seat.

'Fuck off,' Cerise told him.

Parkin looked at Jessica. 'She's not happy,' Jessica explained. 'Is the door open?'

'I took the liberty of informing the house of your arrival,' Parkin said.

And at that moment the front door swung in to reveal both the butler and Barbara. 'Is there a problem?' she asked. Then she too looked at Cerise. 'Shouldn't you be with the princess?'

'I wish a hot bath and some decent food,' Cerise said, and marched past her into the house.

Barbara looked at Jessica. Who shrugged. 'She's free to do whatever she likes as far as we are concerned, as long as she does it here. We need to have a word with Sir William.'

'Well...' Barbara was doubtful.

'Police business.'

'You'd better come in. Oh, do lock up those dogs, Parkin.' Parkin touched his cap, and chased the dogs towards their kennels. The butler stood aside and allowed the two policewomen into the house while looking censoriously at their pants; if Jessica was wearing a jacket, Andrea was in jeans and a loose shirt. 'Sir William and the sultana are in the small sitting room,' Barbara explained, leading the way and opening the door. 'Detective-Sergeant Jones and Detective-Constable ... ah...'

'Hutchins,' Andrea said.

Sir William and the sultana were drinking cocktails. Both were dressed for dinner, Sir William in black tie and Vanessa in a very low-cut long gown. Neither rose. 'Did you wish something?' Sir William asked.

'Is my daughter now in safe hands?' Vanessa demanded.

'The princess was always in safe hands, Your Highness,' Jessica said. 'I have returned Cerise.'

'What is she, a library book?' Sir William asked. 'I hope you had a good read. Haw haw haw.'

'As you say, Sir William.'

'But what is she doing here?' Vanessa demanded. 'Her business is to be with the princess.'

'The princess has dismissed her, Your Highness.'

'Dismissed her? My daughter has dismissed Cerise? Cerise is her oldest friend.'

'I have to tell you that, as I thought you understood, Cerise has been in constant contact, down to last night, with the people who have been trying to kidnap the princess.'

'That was what *you* said. Cerise has never

250

admitted it.'

Jessica ignored the interruption. 'As a result of this, she is also involved in the death of one of my colleagues.'

'The death?' Vanessa asked.

'There was something on the television about a policewoman being murdered,' Barbara said.

'Yes,' Jessica said, grimly. 'However, it has been decided not to charge her with any offence at this time. In the interim, as she has been sacked by the princess, you must understand that she is your responsibility.'

'My responsibility? Now you look here—' Sir William's head jerked. 'What is that?'

'A car coming down the drive, at speed.' Jessica stood up. 'Parkin couldn't have shut the gates.'

There was a huge explosion, followed immediately by another.

Despair

The entire house shook; some plaster fell from the ceiling, and the lights dimmed and then came on again. Jessica stumbled as she lost her balance, and sat down heavily on a chair. Andrea, also on her feet, was thrown against Barbara; they fell, together, to the floor. The sultana uttered a high-pitched scream, while her father shouted, 'What the devil...?'

Jessica regained her feet, and listened to the noises coming from outside. The dogs were barking, but as that sound was muted she reckoned they had already been locked up. There were shouts of alarm coming from the kitchen, punctuated by screams. The butler appeared in the doorway, bleeding from a head wound and with his uniform in tatters. 'Sir William!' he gasped. 'Sir William...' Then he fell forward on to his face.

Vanessa screamed. Jessica grabbed her arm and dragged her to her feet. 'Get out,' she said.

Vanessa blinked at her. 'Where?'

Jessica hesitated; she could smell burning. Before she could make up her mind, two people appeared in the doorway. They both wore leather coats, gleaming with wet, and slouch hats. They looked so 1930s she might have been tempted to laugh but for the fact that each carried an AK-74 assault rifle. 'My God!' Sir William shouted, and dived behind the settee.

Vanessa screamed again.

Neither of the intruders was masked, and Jessica, recollecting the identikit pictures Karina had concocted for Moriarty, recognised them. She also realised that she had been caught on the hop, and that, were she to draw her weapon, she would be killed. Andrea realised that as well, and, although her hand was hovering by her bag, she made no move to open it, preferring to wait for her boss to give instructions. Barbara, with less experience of the type of people they were dealing with, stepped forward. 'What do you think you're doing?' she demanded.

Sonia fired a single shot, striking her in the chest. Barbara never uttered a sound; she just fell backwards on to the floor, the front of her black dress already darkened by blood. 'Jesus!' Andrea muttered, and looked at Jessica.

But all Jessica's training was reminding her not to overreact, unless it could be done with profit. The fact that they had killed Barbara meant that she had every right to kill them, just as she had both reason and desire to kill them for the murder of Louise – she had no doubt that this pair was responsible for that – but she couldn't do that if she was dead.

'That's her,' Rosen said. He stepped over Barbara's body and grasped Vanessa's arm, pulling her towards him.

Vanessa screamed, her large, half-exposed white breasts heaving. 'Let me go!'

Rosen swung the butt of his rifle and struck her across the head; Vanessa subsided with a groan and he ducked, thrust his shoulder into her stomach, and straightened with her in a fireman's lift. 'Let's go.'

'Aren't we going to kill these two?' Sonia inquired. Sir William was out of sight behind the settee.

'They have nothing to do with us,' Rosen said. 'They're just two pretty women.'

'They can identify us,' Sonia said.

Jessica saw her finger whiten on the trigger of the tommy-gun. 'Take cover!' she shouted, and herself fell behind the nearest chair, drawing her weapon as she did so. The assault rifle chattered, and bullets crashed into the wall above her head, showering her with splinters. But now she was able to return fire, as was Andrea. Sonia gave a little shriek, and half turned as she was thrown against the wall. She had let go of her weapon, which fell to the floor at her feet.

Jessica scrambled up, Skorpion thrust forward. 'Stop!'

Panting and sobbing, and bleeding – although Jessica couldn't be sure where she had been hit – Sonia still turned for the door. Jessica hesitated; she couldn't shoot an unarmed woman. Andrea ran forward but was checked by Rosen, who was in the corridor, Vanessa still slung over his shoulder. His left arm was round her thighs to hold her in place, but his right hand still held his rifle, and the muzzle was jammed into Vanessa's side. 'Move and she dies,' he said. 'Drop your weapons.' Andrea looked at

Jessica, who had no choice but to nod and drop her gun. Andrea did likewise. 'Are you bad?' Rosen asked Sonia.

'Shit!' Sonia moaned. 'Yes, I'm hurt bad.' She was still leaning against the door, holding her right shoulder in her left hand; the fingers were smeared with blood.

'Get to the car,' Rosen said.

Sonia dropped to her knees, scrabbling for the dropped rifle. 'Not till I've settled with these bastards.'

'Stuff that,' Rosen told her. 'Do you want to bleed to death? Get out to the car. The boss is waiting.' Sonia hesitated, but realised she didn't have the strength to pick up the gun, much less fire it. She heaved herself to her feet and staggered along the corridor. Rosen grinned at Jessica and Andrea. 'I'd like to take you with us, but there isn't room,' he said. 'Just remember I saved your lives. And remember too that if you make any attempt to follow, this bitch gets it.' He kicked the door shut.

'My God!' Sir William said again, emerging from hiding. 'They've taken my daughter!'

Jessica ignored him, and knelt beside Barbara. Andrea was doing the same to the butler. 'He's dead.'

'So is she,' Jessica said.

'You just stood here,' Sir William said, 'while they took my daughter. The Sultana of Kharram.'

'They also killed your mistress,' Jessica said. 'Doesn't that bother you?'

Sir William stood above her. 'She was stupid, challenging them.'

'And we weren't, so we're still alive.' She wasn't terribly proud about that.

'What are you going to do?'

They listened to the roar of the car engine on the forecourt, and heard several more shots. Then they smelt burning. 'Jesus,' Jessica muttered. She picked up her gun and ran along the corridor, Andrea at her shoulder, both pausing as they came upon the wrecked front door and the shattered hallway; potted plants and suits of armour were scattered about in pieces, the ceiling sagged, and all the lights had been blown out, although there was a glow from the flickering flames. The two women grabbed collapsed drapes to beat out the fire, while Jessica also looked at the car driving away. In the darkness any reasonable identification was impossible; it had already gone too far for the number plate to be read.

A figure emerged out of the gloom, and Andrea brought up her gun, then checked as she recognised Parkin. The big chauffeur was shivering. 'Those people shot at me,' he said. 'They shot at me.'

'Lend a hand,' Andrea suggested.

Parkin went past her to where there was a

fire extinguisher, and a moment later the flames had disappeared. Or at least, *these* flames. 'Oh, hell,' Jessica said. Beside the house, the Land Rover was burning. 'Bastards.'

'What do we do?' Andrea asked. 'Pursue? We can use my Clio.'

'We'd never catch them now, and if we did, they could well do the sultana.' Who was now in the hands of the thugs who had tortured Louise to death, she realised.

Sir William arrived behind them. 'I demand action. Two of my staff are dead, my daughter has been kidnapped...'

'You'll get action,' Jessica told him, and used her mobile.

Sonia made sobbing, growling noises as she half fell into the back of the car. 'What in the name of God...?' Burke asked. He was seated in the front beside Loman, who was driving, waiting with his hands tight on the wheel.

'She stopped one.' Rosen threw his rifle into the back of the car, then dumped Vanessa on the back seat; her head fell on Sonia's lap.

'Those bitches,' Sonia moaned. 'I am bleeding to death.'

'What bitches?'

'Let's get out of here,' Rosen said, scrambling into the back beside the two women.

'Those people who turned up just before we went in. They weren't guests; they were policewomen.'

'Drive,' Burke commanded, and Loman swung the car and sent it towards the gates. 'Policewomen?'

'You said there would no longer be any bodyguards, with the princess gone,' Rosen accused. 'But these were plainclothes. They had to be the bodyguards.'

'If they were not in uniform, how can you be sure they were policewomen?'

'Because they were both armed,' Sonia shouted. 'Automatic weapons, which they knew how to use. God, I am in agony. Are you going to let me bleed to death?'

Burke turned round and shone his flashlight on her. 'You don't look good,' he agreed. 'See what you can do, Rosen.'

Rosen pushed the still unconscious Vanessa against the rest, and shifted himself along her body to be beside Sonia.

'Don't you touch me,' she snarled.

'You stupid bitch, how can I help you if I don't touch you?'

'Here.' Burke had opened the glove compartment, and from it took both a first-aid box and a flask. 'Give her a drink.'

Sonia took the flask in her left hand. Rosen released the cap for her, and she drank deeply. Then she subsided, her eyes shut, but started again and screamed as Rosen opened her jacket. 'Oh, my God! The pain!'

'Have another drink,' Burke recommended, and she did so. 'Well?'

Rosen sat on Sonia's lap to stop her kicking, and pulled the jacket away from the shoulder. Sonia screamed and moaned, and drank. 'It's not good,' Rosen said.

'You think the bullet is still in there?'

'I don't know, Mr Burke. But the shoulder is a mess. There are bits of bone hanging about.' Sonia moaned. 'She needs a doctor, and quickly.'

'Ruby will know what to do,' Loman said. 'She trained as a nurse.'

'She'll have to wait until we get there. Bind it up to stop the blood. These policewomen, they're dead?'

'No.'

'He wouldn't do it,' Sonia groaned. 'He wouldn't shoot.'

Burke flicked the flashlight beam on to Rosen's face. 'As Sonia said, they had guns, which they knew how to use. I couldn't kill them both without being shot myself,' Rosen said. 'Where would we have been then?' He preferred not to tell Burke that he had had them at his mercy when they had dropped their weapons; he didn't suppose the boss would have understood that they were both simply too good-looking to kill.

'But they got a good look at you.'

'Well, I suppose they did.' Burke tore away

some of Sonia's clothing to further expose the bloody flesh, then applied lint and antiseptic – which brought more screams of agony – before taking a roll of bandage from the box and tying it as best he could round the shattered shoulder. The bandage immediately turned red. 'But going by the identikit pictures they showed on TV today, everyone in the country knows what we look like.' He returned his attention to Sonia's shoulder. 'This is very bad.'

'Like I said, she'll have to wait. What about her?' He turned the flashlight beam on to Vanessa.

'Just a bump on the head.'

At that moment Vanessa started to groan and move. Rosen held her shoulders, and pushed her into an upright position. Vanessa's eyes opened. She stared at Rosen, and screamed. 'Not another fucking screaming woman,' Burke said.

'Listen,' Rosen said, shaking Vanessa's shoulders. 'Shut up or I'll hit you again.'

She blinked at him; tears were pouring down her cheeks. Then she realised that the bodice of her gown had come down, and hastily pulled it up. 'Where am I?'

'With friends. Just sit still and you won't be harmed.'

'But ... my father. That noise...'

'I never saw your father.'

'But what do you want from me?'

'The same thing we wanted from your daughter.'

'When my husband finds out what has happened—'

'He'll do exactly as we ask,' Burke said.

'Now shut up,' Rosen told her again. 'Well, Mr Burke...' He was determined to be cheerful. 'At least we've completed the job, eh?'

'Not yet,' Burke said.

'Oh, I know the sultan still has to give in to our terms. But surely he'll do that now we have the lady.'

'Maybe he will,' Burke said. 'But I still want the girl.'

'The princess? Do we need her as well as her mother?'

'Probably not. But I *want* her, Rosen. Because she is a two-timing bitch.'

'Check on Cerise,' Jessica told Andrea. 'Bring her down here.' She smiled encouragingly at Sir William, and used her mobile, calling the commander first of all.

'Really, JJ,' Adams said. 'My wife and I are just going out to dinner.'

'Something has come up, sir.'

'Not again! Oh, well, tell me about it.' Jessica did so, and was rewarded with a stunned silence. Then he said, 'Let me get this straight. These thugs blew in the front of Sir William's house with dynamite?'

'I don't think they used dynamite. I think

they used some sort of hand grenade, like a Mills bomb. Or rather, two Mills bombs,' she added, looking through the shattered doorway at her still burning car.

'And you say they have shot two people?'

'I said there are two fatal casualties, sir. One was shot, the other was fatally injured in the bomb blast.'

'And they took away the sultana?'

'I'm afraid so, sir.'

'What about Sir William?'

'He's right here, sir,' Jessica said maliciously.

'Give me that!' Sir William virtually snatched the phone from her hand. 'Now look here, Adams, what the hell is going on?'

'Well, Sir William, they seem to have taken us by surprise.'

'You told me—'

'That Princess Karina would be placed in a safe house – at your request, sir. That has happened. We both then assumed that Blandlock no longer needed protection. That two of my operatives were at the scene is purely fortuitous.'

'And a fat lot of good they were. They didn't fire a shot until it was too late.'

'I should remind you, Sir William, that my people are required primarily to *save* life, not take it. I would say they have probably done that.'

'And my daughter, the Sultana of Kharram?'

'We are going to act on that now. Give me Sergeant Jones.' Sir William looked as if he would have said more, then changed his mind and handed the phone back to Jessica. 'JJ, I want you to hold the fort until I get there. I'll be coming mob-handed.'

'We also need an ambulance, sir.'

'There'll be one. I'll be with you in an hour.' Before he hung up, they heard him say to his wife, 'I'm afraid dinner is off, darling,' which brought a squawk of annoyance from the distance.

Jessica switched off, and gazed at a clutch of anxious faces as the servants regained enough courage to venture into the house. 'Ooh! What a mess,' commented an upstairs maid.

'Shot at me, they did,' Parkin said.

'Ooh, Mr Parkin!'

'What Mrs Harley is going to say—'

'Mrs Harley isn't going to say anything,' Sir William told them. 'She's dead.'

They gaped at him, then the housemaid groaned, and fainted. One of the footmen caught her. 'Put her to bed,' Jessica suggested. 'And then sit down, have a drink, and try to calm down. The police will be here in a little while.'

'But what about dinner?' the chef inquired. 'Mr Brower isn't going to like us not serving dinner.'

'I'm afraid Mr Brower is also dead,' Jessica told him.

There was another chorus of oohs and aahs. 'We have to have dinner,' Sir William said.

'You're not serious,' Jessica said. 'With two people lying dead in your sitting room, and your daughter—' She checked; Sir William did not know what had happened to Louise, and she didn't want to find out how he might react to the idea that his daughter might be being tortured with a length of thin wire.

'We'll get her back,' Sir William said confidently. 'Commander Adams said so. And we must keep up our strength. I'd be happy if you and your, ah, associate would join me. In the circumstances, there's no need to dress.'

Jessica forgot her promise to Andrea and lost her temper. 'You,' she said, 'are just about the most unutterable bastard I have ever known. Go and have your fucking dinner, and I hope you choke.' She walked past him, and encountered Andrea coming down the stairs behind Cerise, who was once again in a nightdress, although she had changed to a clean one. 'In there,' Jessica said, pointing at the small sitting room.

'I heard a noise,' Cerise said.

'So have a look at what your friends have done.'

Cerise peered through the door at the bodies of Barbara and Brower, gave a gulp, and her knees seemed to give way. Andrea, still standing behind her, caught her and deposited her in a chair. 'What do you want done with her?'

'Nothing. I want her to sit there until the commander arrives. Contemplate, Cerise,' Jessica suggested. She picked up Sonia's abandoned rifle, using her handkerchief to grasp the barrel, went to the door, and beckoned Andrea to follow her.

'You can't leave me alone in here ... with *those*!'

'I told you, think about it.' She closed and locked the door.

'She's not going to go mad or something?' Andrea asked.

'Not her. She's a lot tougher than she looks. Or pretends to look. Well...' She thumbed her mobile again. 'Hello, Charlie. Jessica Jones. Any of my mob in there?'

'Oh, yes, Sergeant, several. They said they were waiting for you.'

'Yes. Is Tom there?'

'He's right here.'

Tom came on the phone. 'Don't tell me: you're going to be late.'

'It could be very late. Stay sober and I'll try to get to you before closing. If I can't, I'll call you back.'

'Some birthday party,' he complained.

'We can always have it tomorrow.' She blew him a kiss down the line.

'He's not happy,' Andrea suggested.

'Not in the least. I need to have a word with Parkin.' Although there was another, bigger idea roaming around her brain. She leaned the rifle against the wall.

'Ah ... when *do* we eat?'

'Don't you start.'

'Well, it's been a long time since lunch...'

'You have my permission to dine with Sir William. I know that will make him happy. Just sit at the other end of the table.'

'But you won't.'

'Not right now.' Andrea, she reflected, had not seen Louise's body, nor did she know what had happened to her – and could well be happening to the sultana right now.

She went outside and up to Parkin's flat. 'Terrible, it was, miss,' Mrs Parkin said. 'They shot at my Peepee. Shot at him, they did.'

'Fortunately, they missed,' Jessica pointed out. 'Others weren't so lucky. Why didn't you shut the gate, Parkin, after we were in?'

'Well, Sergeant...' The chauffeur looked embarrassed. 'I thought you'd be going back out again right away.' Jessica supposed that was a reasonable explanation; she didn't really distrust the chauffeur, anyway. 'Shall I close them now?' he asked anxiously.

'Rather a stable-door situation, isn't it?

Anyway, there'll be all manner of vehicles coming through them in a little while.'

In fact, there were seven, including the ambulance. They all arrived about forty minutes later. By then Andrea had indeed joined Sir William for a meal, and even Jessica had succumbed to the calls of nature sufficiently to have a sandwich, prepared for her by an anxious chef. Everyone moved very quietly, and there was little conversation – although there had been, it seemed, in the dining room. 'He propositioned me,' Andrea said. 'Would you believe it? With his daughter snatched and two stiffs in his sitting room ... Was the housekeeper really his mistress?'

'Yes, she was. Did he want you as a replacement?'

'He wants me as his personal bodyguard.'

'For every moment of the day or night, I imagine, especially when he's in bed. It's your own fault for being so good-looking. Did you tell him you weren't into men? Or is that a secret?'

Andrea flushed. 'I just simpered girlishly. After all, he *is* a millionaire, isn't he?'

'And you reckon you could run Chloe on the side. Take my advice, and continue to simper girlishly.'

There was also Cerise to be coped with; she might not be going mad, but she was certainly in an extremely depressed state.

Jessica was very happy to see the commander. He was accompanied by a forensic team as well as a CID team as well as a medical team, and they took over the house. Everyone, including the two police officers, had to make statements while the bodies were examined by a doctor and then removed by the ambulance crew. The attention to detail, Jessica knew, was essential if any case was ever going to be presented to a court of law, but it was intensely irritating that Adams would not speak with her, privately, until he was satisfied that everything was going according to the book; he spent most of his time placating Sir William.

It was nearly midnight before they sat down together. By then she had already called Tom back, and told him that the only worthwhile place to wait for her was in bed, which didn't make him very happy, at least not in the short term. 'Now, JJ,' Adams said, sitting beside her in another of the small sitting rooms with which Blandlock abounded. 'Bit of a mess, eh? Doesn't do our reputation any good.'

'With respect, sir, I don't think our reputation comes into it. We were required to protect the princess, not her mother, and we have done that successfully.'

'But now we have lost the sultana. Under the noses of two of our officers. I know there was nothing you could do, JJ, without

268

further endangering the woman's life, but that isn't how the media are going to see it. There is going to be the most frightful stink when this breaks tomorrow. It is very possible that there may be a call for heads to roll. And you know who I suspect will lead the call? Bland.'

'The head in question being mine,' Jessica remarked.

'Well, he doesn't like you, and that is a fact. As for what will happen if the body of the Sultana of Kharram is found floating in a canal...'

'Then our best bet is to get her back before that can happen, sir.'

'She's probably already dead,' he said gloomily.

'I don't think she is, sir. Isn't this whole thing based on forcing the sultan to give the new lease to whoever these people represent? They intended to use the princess for that purpose. But now they realise they can't get hold of her, they have gone for the sultana. I think she will stay alive, at least until the sultan has refused to sign over the lease. And if he does surrender, then I would expect her to be returned unharmed.' I hope and pray, she thought.

'Does that put us any further ahead? She has still been kidnapped, in the presence of two police officers. We don't have a clue where she is, where they have taken her,

269

what vehicle they are using. You can't even give us a description, much less a number.'

Jessica kept her temper with difficulty. 'I considered it my first duty to tend to the casualties, sir, and see if they were still alive and could be helped. As for the vehicle, I only saw the back of it, but I think it was a Mercedes.'

'Of course, of course, JJ. I'm not blaming you...'

Liar, she thought.

'But we have to face facts.'

'Yes, sir. However, I believe I am in possession of a fact which may lead us to these people.'

'Eh?'

'The research undertaken on my behalf by Inspector Moran turned up a Russian émigré named Stanislav Tarnowski as the most probable principal in this case. He is a contract enforcer of illegal transactions or blackmail threats who uses explosives as his deterrents or paybacks.'

'A Russian? Why wasn't I informed of this?'

'When I discovered the identity of this man, I was still under the impression that I was on a simple protection assignment. And it appears that, under the assumed name of Burke, he has been living in England for some time. This was known to us, but there was nothing we could do about it. He came

270

here with genuine papers, as an Irishman, and has lived in perfect propriety. According to Inspector Moran, he has never even received a parking ticket.'

'How do we know he is really Tarnowski?'

'Liaison with the FBI, sir. He's wanted in the States. But they have never had sufficient evidence against him to apply for extradition.'

'And you think he may have broken cover to be involved in this? I'm not sure how this helps us. We don't even know where he is.'

'I think we do, sir. One of the kidnappers, a Spanish hit man whom we have identified as Jaime Sanchez, and who is presently operating under the name of Rosen, was here this evening.'

'You know this man?'

'I have seen an identikit of him, made up by the princess. Well, when his woman companion was wounded and she wanted to take it out on us, he told her she couldn't, because, and I quote, "The boss is waiting." To me that suggests that this man Burke was actually in the car outside the house.'

'Which has now driven away, God knows where.'

'Sir, Burke lives in England. He has an address.'

'You're not suggesting that he would be so stupid as to take the sultana to his own home?'

'No, sir, I am not. But wherever he has taken her it had to be arranged, and as he did not know he was going to be operating in England at all until after his first attempt to snatch the princess failed, the arrangement had to be at short notice. I believe that a search of Burke's home may well turn up some indication of where the sultana is being held.'

'Hm. A long shot.'

'Yes, sir. But it's the only shot we have.'

'Based on pure supposition. You say that Burke has never been involved in any criminal activity in this country, and also that he is a bona fide resident. That means he is entitled to all the protection of the law as regards his behaviour and property, until he can actually be proved to have broken the law. You have no proof, only supposition based on the fact that this man, very vaguely, fills a profile of the man you are after. I'm afraid there is nothing there that would stand up in a court of law.'

Jessica experienced a growing sense of desperation. 'I am not suggesting we put him in court right this minute, sir. I'm suggesting we search his house.'

'We'd still need a warrant. Which would require offering a magistrate reasonable cause for suspicion. I don't think you have that yet, Sergeant.'

'Sir, a woman's – the sultana's – life may be

at stake here.'

'Hm. Yes. Well, I'll discuss the matter with Inspector Moran tomorrow morning. You say he has all the gen.'

'Tomorrow morning?'

'Well, for God's sake, it's pushing midnight. You don't expect me to get him out of bed?'

'No, sir,' Jessica said obediently.

'I can see that you are overwrought,' Adams said sympathetically. 'I don't blame you. I have promised to do all I can to save your rank. Or at least your neck. Now you are officially off this case. It's just bad luck you happened to be here when those thugs broke in. As of now you, and DC Hutchins, are on leave. Take the rest of the week off, and report for duty on Monday morning. And use the time to relax and get fighting fit again.'

There is nothing the matter with me, Jessica wanted to shout. But that would be self-defeating. 'Yes, sir,' she said.

'We could still tie one on,' Andrea said.

Jessica's Land Rover being a write-off, they were returning to London in the Clio. 'The pubs are shut,' Jessica pointed out.

'Well, why don't you come to our place? We've a bottle of gin. I'll bet that's where Chloe and Prissy are.'

'Thanks, but I'll pass it up. Tom's waiting

273

for me at home.'

'Oh. Right.' Andrea was silent for a few moments, then she said, 'Are we really done with it?'

'That's what the man says. I imagine he feels that, after Louise, we're no longer capable of a rational judgement of any situation that might arise. Who's to say he's not right? I certainly didn't behave very rationally with Cerise this afternoon.'

'I think you behaved very rationally this evening.'

Jessica glanced at her. 'You think I should have started shooting sooner?'

'Our pistols against two assault rifles? Thank God you didn't, or we'd both be dead. What I'm trying to say is, I hope you don't feel that I've let you down. Or any of us.'

'You've all been great. Especially you.'

'Because I'd like to work with you again. Please. Any time, any place, any job.'

'You will,' Jessica promised, wondering if she was making an advance, and suddenly wondering what Andie – so beautiful, so laid back, so soignée – would be like in bed. She reckoned Chloe was a lucky girl.

But she had Tom.

He woke up as she entered the bedroom. Predictably, he was sprawled on the bed, naked, his lank black hair disarranged, but his rugged face and muscular body were, as always, a compelling sight. At least to her. She found herself wondering if Andrea would find it so. She had obviously given at least a passing thought to the profits that might be made from working for Sir William. But now was surely not the time for too much introspection.

He looked at his watch. 'You missed your birthday.'

'Yes,' she said, hanging her jacket in the wardrobe and kicking off her shoes.

'And you're not a happy bunny.'

'No,' she said, dropping her pants and hanging them beside her jacket.

'Too unhappy even to give her long-lost lover a kiss?'

'Oh, sorry.' She sat on the bed, and he put his arm round her waist, kissing her mouth while he slid his hand inside her knickers to give her bottom a squeeze.

'Tell Daddy.'

'I may just do that.' She freed herself, finished undressing.

'Did I ever tell you that you are the biggest turn-on I have ever known?'

'I don't feel like a turn-on at this moment.' She went into the bathroom.

He waited until the various waters stopped running, then asked, 'Who's this Brian?' She came to the doorway. 'Well,' he said. 'I flicked through the e-mails. I always do.'

'Brian is the name of my ex-husband. I'd

have thought you'd remember that.'

'Good God, so it is. He been troubling you?'

'He invited me out for a drink on my birthday.'

'And?'

'I accepted. You weren't here, and I was feeling lonely. I had no idea that this job was going to blow up in my face.'

'Supposing it hadn't, and I had still come home today?'

'Yesterday. I would have broken the date.'

'I'm glad of that. Now, tell me about this blow-up.'

'Later,' she said.

It is remarkable, the mental impulses that stimulate sexual desire, she thought. She was very tired and really only wanted to sleep. Every time she thought of Louise she felt physically sick, but it was the sickness of stimulation, spreading from her groin up through her stomach to her throat. She couldn't stop herself wondering what it might feel like, mentally and physically, to be stripped naked and tied up or held down, at the mercy of two unutterable thugs, and feel a length of wire passed between your legs, knowing that the initial sensation was going to be replaced by the purest agony ... and then Andie!

She clung to Tom as if it was their first

night together, working her body against his, feeling the reassuring touch of his hands, roaming from her shoulders down to her bottom and then round in front, to go between her legs to bring her to orgasm before rolling her on to her stomach and spreading her legs. As always, he handled her rather like a sack of potatoes, but tonight she was in the mood to want even that, while she wondered at the so narrow margin between the pure bliss of being manipulated by Tom and the sheer horror of being manipulated by, for example, Rosen. The way he had looked at her, contemptuously sparing her life because she and Andie were pretty women, the way he might even now be looking at the sultana, who was entirely in his power...

She rolled over, so violently that she almost threw Tom off the bed. Fortunately, he had just climaxed himself. 'What the hell...?'

'I'm sorry.'

He put his arms round her, and drew her back to him. 'Tell me.' She brought him up to date. 'Shit,' he said. 'That lovely girl. But you'll get them.'

'No, I won't,' she said. 'I've been taken off. Too emotionally involved. You're damned right I'm emotionally involved.'

Knowing as much about the requirements of their profession as she did, he had nothing to offer except for saying, 'Try to get some sleep.'

This she did, nestling in his arms, only to be awakened with a start when the entry-phone rang. 'For God's sake...'

Tom was out of bed and going into the lounge to answer it. A moment later he was back in the doorway. 'It's the princess. She's downstairs and wants to come up.'

The Proposition

'Oh, God!' Sonia moaned. 'I'm dying!'

They had been driving for over an hour, and the sedative had worn off. But now they were among houses. 'We'll be there in five minutes,' Loman assured her.

'I am so cold.'

'Wrap her in a blanket,' Burke suggested. 'There is one behind the seat.'

Rosen reached behind himself, then leaned across Vanessa to shroud Sonia's shoulders. Vanessa glared at him, but chose not to say anything; still recovering from the blow she had received, she had kept silent throughout the drive, apart from the brief outburst on awakening.

A few minutes later they turned into Loman's drive. Burke glanced at his watch.

'Not yet ten,' he said, and looked at the houses to either side and across the street, every one ablaze with light. 'Is it safe?'

'At this hour everyone will be either finishing dinner or watching telly,' Loman assured him as he braked before his closed garage door. 'If that goddamned van wasn't in there, we'd be absolutely safe.'

'We must make do with what we have,' Burke said with his invariable equanimity. 'Now, this must be done quickly and slickly. Loman, you go first, open the door, and alert Ruby that she has work to do. Rosen, you'll help Sonia into the house. Try to stay on your feet, Sonia.'

'And her?' Rosen jabbed Vanessa in the ribs, bringing a gasp.

'I'll stay here with her until you come back for her.' Loman hurried off. Rosen got out of the car, went round to the other side, opened the door, and helped Sonia out. Burke turned round in his seat to look at Vanessa. 'I hope you will not try anything stupid,' he said.

Vanessa licked her lips. 'What are you going to do to me?'

'That depends on how you behave. How well you do what you are told to do.'

'Do you suppose you can get away with this? All the police in England will be looking for you.'

'I once had most of the police in America

279

looking for me,' Burke reminisced. 'And I'm still here.'

'And you think you can keep me a prisoner in a small house in suburban London?'

'Think of Edgar Allan Poe,' Burke recommended. 'He wrote a short story called *The Purloined Letter*. I won't bore you with the plot, but it centred around this extremely important letter. In an effort to find it, the police searched this fellow's flat from top to bottom, without success. What they didn't reckon was that the letter was stuck in an incoming mail slot, with a lot of other letters. So there it was, right under their noses, but they never thought to look there because it merged so completely with its immediate surroundings.'

'That was a story,' Vanessa said.

'Fiction – *good* fiction – is always a reflection of fact. Loman's little house conforms very well to the pattern of belonging. Anyway, you're not going to be there very long.'

'What do you mean? Where are you taking me?'

'Never anticipate,' he recommended. 'Rosen.' Rosen opened the car door. 'Please get out, Your Highness,' Burke invited. 'But remember – behave yourself.'

Vanessa eased herself forward, got her feet out of the door – which had been opened on the house side of the car so that it was at least partly concealed from the street and the neighbouring houses – and then hurled herself forward, as Karina had done in Kharram. But this time Rosen was ready for her, and he was not handicapped by any instructions to treat her gently. He side-stepped, and at the same time hit her as hard as he could in the stomach. Vanessa gave a great moan and fell to her hands and knees. 'Get her inside,' Burke said, also getting out, and reaching into the back for the rifle.

Rosen thrust his hands into Vanessa's armpits, and heaved her up. She was gasping for breath, and had vomited; saliva was still dribbling from her mouth. Rosen turned her round so that he was behind her, and half carried, half pushed her towards the door.

Burke followed, holding the rifle against his side, giving a quick glance up and down the street to make sure it remained empty. Loman held the door open, and Vanessa was forced into the hall and then the lounge. Sonia lay on the floor, panting and groaning. Ruby knelt beside her; she had stripped Sonia to the waist and was removing Rosen's hasty bandage. Blood dribbled down on to the carpet. She raised her head as the men came in, and looked at Vanessa, who was only half conscious. 'Don't tell me there's another would-be stiff.' Sonia gave a shriek, this time of mental anguish.

'She'll recover,' Rosen said, and threw

Vanessa on to the settee, where she sprawled on her back, arms and legs flung wide, staring at him, still unable to speak. 'Did you ever see such tits?' he asked. 'I know Arab men like them big, but she is a whopper.'

'One day your obscene tastes are going to get you into trouble.' Burke stood the rifle against the wall. 'Where is the other one?'

'She dropped it,' Rosen said.

'And you left it, with her prints all over it? Shit.' He stood above Sonia. 'Well?'

'It's not good, Mr Burke,' Ruby said. 'I can just about stop the bleeding, but the bones are all shattered. What did this?'

'A single shot from a high-velocity machine pistol,' Rosen said.

'Who fired it?' Burke asked.

'The little blonde bit,' Rosen said.

'You mean one of those so-called police-women? Do you know her name?'

Rosen slapped Vanessa's face, twice. Just getting her breath back, Vanessa gasped in pain. She tried to sit up, and Rosen pushed her down again. 'Tell us the name of the blonde policewoman,' he said.

'You bastard,' Vanessa spat.

Burke stood above her. 'Answer the question, or I will let him have you. He is very rough on his women.'

Vanessa sucked air into her lungs. 'Jones.'

'Oh, come now. You can do better than that.'

282

'Her name is Jones,' Vanessa shouted. 'Detective-Sergeant Jessica Jones. We were told she is one of their best people.'

'Jessica Jones,' Burke said, committing the name to memory.

'We need a doctor, Mr Burke,' Ruby said. 'And quickly. Otherwise...'

'Is she going to die?'

'I don't think she will die. But she could lose the arm.'

'No!' Sonia shouted. 'You must help me.'

'For God's sake give her another sedative,' Burke said.

Ruby filled a hypodermic needle. 'Listen,' Sonia begged. 'You must help me, Mr Burke, you must!'

'I know a good man...' Loman ventured.

'No good men,' Burke said. 'Not until this business is finished.'

'No,' Sonia said. 'Please get a doctor. Please ... Don't touch me!' she screamed. But Ruby thrust the needle into her arm, and a moment later she subsided, eyes drooping shut. Ruby looked at Burke.

'Get her out of here. Put her to bed,' Burke said.

'Yes, Mr Burke. There's been a telephone call. He didn't give his name, but he left a mobile number. Foreign, he sounded.'

'Ah,' Burke said. 'So he got here.'

'Who?' Rosen asked.

'That is not your business. Get that woman

out of here.'

'You'll have to carry her, Rosen,' Loman said. 'She's a big woman, too heavy for me.'

Rosen glanced at Burke, and received a nod. Reluctantly, he left Vanessa's side and scooped Sonia from the floor. She was quite out, her head hanging loosely, her hair trailing. Loman and Ruby followed him up the stairs. 'In here,' Ruby said, opening the spare room door. Rosen carried Sonia in and laid her on the bed. 'Wait,' Ruby said. 'Lift her up again.'

'Shit!' Rosen muttered, but he did as she wished.

Ruby took a blanket from a cupboard and spread it over the sheet. 'We don't want the bedclothes ruined.'

Rosen laid Sonia down again. 'You mean she's going to continue bleeding?'

'Look at your jacket,' Ruby suggested.

Rosen looked down at the bloodstain. 'Shit!' he commented again.

'What are we going to do?' Loman asked.

'That's Burke's business.'

'He means to let her die.' Rosen frowned at him. 'She is your partner,' Loman said. 'Doesn't that bother you?'

'She was a fucking nuisance.'

'Well, it bothers me. I know Burke. He is going to get what he wants, and then just disappear. Oh, he'll pay us exactly what he owes us. He is very scrupulous about that.

284

But he'll still reckon it's *our* business to get rid of the body. Both bodies.'

'Eh?'

'You don't imagine he is going to turn the sultana loose? She knows everything about us now, from what we look like to where we live.'

'Shit!' Rosen muttered again. He was not in the least averse to taking life, but if they killed someone who was in effect a reigning queen – and who was, for all her age, still a damned good-looking woman into the bargain – they would be hunted to the ends of the earth. And from what he had heard of Kharrami justice... 'I'd better talk to him,' he decided.

Burke used the phone in the lounge. 'Tell me,' he said, and listened. 'You do not have the address? What use is that? Well, give me the phone number. A mobile? Belonging to Sergeant Jones? That is interesting. Very well. I will be in touch.' He replaced the phone, sat on the settee next to Vanessa, and then carefully, and delicately, restored the bodice of her gown to its proper position. 'Must be dignified, Your Highness.'

'I am going to watch your head being cut off,' Vanessa said, her voice loaded with venom. She had watched him use the phone, but had not attempted to move; he assumed she was still in some pain.

'You people are so *violent*,' Burke remarked. 'Why do you not co-operate? Then no one else will come to any harm.'

'My husband will never give you that concession,' Vanessa said. 'Never, never, never.'

'Surely the decision should be his. I am prepared to wait for that. What I want from you, in the short term, is the whereabouts of your daughter.'

'What do you want her for, if you have me?'

'Your Highness, I hate to be indelicate, but it seems reasonable to suppose that your husband will be more interested in preserving the life of his daughter, who is also his only child and his heir, than that of an ageing woman who has shared his bed for nineteen years. I am assuming that you still do share his bed?'

'Bastard!'

'I see. But men will be men, especially when, like the sultan, he has so much willing nubility at his command. However, quite apart from twisting his arm, the princess and I have some unfinished business to complete.'

'What unfinished business?'

'At the moment, that is not your concern. Now, tell me where Karina is.'

Vanessa tossed her head. Her confidence was slowly returning, now that she appeared to be dealing with a gentleman rather than a thug. Not that she did not still intend to have him taken back to Kharram and executed in the most rigorous manner allowed by law. 'I do not know where she is.'

'Oh, come now. Your daughter? Listen, we know she left Blandlock, suddenly, on Monday afternoon. Did she do this on her own, or in the company of a policewoman?'

'She left with Sergeant Jones.'

'Ah, the ubiquitous Sergeant Jones. She is someone I simply have to meet. So where did Sergeant Jones take the princess?'

'I assume to her flat.'

'So give me the address.'

'I do not have the address.'

'I see. But the princess is still there, is she?'

'No. I objected to that arrangement, and she was moved, this afternoon, to a police safe house.'

'Tell me that address. I am sure you know it.'

'I do not,' Vanessa said, looking him in the eye.

'Your Highness, you are trying my patience. Do you expect me to believe that your daughter has been placed in a safe house, but you do not know where that is?'

'I do not know where Karina is right now,' Vanessa said. 'I was to join her tomorrow morning. The police were coming for me, to take me to her.'

Burke regarded her for a few moments,

then said, 'All right. I'll accept that. But I assume she is still in the care of Sergeant Jones?'

'As far as I know,' Vanessa said.

'And of course Sergeant Jones has a team, has she not? So that she can take some time off her duties. Now, I have obtained her mobile number from a friend who happens to possess it, so you will telephone her, and tell her to remove the princess from the safe house for an outing tomorrow morning, at a place I will describe to you, where she is to meet you. Whereupon we will exchange you for her.'

'I will not lure my own daughter into a trap,' Vanessa declared.

'She will come to no harm. As I have explained, I feel that the sultan will be more amenable to reason if we have Karina rather than you. Listen very carefully. I strongly advise you to co-operate. Otherwise I shall give you to Rosen for a while. You will remember that he has a way with women. Sadly, it is not generally a way that appeals to women.' He took his mobile from his pocket. 'We will use this, so the call cannot be traced.'

'I will see you damned,' Vanessa said.

'Ah, Rosen,' Burke said as the big man came down the stairs. 'I have a little job for you.'

★ ★ ★

Still only half awake, Jessica blinked at her watch. 'Karina? Here? At one o'clock in the morning?'

'I told her to come up,' Tom said.

'Well, for God's sake put on some pants.' Jessica got out of bed, pushed her hair into some sort of order, and pulled on a dressing gown. Tom, wearing shorts, was opening the door to admit a very bedraggled-looking Karina, her shirt and jeans and hair soaked. 'Looks like it's raining out there,' Tom remarked.

Karina peered at him. 'Who are you?'

'Mine host.'

Karina looked past him at Jessica. 'Thank God! I was beginning to think I'd got the wrong flat.'

'Come in and shut the door,' Jessica said. 'What in the name of God are you doing here? You're under guard.'

'Oh, them,' Karina snorted. 'Can I have something to drink? Alcohol?'

The gin bottle was still on the sideboard. Tom moved towards it, instinctively, then checked and looked at Jessica. 'Is she supposed to? I thought she was a Muslim.'

'She makes up her own rules as she goes along,' Jessica said. 'Right, have your drink and then get out of those wet clothes before you wind up in hospital. Have you the number of your house?'

Karina took a gulp of gin and tonic. 'Brrr!

289

No I don't. And what do you want it for?'

'To tell them that you're safe. They'll be going spare. I'll call the Yard. They'll have it.'

'No,' Karina said. 'Please.'

'How did you get out, anyway?' Tom asked, taking her empty glass, and glancing at Jessica, who shook her head.

'I climbed down the drainpipe outside my bedroom window.'

'You...' Tom had never met any royalty, but he tried to conjure up a mental picture of one or two English princesses shinning down a drainpipe, and simply couldn't. 'How high up were you?'

'Three floors.'

'Holy hell. And then you walked, alone, through the streets of London in the pouring rain...' He looked at Jessica. 'Weren't you happy there?'

'I had to get out,' Karina said. 'When they told me what had happened to Mummy ... I had to come to you.' She sneezed.

'In the bedroom,' Jessica commanded. 'Strip off and have a hot shower.'

Karina hesitated. 'You won't call the police? Please!'

Once again Jessica and Tom exchanged glances. 'Okay,' Jessica said. 'I won't call anybody until after we've talked. But go and have that shower. At least that way I may not have to call a hospital as well.'

Karina hesitated a last time, then went to

the bedroom door.

'Mind if I go back to bed?' Tom asked.

'Of course not,' Karina said over her shoulder.

'He's a total lecher,' Jessica pointed out. 'What he really means is, he wants to keep an eye on you.'

'Who wouldn't?' Tom asked.

'Be my guest.' Karina went into the bedroom.

'I ought to lock you up,' Jessica said. 'Haven't you had your ration for tonight?'

'She's a good-looking girl,' he said, apparently seriously. 'I don't intend to touch.'

'You'd better not. And kindly keep your pants on.'

Karina had already disappeared into the bathroom, apparently undressing in there. 'Anyway,' Tom said as he got beneath the sheets, 'it strikes me this might be a team job. Getting her back, I mean.'

'Keeping my job, you mean. It's already on the line.'

'Tell you what: if you're fired, I'll marry you.'

'You're so kind.' The bathroom door was opening, and she ran forward, taking off her dressing gown as she did so to wrap it around Karina when she emerged. 'Does that feel better?'

'I suppose so.'

'I'll get a clean towel for your head.' Jessica went into the steaming bathroom. When she came back, Karina was sitting on the bed, fortunately on the far side from Tom. Jessica wrapped her head in the towel. 'Now, tell me what's got to you.'

'They told me about Mummy.'

'I feel like shit about that,' Jessica confessed. 'But it was so unexpected. We were taken completely by surprise. We all thought they were after you, and only you.'

'They were. Are,' Karina said miserably.

Jessica looked at Tom, who waggled his eyebrows. 'We're not with you,' Jessica said. 'They want to force your pa to make over the concession to their principals, right? So they went for you, to twist his arm. Now they have your ma, who is surely the next best thing.'

'Oh, that's part of it,' Karina said. 'But the object was to force Daddy to abdicate more than the oil.'

Jessica frowned as all those hitherto formless suspicions that had been chasing themselves around her brain began to take shape. 'You knew this?'

'I set it up. Well, I agreed to go along with it.'

'You...'

Tom sat up. 'I think you need to explain that, Princess.'

'Daddy is old. And, well, decrepit. You

292

must understand. He's terribly nouveau riche. Down to twelve years ago, Kharram was the poorest state in all Arabia, not merely in the Gulf. And then, suddenly, bingo. The old dear entirely lost his head. In the first place, he gave away the concession for peanuts. Oh, everyone became very rich, certainly compared with anything they had known before, and he became a multi-millionaire, but it was, and is, still peanuts when you consider what's down there. And Worldoil are naturally expecting to renew their lease on the same terms as before. Everyone has tried to tell Daddy that he should up the ante, at least to double, but he won't hear of it. He actually thinks that they might pull out if he asks too much.'

Jessica scratched her head. The only serious negotiating she had ever done in her life had been when buying the second-hand Land Rover, which down to last evening had been her favourite toy.

'And then,' Karina went on, 'there's the money he's spent, on rubbish. The opera house. When I was there on Saturday, there was an international cast, plus the fact that I was going to be there, which was well publicised ... And the place was only half full. It cost millions to build.'

'I thought the Kharramis were very happy with their situation, even if there is a bit of waste,' Tom said. 'It isn't as if there are still

293

any slums, or poor to be taken care of. Everyone has electricity and good water, good plumbing...'

'But not everyone wants that,' Karina said. 'Some of our people had lived in the same house for generations, and then suddenly they were told that they had to move out so that their home could be bulldozed to make room for a high-rise. Our people don't like living in high-rise apartments. They like to be near the ground.'

'Well,' Tom said, 'to paraphrase old Abraham Lincoln, you can please all of the people some of the time, and you can even please some of the people all of the time, but you cannot please all of the people all of the time.'

Karina clearly had no idea what he was talking about. 'And then there's Mummy,' she said.

'I thought she was very popular,' Jessica ventured.

'She is. With any woman aged between fifteen and thirty. And quite a few men in that age group as well. Everyone else thinks she is too liberated, and has tried to make everyone else too liberated too. Her views on dress, and alcohol, and a whole lot of things have offended the ayatollahs.'

'And you don't approve either?' Tom asked. 'But you drink.'

'That's my business.'

It was Tom's turn to scratch his head.

'Let me get this straight,' Jessica said. 'Are you telling us that there is some kind of conspiracy against your father, intended to destabilise the regime, so that he can be deposed?'

'Well...' Karina licked her lips.

'And you knew this?'

'Well, I had to do what was best for my country.'

'Great God in Heaven!' Tom commented. 'And you would succeed him.'

'I am his heir.'

'Would your people accept you? A woman?'

'Of course. There have been several ruling sultanas in our history. I would be required to marry, of course.'

'You mean you agreed to have people blown up, murdered?' Jessica was aghast. But she was also aware of a slowly growing anger. She was thinking of Louise.

'No!' Karina said vehemently. 'I was not told of any killing. I was told there would be an alarm, and I should flee out of the rear of the building, where a car would be waiting. No one said anything about a bomb and shooting.'

'You said the people who snatched you roughed you up, and you had to fight your way clear.'

'Well, they did. They didn't know of the

arrangement. We had to keep it as secret as we could. But I meant to get away from them anyway, once the bomb had gone off and Manfred had been shot. I was very upset about that.'

'I'm glad of that,' Jessica commented sarcastically. 'So you decided to terminate your arrangement. But you didn't feel up to telling your pa about it.'

'Well, he would have been very angry.'

'You could be right.'

'And it would have meant betraying my associates. They would have been arrested, and, well...'

'Had their balls burned.'

'What did you say?' Tom asked.

'That's what they do to people who conspire against the sultan,' Jessica explained. Tom swallowed. 'Just who are these people, anyway?' Jessica asked.

'I really don't wish to say.'

Jessica considered her for some seconds, then decided against pressing that point, for the moment. 'But this man Burke is one of them.'

Karina snorted. 'He's the hired help.'

'Have you met him?'

'No. And I don't want to meet him. I didn't know I was dealing with a mass murderer.'

'But didn't you contact him to let him know you'd changed your mind?'

'I *was* going to contact them, and tell them

the deal was off. But then Daddy sent me over here. Just like that. Before I had the time to think.'

'And they were already committed.'

'I thought they'd just pack it in when they realised I wasn't going to co-operate. I didn't believe they'd follow me here. I didn't see how they could know where I was. That bitch Cerise...'

'She was in it too?'

'Yes. But I told her it was off. And then she got in touch with them, anyway.'

'I can understand that you were annoyed with her. She was too fully committed as well. And Henri?'

'Well...'

'Is he your lover?'

'Well, he is the representative of the international consortium which was backing us.'

'Which is *still* backing you, you mean, whether you want it or not. So what exactly have you arranged with Henri?'

'You told me I could not see him.'

'Princess,' Jessica said, 'I think you should know that I am operating on a very short fuse. You were alone here yesterday morning, for over an hour, before Chloe arrived. Are you trying to tell me that you didn't call Henri during that time?'

'How was I to do that without his number?'

'Because he gave you his number when he

called you earlier.'

'Well...' Karina screwed up her features. 'I did call him, yes. But I told him not to do anything until I had got you off my back.'

'But you gave him this address.'

'No, I did not. I was afraid that if he came here you might shoot him or something.'

'You could have been right. Well, you have really landed everyone in it now. Including yourself. I am going to have to place you under arrest.'

'I have committed no crime in England.'

'You have committed a crime in Kharram. A sufficiently serious crime for you to be returned there, to face your father.'

Now Karina's face puckered, and she looked about to burst into tears. 'He will beat me, and then lock me up.'

'That sounds very mild to me.'

'All right.' Karina grasped Jessica's hands. 'Do what you like with me. But rescue Mummy first.'

'So you really think she's in danger?' Jessica was quite sure she was, but she wanted to hear the princess's opinion. 'All she has to do is persuade your pa to grant the concession, right?'

'She'll never do it. And even if she agreed, Daddy would never do it.'

'But you reckoned he'd do it to save you.'

'Well, I am his heir. And...' She bit her lip. 'If anything were to happen to Mummy, he'd be able to marry again.'

'And perhaps beget another heir. A male heir,' Jessica said thoughtfully, 'who would replace you in the line of succession. I can see that you want your ma to stay alive. You'll forgive me for not having a very high opinion of your family, Princess. Or you. But could your pa not just divorce your mother if she no longer turns him on? I thought that was a simple matter in a Muslim country.'

'It is, in theory. But as I said, Mummy is very popular with the youth of the country. They would not like her to be put aside.'

'But if she got herself murdered by a bunch of thugs ... You really have dug yourself a hole, Princess. And there is nothing we can do about it.'

'Nothing? You, with all your experience, all your successes...'

'I may have some ideas, but I have been taken off the case. Thanks to you, my job is on the line. Certainly my rank is.'

Karina squeezed her fingers. 'Please help me, JJ. Help me, and I will do anything you wish. Ask anything of me.' Her tongue circled her lips, and she glanced at Tom.

'Down, boy,' Jessica recommended. 'Even if I wanted to help you, Princess – and it *would* probably cost me my job – I have nothing to go on. I don't have a clue – no one appears to have a clue – where your mother may have been taken.'

'But you know where Burke lives in this country, don't you?'

'Yes. And I have already suggested that a search of his house might be useful, but my superiors don't think we'd get a warrant. There is nothing to connect Burke with the kidnapping of your mother, or the attempted kidnapping of you. Just a hunch.'

'But you and I know it is more than a hunch.'

'Try convincing Commander Adams of that.'

'Couldn't we go there without a warrant? He's not likely to be there. Unless he's taken Mummy there. And if he has, well, we could wrap the whole thing up.'

'You are really trying to get me thrown off the force. Anyway, he certainly won't have taken your mother there.'

'But we'll find a lead. I know we will. Please!' Karina said. 'Listen, help me get Mummy back, and I'll confess to everything. I'll say I made you do what I wish. I am the Princess of Kharram. I did not ask for you to be replaced. I did not *want* you replaced. I will insist that you not be punished.'

Jessica looked at Tom. And Jessica's mobile rang.

Jessica and Tom both reached for it, but Jessica let Tom pick it up. 'Yes?'

'Excuse me,' a man's voice said. 'Would

300

this be the residence of Detective-Sergeant Jessica Jones?'

'It could be,' Tom said.

'Is Sergeant Jones at home?'

'At one o'clock in the morning? Where did you expect her to be?'

'I would like to speak with her, please.'

Tom raised his head. 'Shall I tell him to bugger off?'

'Let's hear what he has to say.' She took the phone, smiling reassuringly at Karina, who was sitting with fists clenched. 'Who is this?'

'We have never met, Sergeant. But we have what might be called an acquaintance.'

'Would you be Mr Rosen, or Mr Burke?'

'Brilliant, Sergeant. My name is Burke, yes. I was under the impression that you had already met Mr Rosen. Now, I wish you to listen to me very carefully. Oh, incidentally, I would not waste your time attempting to trace this call. I am using a mobile.'

'I thought you might be.'

'Very good. Now, as I am sure you are aware, we hold the sultana.'

'Yes.'

'But it is not her we wish. We wish the princess. So, as we have the sultana, and you have the princess, we are willing to trade.'

'I no longer have the princess,' Jessica said, gazing at Karina.

'I did not telephone you to play a game, Sergeant. I know you have, or can gain,

301

access to the princess. If you wish the sultana to survive, then you will obey my instructions. You will take the princess from where she is currently placed, at nine o'clock tomorrow – I mean, *this* – morning. This is for the purpose of giving her some fresh air, you understand. Immediately before you leave for the princess, at a quarter to nine, I will telephone you and give you my instructions for her delivery. I trust you will keep this call and my wishes to yourself, and obey them implicitly. Please understand that I will not hesitate to execute the sultana should we perceive anything suspicious about your activities. When you have carried out all of my instructions, the exchange will be made.'

'I see,' Jessica said. 'And what then happens to the princess?'

'Nothing will happen to the princess, provided the sultan agrees to our terms. I give you my word.'

Which he would probably keep, Jessica thought; however angry he might be at what he would consider Karina's defection, he needed her as a figurehead behind which to mount his *coup d'état*. 'I will need time to consider this,' she said.

'There is no time for consideration if you wish to save the sultana's life,' Burke said. 'She would like to speak with you.'

Jessica found she was holding her breath as she listened to the voice at the other end of the line. 'Please,' Vanessa begged. 'Please help me, Sergeant Jones.'

It was definitely Vanessa, although all the arrogant confidence she had earlier displayed was gone. 'Are you all right?' Jessica asked. For a reply there was an unforgettable whimper. Karina opened her mouth, and had it shut again by Tom, clamping her jaw. 'Your Highness?' Jessica asked.

'I think she has said enough,' Burke said.

'What have you done to her?'

'Nothing serious. Rosen has been amusing himself, that is all. She will be returned to you with no external damage, I promise you. Perhaps she will be a little more, shall I say, introspective in the future. But that is surely no bad thing. A quarter to nine tomorrow morning, Miss Jones.'

The phone went dead.

Tom took his hand away, and Karina wailed, 'Mummy! What have they done to her?'

'I'd try not to think about it, if I were you. You heard the deal he was offering?'

'Yes. Yes, we must go through with it.'

'Right. We'll offer you all the protection we can. I'll get on to the commander right away...'

'No!' Karina cried. 'You can't. They'll mess it up. And Mummy will die. They'll do it. I know they will.'

Jessica looked at Tom. 'She has a point,'

he said.

'And just what do you propose we do?'

'I'm prepared to make the exchange,' Karina said.

'Because you feel the need to atone for the mess you've caused?'

'Because it's my mother's *life*!'

'And what about *your* life?'

'He said I wouldn't be harmed, as long as Daddy accepts his demands.'

'If you believe that, you'll believe the earth is flat. Harm is a matter of interpretation. Don't you realise he has it in for you now, for reneging on the deal? At the very least he'll give you to that thug Rosen.'

'I'm prepared to risk that,' Karina said with dignity.

'Well, I'm not. And have you considered *my* position? I'm sticking my neck out as it is, in having you here for this length of time without reporting it. You are now asking me to keep you here for another eight hours, and then hand you over to the opposition. I'd be drummed out of the force.'

'I said I'd protect you. Please. We must help Mummy.'

Jessica glared at her, then looked at Tom. 'Have you considered taking them out?' he asked.

'Have I *what*? My job is to protect the princess, not get her killed.'

'Taking them out would be the best way of

protecting her.'

'Tom Lawson, you have got to be stark staring mad.'

'If,' he said, 'and I know it's a big if, we were to get to the sultana before the rest of the squad, it would do your position a world of good, JJ.'

'Are you saying you wish to be involved?'

'I *am* involved. With you.'

'You'd be putting your own job on the line. Especially if we break a few laws.'

'You've trained with the SAS. So have I. Who dares...'

'Wins.'

Karina clapped her hands.

'And you reckon the two of us can take on Burke's mob?'

'Three of us,' Karina said.

'Princess, there is liable to be shooting.'

'I'm not afraid of being shot at. And anyway, if I'm not there, they won't play at all.'

Jessica looked at Tom. 'Again, she has a point. But we'd need a back-up.'

'And where are we going to get that?'

'Well, what about your team? They were in on the ground floor. And if your job is on the line because of that foul-up at Blandlock, so is Andrea's.' Jessica stared at him, and then remembered Andrea saying, Call on me, any time, for anything. Presumably something like this was not what she had in mind, though. 'And wherever Andrea goes, Chloe will want to go too,' Tom added.

'I'll have to put it to them, put them in the whole picture.'

'Don't you trust them?'

'Of course I trust them. But I have to give them the right to refuse.'

'Try them,' Tom suggested.

The Assault

'We need more people,' Burke said. 'Thanks to that stupid bitch getting herself shot. Can you raise anybody, Loman?'

'Well, why do we need more people, Mr Burke? If it is going to be a straight swop?'

'For two reasons. The first is that it is not going to be a straight swop. I want that police sergeant as well. The second is that she is unlikely to play it straight either. She'll have something up her sleeve. So we need to cover ourselves. Who can you raise?'

'Well, sir, it's pretty short notice...'

'I know that. I had hoped to be able to complete the business with what we had, but as that can't be done...'

'I could try the Dorrell brothers. They're just out, and I believe they haven't got stuck into anything yet. They'd be glad of the work.'

'You know these men personally?'

'We were friends as kids.'

'And they are reliable? And capable of taking executive action?'

'They went down for GBH. And they know how to keep their mouths shut. What do I tell them?'

'That you require them to oversee the delivery of some extremely valuable goods, at which someone may try to pull a fast one. Get them here, and I will tell them what they have to do. Tell them to bring shooters.'

'They will have to be well paid.'

'They will be well paid. Now get hold of them.' He went upstairs and into the bedroom, where Ruby was sitting by Sonia's bedside. There was a blood-filled bowl on the floor beside her. Sonia was unconscious. 'Well?' Burke asked.

'I've changed the bandages, Mr Burke. But as you can see, she's losing blood. She needs a hospital and a transfusion. She's bad.'

Burke looked at his watch; it was just coming up to dawn. 'She can wait another couple of hours, Ruby. Then it'll be done.'

'I'm not sure she *can* wait another couple of hours, Mr Burke.'

'See that she does,' Burke said, and went into the other bedroom, where Vanessa lay on the bed, naked and with her wrists tied to the bedpost above her head. There were red blotches on her body, and red weals as well. She moved restlessly, although she was only half awake. Rosen sat in a chair beside the bed, dozing. 'What?' Burke commented. 'Have you run out of steam?'

'Just resting,' Rosen said. 'And she has become boring.'

'Never mind. You will soon have some fresh material to play with.'

'Are we ready?'

'Another couple of hours. But she will have to be dressed and looking as well as possible. Give her a bath. You will enjoy that. And then make her eat something. It might be a good idea to give her a shot of whisky as well, to cheer her up. They have to believe we're on the up and up, until we make our play.'

'Have we got enough people, with Sonia out of action?'

'We will have.'

'What about Ferrière?'

'I am going to contact him now.'

Jessica surveyed the faces in front of her. The three women looked more anticipatory than anxious; Louise had been a friend to all of them. 'I don't want any of you to be in any doubts about what we're up against,' she said. 'Andie will confirm that these people are absolutely cold-blooded killers.' Andrea nodded. 'You also need to bear in mind that what we are doing is outside the law. If it comes off, we shall all be heroines. If it fails, at the very least we shall be turfed off the force, if we don't face criminal charges. So if anyone wants to drop out before the going gets rough, I'm not going to hold it against them.'

No one moved.

'Right. And thanks. Now, we can't make any concrete plans until we get our final instructions from Burke. But one or two things are obvious even at this stage. His MO is to do things in public, distracting the people around. However, he is also very careful. He can't tail us from the start, because he anticipates that we will start from wherever the princess is being held, and he doesn't know where that is. But we can be certain that he will have the exchange point staked out, to make sure I don't turn up mob-handed. So we are going to have to be very smart about this. I have no doubt at all that he will, if necessary, carry out his threat to kill the sultana. He's in this so deep, whatever he does now is not going to affect the outcome if he's caught. But we do have one asset.' She smiled at Karina, who *was* looking anxious. 'He wants the princess, alive. So now we wait. We'll make our final dispositions when he calls back.'

'Grub up.' Tom had been cooking. 'I

309

recommend that all the condemned eat a hearty breakfast.'

'What about Henri?' Karina whispered to Jessica as the other women helped themselves to bacon and eggs.

'What about Henri?'

'Well, he might be useful.'

'Princess, Henri is on the other side. Where do you suppose Burke got my mobile number – from Directory Inquiries?'

'Henri would never hurt me.'

'I'm sure you're right. But as I have just said, I don't believe Burke means to hurt you either, at least not seriously, until he's obtained your father's surrender. But can you be sure that Henri would object to your mother being hurt?'

Karina bit her lip. 'She does not like him.'

'And I'm sure he knows this. See what I mean? Have something to eat.' The phone rang, and everyone turned towards it. 'No one makes a sound,' Jessica said, and picked it up. 'Yes?'

'JJ?!'

'Shit!' Jessica muttered under her breath. But she supposed it had to happen.

'What was that?'

'Nothing, sir. Good morning, sir. It's just that I am supposed to be on leave.'

'You are. But the most terrible thing has happened.'

'You've found the sultana's body?' She

waggled her eyebrows at the watching faces.

'Good lord, don't even think of it. It's the princess. She's absconded.'

'Would you repeat that, sir?'

'She's gone. Sneaked out. Sometime last night.'

Jessica allowed herself a whistle of stupefaction. 'With respect, sir, wasn't she fully protected?'

'Of course she was. No one could possibly get into the building.'

'But someone could get out.'

'Well, it never occurred to us that she might wish to do so. She seemed quite happy with the arrangement.'

'May I ask when this happened? The time she left?'

'No one has any idea. She said goodnight to the duty officer; her door was locked, and he left her, so far as he knew, watching television. She had had her supper and he presumed that she would, in the course of time, go to bed. One of his men was on duty in the corridor all night. But when the maid took in her breakfast an hour ago, in the company of a policeman, she wasn't there.'

'She can't have vanished into thin air.'

'She seems to have shinned down the drainpipe.'

'Weren't the windows barred?'

'Yes. But again, they were designed to keep people out, not keep someone in. The bars were screwed in from the inside. The princess simply unscrewed them with a nail file.'

'And then climbed down a drainpipe ... how many storeys?'

'Three. As I told you, she is one feisty young woman.'

'In the pouring rain. She must have had an urgent meeting somewhere.'

'She must be found.'

'Of course, sir. Are you telling me my holiday is over?'

'No, no, JJ. It's a job for the uniformed branch. However, it has occurred to me that she might come to you.'

'Why should she do that? If she's taken all this trouble to escape one protection unit, she's not likely to turn herself in to another.'

'I have an idea that she regards you as a friend more than a police officer.'

'It's very nice of you to say so, sir. But she also knows I play by the book, and if she turned up here I would immediately contact you.'

'I just want to be sure you do that, should she turn up there.'

'Of course, sir.'

'Because the alternative is that she's gone off looking for her mother on her own. It gives me the shits just to think of it.'

'It would upset me as well, sir. I'm sure she'll turn up. There's just one thing: has the fact of her disappearance been released to the media?'

'Good lord, no. They'd crucify us. This is strictly an internal matter, at least until, God forbid, we discover that something has happened to her.'

Jessica gave a sigh of relief. Burke should have no idea what had happened. 'What about Sir William?'

'I haven't told him yet, either.'

'Very good, sir. Well, if she should turn up here I'll be in touch.'

'Mind that you do. Right away, JJ. Right away.'

'Yes, sir.'

'Oh, by the way, Pleyell's funeral has been arranged for Friday. Full honours. I'd like you and your people to be there.'

'We will be, sir.' Jessica replaced the phone. 'I have just burned my very last bridge,' she said. 'This had better work.'

They had just finished breakfast when the phone rang again; the time was a quarter to nine. 'Yes?' Jessica asked.

'Detective-Sergeant Jones?'

'I am she, Mr Burke.'

'When are you picking up the princess?'

'I was about to leave.'

'Very good. When you have done that, drive out of London, to the south, and go to the town of Dorking. You know this place?'

'I've been there. But I'm not sure I can get there quickly from central London.'

'Try. What will you be driving?'

Jessica had already arranged with Tom that she would use his car. 'A blue Peugeot five-oh-five estate.'

'Very good. Coming from the London direction you will approach the town down a shallow slope. At the foot of the slope, on your left, there is a considerable hill, below which there is an hotel. Do you know this?'

'Yes. The hill is called Box Hill.'

'Very good. As you reach the hotel car park, which is adjacent to the road, you will slow down, and allow a car to leave the park in front of you. This car will be a Ford Mondego. You will follow this car into Dorking High Street, and when it stops you will stop behind it. Understood?'

'Yes. What happens if, because of traffic, I am late?'

'We will allow you a few minutes. If you are not outside the hotel car park at ten o'clock, we will call you on your mobile. When we call you, you will give us your exact position, and we will judge how much extra time to allow you. We will only do this once. Understood?'

'Yes.'

'Then I look forward to seeing you. And the princess, of course. Let me reiterate that if you and she are not alone in the car, or if you are accompanied in any way, the sultana will die. By being alone I mean any kind of surveillance, including that by helicopter. If any aircraft is seen, she will die.'

'I cannot be held responsible for all the aircraft movements in England, Mr Burke. That is absurd.'

'My conditions stand. Perhaps you had better pray. Good morning.'

Jessica replaced the phone. 'The bastard! He seems to have it all thought out, with one vital exception: he doesn't know that I don't have to drive into London and collect the princess, and that therefore we have a head start.'

'Won't he expect you to be mob-handed, in some way or another?' Priscilla asked.

'No. The reason he is playing it this way is he figures the schedule is so tight I have no time to do anything but get Karina and rush down there. The only option I would have of bringing force to bear would be to call in a chopper, which is why he stressed that point. But as I say, we can steal a march. I need a volunteer to come with us.'

'Me!' As always, they all spoke together.

Jessica smiled at them. 'Andie, you're elected. You'll have another chance to blow their heads off. Whose car were you guys using?'

'My Clio,' Andie said.

'Right. Tom, will you drive? You and Chloe

315

and Priscilla get down to Dorking right away. Drive as fast as you can until you're outside the town, then enter it as casually as you can. Park the car and meander on to the high street until we arrive, following our guide. We have to play it by ear from then, but do not do anything until I press my alarm. Then take whatever action seems appropriate, remembering that there may be innocent bystanders about, and we don't want any of them hurt. Got it?' They nodded. 'So, go, go, go.'

Tom kissed her. 'Take care.'

'And you.' Andrea and Chloe hugged each other. Then Tom and Chloe and Priscilla hurried out of the flat. 'We'll give them five minutes,' Jessica said. 'Collect those blankets.' Andrea and Karina folded the blankets, and they took them down to the estate car. Jessica disengaged the two rear rows of seats and laid them flat; Andrea got into the hatchback, spread a blanket on the metal floor, and lay down. Jessica then covered her with two more blankets. 'You can leave your head out until we're nearly there,' she said.

'Thanks a bunch.' Andrea laid her shoulder bag against her stomach, but took out her pistol and held that against her breast.

'Just be patient,' Jessica recommended. She got behind the wheel, Karina seated beside her, and started the engine. 'Now, Princess,' she said as they turned into traffic, 'let's get one or two things straight. I believe that you are genuinely concerned about your ma, and are anxious to do all you can to get her back unharmed. However, I'm sure you'll agree that your confession has made you, shall I say, a little unpredictable. I want you to be absolutely clear in your mind about one thing: if you have another change of heart, at any time – and I am thinking mainly of after we have regained your mother – I am not going to hesitate for a moment about shooting you, if I consider it necessary.'

Karina gulped, and then said, with some dignity, 'I will not betray you.'

'Thank you. I should also point out that your record of keeping your word to obey me is abysmal. Now I am going to tell you again. You just sit there. You move only if and when I tell you to, and you move in the direction I tell you to. The only exception to this rule is if any shooting starts, and I am otherwise occupied, you get down on to the floor, out of sight, and you stay there until I tell you to get up. Because if you do or say anything that could endanger the life of one of my people I am going to take it as an act of betrayal. Right?'

'Right,' Karina agreed. 'I will obey you.'

'Then let's wrap this up.' It was still raining, quite heavily, which Jessica decided would be more to Burke's advantage than hers. She concentrated on the road rather than on what might lie ahead. As she had told her team, she could only play it by ear, and she trusted in her, and their, professional nous to deal with whatever problems were going to arise.

It was a quarter to ten when her mobile buzzed. 'We are in position, looking at prints in a local art gallery,' Tom said. 'We have a good view of the high street.'

'Anything worth mentioning?'

'I can't say there is. There aren't too many people about. It's raining pretty heavily here.'

'Snap,' Jessica said. 'See you.'

A few minutes later they reached the top of the hill.

'Did you see that?' Rosen asked Burke, who was seated beside him in the Mondego parked in the hotel car park. Burke had opted to leave Loman to position the Dorrell brothers, as he was the one who knew them.

'See what?'

'That car that just drove by.'

'It wasn't a blue Peugeot estate,' Burke pointed out. 'It was a little red thing.'

'It was a red Renault Clio,' Rosen said.

'So?'

'The car that passed us when Sonia and I were staking out Blandlock on Monday afternoon was a red Clio.'

'Do you have any idea how many small red cars there are in England?'

'That car was driven by a blonde woman, with the princess as her passenger. Sonia was sure of it.'

'And this car was driven by a man.'

'With two women passengers.'

'So he's a popular fellow.'

'The point is, Mr Burke, that we know this Jones woman owns, or has the use of, a red Clio. Now she is on her way to surrender to us, so she says. If she were intending to use a back-up, despite your warnings, isn't the most likely car for her to use a red Clio?'

'Your nerves are showing, Rosen. That is pure coincidence.'

'Can we afford to risk a coincidence, Mr Burke?'

'Hm.' Burke considered. Then he thumbed his mobile. 'Loman, a small red car has just driven into town. Did you see it?'

'A Clio. Yes.'

'What is it doing?'

'Turning off into the Municipal Car Park.'

'Can you see it from where you are?'

'No.'

'Well, keep an eye out for any people walking up from the park, and call me back.'

'Will do.'

Burke called Jessica. 'It's not ten yet,' she said.

'Five to. Where are you?'

'Just topping the hill.'

'You made good time. Come down slowly.'

'I see her,' Rosen said.

Burke rolled down his window and levelled his glasses; the rain was coming from the other side. 'One blue Peugeot estate, two women, one fair and the other dark. She's behaving herself. Start your engine.' Rosen obeyed, and the mobile buzzed. 'Yes?' Burke asked.

'Three people have just come up from the car park,' Loman said. 'They have gone into a picture shop.'

'Okay. Forget them. Whoever they are, it'll take them too long to catch up. Are your friends in position?'

'Yes.'

'And they know that I want this pair alive and, if possible, unhurt?'

'Yes.'

'Then get into your car and go.'

'Will do,' Loman said.

The Peugeot was close. Rosen released the handbrake and drove out of the hotel car park. The Peugeot braked to allow him space, and he drove slowly into the town. To Jessica's dismay the Mondego did not stop there, but drove straight through the shopping centre and out the other side, still very slowly. They twisted through some corners, and reached the suburbs. Still Rosen didn't stop, although he increased speed, and in front of them Jessica now saw a large black Mercedes. The car she had last seen driving away from Blandlock! 'Shit,' she muttered.

'Problem?' Andrea asked from behind her.

'The bastard has out-thought us,' Jessica growled. 'So far.' She had been so sure he would make the switch in the centre of the town, relying on his methods of distraction and on their reluctance to risk hurting any innocent bystanders, but his deliberate procedure was at least giving Tom and the girls a chance to regain the Clio and follow. Although obviously Tom would intend to stay out of sight until he got her call.

Now they were out of the houses and on the open road, and on their left there was a lay-by, vacant save for a single small green car. 'Fuck, fuck, fuck,' Jessica growled.

'Wasn't that the car Henri was using?' Karina asked.

'I think it is still the car he is using,' Jessica said. But there was no way the plan could be changed now. The Mercedes signalled and pulled in behind the parked car, beside which a man lounged. He was wrapped in a raincoat and wore a slouch hat. 'Henri!' Karina snapped.

'Seems to me we've been scuppered right, left and centre,' Jessica remarked, brain whirring as she signalled and followed the Ford into the lay-by.

'Do you want action?' Andrea asked.

'No. We can do nothing until they produce the sultana. Cover yourself up. And you, Princess, sit absolutely still.' Andrea pulled the blanket over her head and did her best to look like a duffel bag.

Jessica had parked some fifty feet behind the Ford, and now she got out, standing behind the open door, her pistol held in both hands and pointing at the three cars in front of her.

Burke also got out. 'This is not nice of you, Sergeant,' he said.

'Just don't come any closer, until you produce the sultana,' Jessica said.

Burke shrugged, and snapped his fingers. Loman got out from behind the wheel of the Mercedes, and opened the boot. He reached inside, and dragged Vanessa out. She was fully dressed, although her evening gown was sadly the worse for wear, and her hands were bound behind her back; she was clearly only half conscious. When he set her on her feet her knees buckled, and Loman had to catch her before she fell. 'Mama!' Karina cried, getting out of the car and running forward.

'Shit!' Jessica snapped. 'Come back!' she shouted.

Karina checked, looking over her shoulder. But she was too far advanced. 'Keep coming, Your Highness,' Burke said, 'or you'll get a bullet in your leg.' He levelled his own pistol while Rosen also got out of the Mondego, carrying his assault rifle.

Karina licked her lips, uncertain what to do. Jessica felt equally adrift, thanks to the stupid girl's disobedience. She was very tempted to shoot it out there and then, but that would certainly cost the sultana's life, as would pressing her alarm button to call Tom into action. While she tried to consider her options, she heard movement behind her. 'Keep out of sight,' she told Andrea without turning her head, and was struck a paralysing blow where her right shoulder joined her neck.

Jessica found herself lying on the wet ground, with water seeping into her pants and threatening even her anorak. She knew she had lost consciousness for a few seconds, and for a moment her brain was consumed by the agonising pain in her shoulder, which was spreading up her neck and into her head. Then she saw a man's foot kicking her Skorpion away, and knew that she had jumped into some very hot water. At the same time she heard a scream, and understood that Karina had also been captured.

Hands were wrapped round her chest, and she was dragged to her feet, fingers eating into her flesh. She was still having trouble with her breathing as well as her head, and she couldn't focus clearly, but she could see, through the mist that covered her eyes, Karina being confronted by Henri, and a man, who she presumed to be Burke, walking towards her. Rosen was behind him. Cars were passing them on the road, but they were all travelling at speed now that they were out of the town; moreover, their drivers were likely to be concentrating on the wet surface. She doubted any of them cast more than a glance at the lay-by, where it would appear that some friends were chatting – Jessica knew she could not be seen from the road, as she was lying on the other side of the estate car.

But no one was paying any attention to the estate car itself, or what might be in it. Andrea was a slim woman, and it did look as if the back contained only a pile of blankets. If Jessica had been caught out by Burke's elaborate preparations, he could still be caught out by hers. If Andie played it right.

Burke stood in front of her. 'The famous Sergeant Jones.' He stretched out his hand, and stroked her cheek. Instinctively her head jerked away from him. 'I am only removing some mud from your face. You are too handsome a woman to be disfigured by mud. I would rather disfigure you personally.'

Jessica stopped panting. She still had her wrist alarm, and desperately wanted to summon Tom. But for Tom to turn up now would mean her death, not to mention the sultana's. In any event this last option was removed, as Rosen stepped forward and unbuckled the alarm from her wrist. 'We need to get out of here,' he said. 'That red car *was* a back-up.'

'I still doubt that. But I agree we should move. You gentlemen are still required.'

For the first time Jessica had a chance to look at the man who had struck her and his companion, who had also been staked out in the bushes. Their possible presence had never occurred to her, so firmly had she been focused on what was in front of her. They were not faces she knew, although she recognised them as typical products of the London underworld, and that they were obviously related. 'Anything you say, Mr Burke,' they agreed.

'Do you have transport?'

'Down a side road, half a mile along.'

'Very good. I have another job for you. Take the Mondego, pick up your car, and then dump the Mondego somewhere. Then come to Loman's house. You know where it is?'

The first man nodded. 'Number twelve, People Hill, Wandsworth.'

Jessica felt a surge of joy. Oh Andie, she prayed, just keep still. But then the other brother motioned to the Peugeot and asked,

'What about this one?' She held her breath.

'Leave it,' Burke said. 'She's a police-woman. It'll be too easy to trace.'

'You mean this little bit is a copper?' asked the other brother. 'Do we get to knock her about a bit?'

'Perhaps,' Burke said. 'When I've finished with her. Bring her over here.' Hands tightened on Jessica's arms, and she was forced along the lay-by to the Mercedes. Again she looked at the traffic streaming by, but to attempt to involve them would doubtless cause casualties; Burke's record indicated that he would shoot his way out of any problem. Her salvation had to lie with Andie.

Karina was standing beside the saloon, her arms round her mother. Vanessa had her head on her daughter's shoulder and was weeping. 'I didn't mean to let you down,' Karina said. 'But when I saw Mummy ... and this bastard...'

Henri was standing on her other side. 'It's for your own good,' he said.

'I spit on you,' Karina told him.

'Now, ladies,' Burke said, 'hands behind backs, please.' Jessica's arms were pulled behind her and handcuffs snapped on her wrists. The same was done to Karina; Vanessa's arms had never been untied. 'Henri,' Burke said, 'you drive your car. Sergeant Jones and I will sit in the back. We

326

have a lot to talk about. Rosen, you're in charge of the two wogs. Please deliver them in one piece. Loman, you'll drive.'

Jessica was forced into the back seat of the smaller car, and Burke sat beside her. Henri got behind the wheel. 'You are taking them to Loman's house? Is that not a risk?'

'No risk at all,' Burke said. 'No one would ever suspect that I have my headquarters in a London suburb.'

'But these people will know,' Henri pointed out. 'This one.'

Burke smiled at Jessica. 'But she is never going to tell anyone, are you, my pretty little policewoman?'

Andrea listened to the cars being driven away, but dared not move for a further five minutes. Then she cautiously pushed her head out from beneath the blankets. The lay-by was deserted. She climbed into the front seat, thumbed Jessica's mobile.

'About time,' Tom said.

'Where are you?'

'A quarter of a mile back, waiting for your signal. Hey, you're not JJ.'

'Andie. Listen, they've scooped the pot.'

'What did you say? Why didn't she signal?'

'She never had time. They had it all worked out. But I have an address. Number twelve, People Hill, Wandsworth. They're going

327

there now. With JJ.'

'Number twelve, People Hill, Wandsworth. Right. We're on our way.'

'No, wait. They've identified my Clio, and they know this car. And we will need a back-up. There were six of them here, and I don't know how many more are at the house. And I think they are all armed.'

'Shit!' Tom muttered. 'Is JJ all right?'

'When last I saw her. Listen, we have to have a car they won't know. Have it waiting on the Portsmouth Road at Putney Heath. And have a back-up squad in position. But they shouldn't do anything until we get there.'

'Just how am I supposed to arrange that?'

'Call the commander.'

'Me?'

'You're the senior officer present.'

'He'll blow his top.'

'He has three lives at stake: a reigning queen, her heir, and his favourite police-woman. He can blow whatever he likes, as long as he has a squad waiting for us there. Now come and pick me up.' She got out of the car and retrieved Jessica's discarded shoulder bag – and the Skorpion.

'You shot my woman, Sonia,' Burke remarked as Henri threaded his way through the traffic on his way back to London.

'How is she?' Jessica asked. She could do

nothing more than keep her nerve, her patience, and her determination to survive until Andrea arranged her rescue.

'Poorly,' Burke said. 'I have an idea she is going to die.'

'There's a pity. Did you say she was your woman?'

'In a manner of speaking. She was my employee. I don't like my employees being shot.'

'I can imagine.'

'So you are going to have to suffer for that.' Jessica gazed at him. He unzipped her anorak and then unbuttoned her jacket. 'This is all muddy too,' he said. 'You even have mud in your hair. It is such pretty hair.' He ran his hand over her head, allowing the strands to slip through his fingers. 'Are you going to scream when I put the wire between your legs? Rosen tells me your colleague screamed – or would have, had she not been gagged.'

Jessica found herself running short of breath again. 'You mean you weren't there?' she asked, cursing her quickened heartbeat; he would be able to see the additional colour in her cheeks.

As he did. 'I think I am getting to you. No, sadly, I wasn't there. If I had been, she wouldn't have died, at least not until she told us what we wanted to know, in which case this whole charade would have been unnecessary. But still, if she had, I might never have made your acquaintance. I would have regretted that.' He unbuttoned her shirt in turn.

'Are you just going to sit there and let him do this?' Jessica asked Henri. 'I had the ridiculous idea that you were a gentleman.' Henri did not reply, although his ears glowed, and she could tell he was watching them in the rear-view mirror.

As Burke noticed. 'Keep your eye on the road, Ferrière. It would be most regrettable if we were to have an accident.'

'I thought he was *your* employer.'

'He represents my employer. But he really is only an office boy.' He plucked at her brassiere. 'I really would have supposed a woman like you, masquerading in a man's world, would have discarded such an old-fashioned female garment. But perhaps you need it because your tits are too large. Would you like me to cut them off for you?' Once again she stared at him, determined to keep her face stony, but uncertain as to whether he was contemplating immediate action – she did not doubt he was quite capable of it. He seemed able to read her mind. 'Oh, I shall not do it until we reach the house. To do it now would be to get blood all over the interior of the car, and the people from whom Henri hired it would ask questions. But there are other parts of you that I am

330

sure are worth exploring.' He released the belt around her waist.

'Come on, come on,' Andrea said. She sat beside Tom in the front of the estate car; the Clio had been left in the lay-by. Chloe and Priscilla were in the back.

'We don't want to get done for speeding,' he reminded her. 'We've time.'

'We don't know that.'

'Listen, if they were going to kill anybody right away, they would have done it at the lay-by.'

'But we don't know what else they might be doing,' Andrea pointed out. 'There are worse fates than death, you know, at least for a woman. But I suppose an MCP like you wouldn't understand that.'

Tom glanced at her in surprise; he had never known Andrea to be so agitated. 'I think I know JJ well enough to know that she can sit through anything, as long as the end result is the one she wants. She's proved that. Anyway,' he added, trying to relieve the tension, 'rape is a tricky business in a moving car on a crowded street.'

Andrea displayed her feelings by fingering the safety catch on her pistol.

Ten minutes later they were pulling to a halt behind a parked BMW. Inspector Manley himself got out. 'Some show,' he remarked.

'Is our back-up in position, sir?'

'It is. Your people haven't arrived yet. What's your plan?'

'Well...' Tom looked at Andrea.

'I'd like to bust in and shoot the lot,' Andrea said.

'Ahem,' Manley remarked.

'That's too risky,' Tom said. 'They have the three women at their mercy.'

'So we'll play it by the book. Negotiation.'

'I don't think these people are prepared to negotiate, sir.'

'We'll find out. Move over, Hutchins.'

'You mean you're coming, sir?' Shit, she thought; that would mean they could no longer act on their own, and carry out her plan.

'Of course I'm coming. That's my woman they have in there.' He glanced at Tom. 'In a manner of speaking.'

Henri swung the car into People Hill – it wasn't really a hill, just a slight upwards incline – and stopped outside the gate of number twelve, leaving the driveway clear. The Mercedes, which had followed them all the way, passed them and turned in to the driveway, parking in front of the garage. It was eleven fifteen, and the street was empty. Burke pulled up Jessica's pants and reclipped her belt. 'Now tell the truth,' he said. 'You enjoyed that, didn't you?'

Jessica's cheeks were crimson, and her entire body was consumed with a combination of angry outrage and equally angry shame. She could only remember that something very similar had happened to her in Istanbul – but then she had been rescued by the SAS, and her assailants had been shot dead. 'I am going to come to Kharram to watch you get yours,' she said in a low voice.

For just a moment he frowned, then he looked past her at Rosen, who was standing at the window. 'Get this bitch into the house,' he said.

'Where in the house do you want her put, Mr Burke?'

'Upstairs with Sonia.'

Rosen licked his lips. He could tell from Jessica's still open shirt and general dishevelled appearance, as well as from her breathing, that his boss had had a busy drive. 'And?'

'Oh, you can have her for a while. I want to have a chat with the princess.'

'Come along.' Rosen opened the door, grasped Jessica's shoulders, and pulled her out of the car. Jessica gave a quick glance up and down the street, but it remained somnolent. She considered screaming, but long before anyone could respond positively she would be dead. She had to keep her faith in Andrea.

The front door was opened by a short,

stout woman. 'Who's this?' she asked.

Rosen thrust Jessica past her and into the narrow hallway. Burke followed. 'A guest. Detective-Sergeant Jones. Apparently she is quite famous – in certain quarters.'

'Detective-Ser— ... A copper!' Ruby was aghast. 'You brought a copper here?'

'Just for a little while. How is Sonia?'

'Bad.' Ruby looked at Jessica, anxiously. She could see that Jessica was handcuffed, and that she had been roughed up, but she was still afraid of her. 'She's going to die, Mr Burke. If she don't get help, right away, she's going to die.'

'Ah, well, she'll have company. Ladies.' Loman and Henri ushered Vanessa and Karina into the house, and Loman closed and locked the door. Karina was supporting her mother, who continued to be unsteady on her feet. 'Take the sultana upstairs as well,' Burke said. 'I want to have a word with you, young lady.'

'Listen,' Karina told him, 'the deal is off. It was off from the moment you blew up those people – *my* people – at Quadrino's. You are a murdering swine.'

'Did you really suppose you could carry out a revolution without spilling a little blood?' Burke asked. 'The deal is on, because you are in too deep to pull out now. If you don't co-operate, I am going to send you back to your father in separate envelopes.'

334

Karina gasped; Burke took off his raincoat and hung it on the stand, then pushed her into the sitting room and closed the door. They heard the key turn in the lock. 'Hold on,' Henri shouted. 'Open up. You can't harm the princess.'

There was no reply. Henri looked at Rosen. Who shrugged. 'He will do what he will do. Upstairs, you. Loman, you'd better give the sultana a hand.' Ruby led the way, and Jessica followed. Rosen was immediately behind her, and Loman helped Vanessa. Henri remained standing irresolutely at the foot of the stairs. Rosen looked down at him and grinned. 'If you listen at the door, monsieur, you may be able to hear her scream.'

'You bastard,' Henri said.

Ruby opened the bedroom door, and Rosen pushed Jessica in. She stared as she saw the woman lying on the bed, bandaged shoulder a mass of fresh blood, while the room stank of disinfectant and other unpleasantnesses. 'Like I said,' Ruby remarked, 'she ain't good.'

'Draw the curtains,' Rosen said, and grinned at Jessica. 'I always knew you and I were going to get together. That's why I let you off the last time.'

Ruby went to the window, which overlooked the street. 'What the shit...?'

'What do you see?' Rosen pushed Jessica into a chair.

'Everyone's getting out. Leaving their houses. Up and down the street. They're just leaving. Chattering at each other. And looking at us.'

Rosen went to the window and stood behind her. Loman pushed Vanessa into the room and then joined them at the window; Vanessa sank to her knees and then fell full length with a thump.

'They're being evacuated,' Loman said. 'The police have got to them.'

'Why?' Rosen asked. 'Is there a fire?'

'It's us, you cretin,' Loman snapped. 'They're isolating us. Get Burke.'

'Watch her,' Rosen said, as nervous as Ruby, even if Jessica was still handcuffed. Then he ran down the stairs.

Jessica had to control her desire to scream, this time with joy. Andrea had turned up trumps. But she knew there was still a long way to go. She didn't suppose Burke would ever surrender.

He came up the stairs, followed by Rosen. 'What's going on?'

'See for yourself,' Loman invited.

Burke looked out of the window. 'There's nobody out there.'

'That's because they've all gone.'

'You're sure you're not imagining things?'

'They was there, Mr Burke,' Ruby said. 'What we have to do is get out while we can.'

336

Burke hesitated, and Loman said, 'Too late.'

From each end of the street two police cars had emerged. The four vehicles stopped, facing each other, each pair some fifty yards away from the house. From each car there emerged three policemen, all in flak jackets, and all armed.

'Shit,' Burke said. 'Right. Out the back.'

'They'll be there too,' Loman said gloomily. 'Show yourself, and they'll shoot you dead.' Burke glared at him.

'We can talk our way out,' Rosen said. 'We've the three women. They'll let us out before they allow them to be killed.'

Burke chewed his lip. Jessica reckoned he had never been in this position before, and had no idea how to handle it. 'They want to talk,' Loman said.

'You in there,' shouted a voice Jessica recognised as that of Superintendent Manley. 'Your house is surrounded by armed police. There is no way you can leave. If you wish to save your lives, send out the three women, and then come out yourselves with your hands up. You have ten minutes.'

'Well,' Ruby said, 'that's it. They mean business. These fucking women are just too high profile.'

'That's the very reason they won't try anything,' Rosen said. 'They can't afford to have any of them killed. It's all a bluff.

Anyway, we can't surrender. Have you any idea what would happen to us if we were extradited back to Kharram? Mr Burke?'

Rosen was asking for leadership. Burke squared his shoulders. 'Open the window.' Loman threw up the sash, and then hastily retreated from any possible line of fire. Burke took his place. 'Now you listen to me,' he shouted. 'We'll come out when we're ready, and when we do, we'll have the women with us. Start anything, and they'll be the first to go. Are you ready to negotiate?'

There was a brief silence. Then Manley said, 'We're willing to listen.'

'Right,' Burke said. 'Here's what we want. First, a helicopter which will take us to Heathrow. Then a fully fuelled aircraft to take us and our hostages to a destination I will reveal to the pilot when we are boarded. When we have reached that destination, the hostages will be released. Come back to me when these arrangements have been made. I will give you an hour.'

'What bloody cheek,' Tom growled. He and Andrea, with Chloe and Priscilla, were grouped behind the superintendent.

Manley lowered his loud hailer. 'He has all the high cards, and he knows it.'

'You're not going to let him get away with it, sir?'

'Not if I can help it. But ... What the hell?'

Horns were blaring and policemen were shouting 'Stop!' A car had just smashed through the ring at the other end of the street, and with blown-out tyres and a crumpled wing was still coming down the street to surge to a halt outside the Loman residence, slamming into the front of Henri's parked car. Two men leapt out, brandishing handguns. 'Do we fire, sir?' asked one of the marksmen.

Manley hesitated, and before he responded the two men were inside the house. 'No one's been killed yet,' Manley said. 'Let's keep it that way as long as we can.'

'You mean no one has been killed at *this* site yet,' Tom said. 'With respect, sir. What about Louise Pleyell? Or the two down at Blandlock? Or the forty in Kharram?'

Manley cleared his throat, and looked relieved to see Commander Adams striding towards them. 'What the hell is going on?'

'A stand-off, sir.'

'Is it true that they have Sergeant Jones in there?'

'I'm afraid so, sir.'

'And the sultana, and the princess?'

'Yes, sir.'

'Fuck, fuck, fuck.' He looked at the three policewomen. 'With respect, ladies. I hope someone is going to tell me who thought up this hare-brained caper. Or would I be right

339

in assuming that it was JJ?'

'It was a joint plan, sir,' Andrea said loyally.

'Which JJ was very reluctant to undertake, sir,' Tom put in.

'Hm. And who were those two villains?' He gestured towards the wrecked car outside Loman's front gate.

They had been joined by several other officers, and one of these said, 'I think I recognised them, sir. The Dorrell brothers. A right pair of thugs. Just out from doing eight for GBH.'

'And carrying shooters. So, we have at least five armed men in there, and at least one armed woman.'

'We can forget about the woman, sir,' Andrea said. 'JJ shot her, down at Bland-lock.'

'Hm. Well, Superintendent?'

Manley outlined Burke's demands.

'Estimation?'

'I'm afraid, sir, bearing in mind what has happened before in this business, that Burke appears to be quite capable of carrying out his threat.'

'Ideas?'

'Well, sir...'

'I have an idea,' Andrea said.

'Well, tell us.' Andrea did so. 'That is absolutely absurd,' the commander declared. 'Someone will certainly get killed.'

'If we are going to consider that kind of

340

direct action,' Manley said, 'we should call in the SAS rather than risk our own officers. Anyway, Hutchins, you are on leave. You're not supposed to be here at all.'

'That's true, sir,' Andrea said thoughtfully.

'So I suggest you push off and leave us to it,' Manley said. 'And hope it works out all right, and that there are no repercussions.'

'Yes, sir,' Andrea said demurely, and withdrew to where Chloe and Priscilla were waiting.

Tom followed them. 'I hope you are not thinking what I think you are thinking?'

'It would have been easier if the brass hadn't interfered, and we'd been able to go straight in,' Andrea snapped. 'Those other thugs wouldn't have arrived yet, either.'

'But you still mean to go in.'

'It doesn't have to involve you,' Chloe said.

'Well, it does. JJ is very important to me.'

'And to me – *us*,' Andrea added hastily.

'So...'

'Let's do it.'

Burke went down the stairs to greet the brothers. Loman and Rosen followed. 'You didn't have to do that,' Burke said. 'But am I glad to see you.'

'Well, Mr Burke, we had to come,' Oliver said. 'We haven't been paid yet.'

'That's true. There'll be a bonus if you stick to the end.'

'Which is what?' Clarence asked.

'Mr Burke has arranged a getaway for us,' Rosen said enthusiastically.

'They'll go for that?' Oliver asked.

'They don't have any choice. Don't you know what we have? Why don't you show them, Mr Burke?'

Burke opened the sitting room door, and they gazed at Karina. The princess lay on the floor with her back to them, her hands bound behind her back. She was naked, and there were several red weals on her buttocks. 'Jesus,' Clarence muttered. 'Is she dead?'

'Good lord, no.' Burke went to her, held her thigh and shoulder, and rolled her on to her back. 'I have just been teaching her a lesson in loyalty. Haven't I, Your Highness?' Karina's eyes opened, and her face twisted with a mixture of pain and repugnance. 'What I want to know,' Burke said, 'is how those bastards got hold of this address.' He looked from Loman to Rosen, almost accusingly.

'I have no idea,' Loman said.

Burke gazed at him for a moment, then snapped, 'Fetch Ferrière!'

Jessica listened to the noises from the street. She couldn't believe it was the police storming the place this quickly. And if it was, she couldn't believe she was still alive. 'What's

342

happening?' she asked Ruby as the men all went downstairs.

'Reinforcements,' Ruby said.

'You were right, you know,' Jessica said. 'The only way you are going to get out of this alive is to surrender.'

Ruby turned towards her, lips drawn back from her teeth. 'Shut up,' she said. 'Shut up or I'll shut you up.'

'Only trying to help,' Jessica said.

Ruby came towards her, and she realised that she might be in for a beating – about which she could do nothing with her hands cuffed – when the door opened and Henri came in. 'They want you in the kitchen,' he said.

'What about these?' Ruby asked, motioning towards the hostages.

'I'm to stand guard.'

Ruby considered for a moment, then she said, 'I'll sort you out later, bitch.' She went outside, and Henri closed and locked the door.

'So, do you want your share?' Jessica asked.

Henri came to the bed and looked down at Sonia. 'Is she dead?'

'She looks pretty close.'

Henri bent over Vanessa. 'And her?'

Vanessa stirred. 'I am so thirsty.'

Henri turned back to Jessica. 'That bastard has been beating Karina. The princess!'

'I thought he might be pretty peeved at her

attempt to back out.'

'You knew that?'

'We've shared a confidence or two.'

'Listen. I can help you to escape. If you'll guarantee me immunity from arrest.'

Jessica's heartbeat quickened. 'I can't guarantee you anything,' she said. 'Except exonerating testimony.' He bit his lip, then took the keys to the handcuffs from his pocket. 'Where did you get those?' Jessica asked.

'They were in Burke's raincoat pocket, hanging by the front door.' A moment later Jessica was rubbing her hands together to restore circulation. 'Here.' From his pocket Henri took a small, snub-nosed revolver. 'Do you know how to use one of those?'

'I'd have liked something bigger. But beggars can't be choosers.' She spun the chambers; there were five bullets. 'Have you one of your own?' He nodded. 'Which I presume you know how to use.' She knelt beside the sultana. 'Your Highness, you must wake up.'

'I am so thirsty.'

There was a washbasin in the corner. Henri filled a tooth-glass and brought it to Vanessa, who drank greedily. 'I could do with one of those,' Jessica said, and also drank deeply before straightening her clothes, tucking her shirt back into her pants and buttoning her jacket.

Henri watched her. 'Did he...?'

'In the circumstances, he couldn't quite make it.'

'You're very calm about it.'

'Been there, done that. Which is not to say that if he gives me the opportunity I wouldn't shoot him in the balls. How many are downstairs?'

'Five. And Ruby.'

'And all armed. Except maybe Ruby. This needs considering, because we have to take care of the sultana as well as getting to the princess.'

Their heads jerked when there was a thump on the door. 'Open up, Henri.' It was Burke himself.

'Shit,' Jessica muttered. 'You've been rumbled.'

'What are we to do?' For a reply, Jessica grasped the sultana's shoulders and dragged her round the bed so that she would have some protection when the shooting started.

'Open up, or we'll break it down and take you apart,' Burke said.

There was a huge noise from the front of the house.

'Now,' Andrea said, 'you all know what you have to do.'

They were seated in the BMW, about fifty yards behind the assembled police cars.

'I'm for the princess,' Tom said.

'I'm for the queen,' Priscilla said.

'I'm for anyone with a gun in his hand,' Chloe said.

'And I'm for JJ,' Andrea said. 'Okay, guys – fasten your seat belts, tight. And as our American cousins would say, let's kick ass!' She started the engine.

'You're sure you can get through there?' Tom asked. He was sitting beside her.

'What's a car, more or less?' She moved forward, slowly. Between the inside police car and the fence of the house just along the street from Loman's there was about nine feet of width, including the pavement. Andrea drove up to it slowly enough, and a uniformed policeman stepped out from behind the car and held up his hand. Andrea placed her hand on the horn, and blew a long blast. He hastily stepped aside, shouting at her, and she put her foot down hard on the gas pedal.

She didn't quite make it, clipping the police car on her side and then being thrown against the fence on Tom's, but then she was through, hurtling down the street before braking violently behind Henri's already damaged car. Again, she didn't quite make it, and skidded into the rear of the smaller vehicle with a crash. The petrol tank immediately ignited, and the flames spread both forward and back; within a few seconds of the impact all three cars exploded, scattering debris across the street.

But by then they were already out, Tom leading the way and running up the path. His chosen weapon was a Magnum, and he used this small cannon to fire two shots into the front door lock before hurling his shoulder against the wood and smashing it in. Then he leapt into the hall, the women immediately behind him.

Only Loman was actually in the hallway, and at the sight of the array of guns being pointed at his chest he dropped to the floor with his hands over his head. Oliver and Clarence were in the lounge; they had been standing on either side of Karina, but had run to the window at the sound of the explosion, which had cracked the glass. Now they turned as the door opened, and were confronted by Tom's Magnum and Chloe's Walther.

Andrea stepped over Loman and looked up the stairs at Burke and Rosen looking down. Rosen levelled his rifle, but before he could squeeze the trigger Andrea shot him in the chest. He came tumbling down, dead before he reached the bottom.

Burke put his shoulder against the door and burst in, confronting Henri. 'Bastard,' he said, and fired. Henri gasped and fell to his knees.

Burke pointed the gun again, and Jessica said, 'Drop it.' Burke turned to face her, gun raised, and Jessica fired. She had already been aiming at his groin.

'I don't know what to say,' Commander Adams said. 'I really don't. But I know what I should do.' He surveyed the five faces standing in front of his desk. 'I should cashier the lot of you. Disobeying orders, taking the law into your own hands, destroying three cars and a dozen windows, risking your lives, not to mention the lives of the hostages, shooting one man dead...'

'He was pointing a rifle at me, sir,' Andrea pointed out. 'That was the second time he had done that.'

'And it got your goat, is that it? And then, this woman dead...'

'She died from loss of blood, sir,' Chloe said.

'After having been shot – by you, was it, Jones?'

'Yes, sir. She also had pointed a rifle at me.'

'Obviously not something to do to you young ladies. This man Ferrière...'

'He was shot by Burke, sir.'

'Oh, yes. At least I am told he will recover.'

'I would like to say, sir, as I put in my report, that he gave material assistance at the end. But for him I would have been killed.'

'I'm sure the judge will bear that in mind. And now this fellow Burke – you know he will be a cripple for life? And as for his, well, prospects...'

'His prospects were suffering from overuse as it was, sir. And he did happen to be pointing a gun at me.'

'The cardinal sin,' Adams remarked. 'What are we going to do about the Kharrami request for his extradition, and that of Ferrière, to face charges there? As I said, you should be drummed out of the force. But this letter...' He indicated the gold-embossed sheet of notepaper on his desk. 'Sultan Yusuf intends to decorate you all with the Order of the Camel, which is apparently the highest award his country possesses. Well...' He suddenly grinned. 'I'd have to say, it's an honour to have you on the force. You'd better take some leave, all of you. And try to stay out of trouble.'

Workmen were busy repairing the front door and hall at Blandlock House, while a repair crew from the local garage was still dismantling what was left of the Land Rover. They stopped to regard the red Clio as it came down the drive, appreciating the two handsome uniformed young women, hair confined in neat ponytails, who got out. The Dobermans immediately started frisking around them, clearly old friends.

Parkin was there as well, to greet them. 'Sir William says to go right in.'

Jessica and Andrea picked their way

through the rubble. Bland was waiting at the inner end of the hall. 'Glad you could come down,' he said. 'I say, I do like women in uniform. Do you know, Jones, this is the first time I've seen your legs? They are superb.'

'Is Her Highness all right, sir?' Jessica asked, determined to keep cool.

'She's under sedation. But hopefully she'll feel better when she gets home. They're flying back tomorrow.'

'And the princess?'

'She's a spunky kid. She's waiting for you upstairs.'

Jessica and Andrea climbed the stairs.

'He seems to have done a U-turn,' Andrea remarked.

'I still wouldn't trust him further than I could kick him,' Jessica commented.

Karina stood at the top of the stairs; her lips were tight, and she moved stiffly, but otherwise appeared unhurt. 'Thank you for coming down.' She looked from one to the other. 'You look just splendid in your uniforms.'

'Thank you, Your Highness. And you...?'

Karina opened the door and showed them into her bedroom. 'I hurt a bit, and I have a couple of scars, but the doctor says they will fade. Can you tell me about Henri?'

'He's going to recover.'

Karina gestured them to chairs. 'Will he be sent back to Kharram?'

'I doubt it. Don't tell me you're still concerned about him?'

'Well...' Karina flushed. 'I must forget him.'

'I think that would be a very good idea. What about you?'

Karina's lips twisted. 'Oh, I am going back. Tomorrow. With Mummy.'

'And Cerise?'

'Oh, yes. Cerise too.'

'What will happen to her?'

'I am sure you would not approve, JJ.'

Jessica gulped.

'May I ask, Your Highness,' Andrea said, 'does the sultana know, well...'

'I have told her everything, yes.'

'Including the names of your principals?'

Karina sighed. 'I had to.'

'And presumably she will tell your father. What will happen to *you*, then?'

'Mummy has already telephoned Daddy, and told him everything. Oh, do not fear for my life,' she said as the two policewomen exchanged glances. 'I am to be married off, to some man of my father's choice. He will be old enough to be my father, and will undoubtedly beat me and keep me in purdah.'

'I'm sorry,' Jessica said.

'Diabolical,' Andrea commented.

'But you think I deserve it. I suppose you are right. I just wanted to thank you for everything you did for me, for saving my mother's life, and to say again how sorry I am about Louise. Can you ever forgive me for that?'

'Yes,' Jessica said. 'We have to. And look on the bright side, Princess. One day you'll be ruling Kharram.'

'That is true. It is something to look forward to. If either of you ever care to visit me, you would be most welcome.'

'We'll keep it in mind,' Jessica said.

They went down the stairs. 'Won't you stay for a drink, maybe lunch?' Sir William asked.

'Thank you, but no,' Jessica said. 'We have an appointment.'

'Do we?' Andrea asked as they drove out of the grounds. 'And what about that invite? Do you think we should take it up?'

'Just keep simpering girlishly. We do have an appointment: Tom and Chloe are waiting in the Wessex Arms. We're going to have that birthday party and that wake, rolled into one.'

'And then?'

'We have a funeral to attend.'

'And then?'

'Try not to think what they will throw at us next.'